Prairie Dawn's
Lakota Moon

Karen Dee Musson

Karen Dee Musson

Copyright © 2025 by Karen Dee Musson

ISBN: 979-8-89397-659-5

Published by EliteScribes Book Writing

Table of Contents

This book is dedicated to my angels, Kim Vergonet, Liz (Medicine Moon) Martinez, Kailyn Hope, and Ruth Dennis.

A very special thank you to Millie Van Gundy Walke and Millie Musson for all your hard work and dedication. I could not have done it without you.

Chapter One

Run to the Hills

White Horse awakens next to the woman whom he has loved for the last six years. He rolls over to kiss her cheek as she sleeps, remembering the night of romance they had the night before. He thinks how he wishes he could bring her another child, but is not willing to sacrifice losing her, and still makes her drink the baby tea when their romance is done, so she doesn't conceive. He quietly comes off their pelt so as not to wake his precious Prairie Dawn. Reaching for his clothes, he begins to dress. Adjusting his waistline, he looks over at his youngest son, Little Foot, just barely six, still sound asleep. He remembers back to the time he was born on that cold winter day and how close he came to losing his mother. Reaching for his tunic and putting it over his head, he looks across at the other pelt where his oldest son, Kikimo, now twelve, lies. He reflects on how fast he has grown and will soon be able to join his Uncle Koawa on the next buffalo hunt. He slips on his moccasins, grabs his flute, and steps out of the flap.

He gazes around at his camp, still in slumber. It has nearly doubled in size over the last year, with warriors and their families, who have moved here from other bands that were destroyed by

Army guns. He inhales the sweetness of the morning air before starting his short walk to the hill overlooking his camp. It is there he will do his morning worship.

It has been a hard few years for the Plains Indians, what with his friends the Cheyenne being hit so hard in Sand Creek and his brothers, the Dakota, in Minnesota. Seems all anyone wants to do anymore is to take away the territory that rightfully belongs to the Indian nation. Much of the land that they once called home has been taken away by the big politicians in Washington and given to settlers who have come east. They were then given permission to cut down the trees, to build their homes, ruin the ground with their wagon wheels, and build their forts. Enough is enough, and now the Plains people are at war. White Horse has counted his blessings as his band has been virtually untouched, allowing his men to help the ones that were harder hit in fighting for their land and way of life.

He finds his usual spot at the top of the hill and sits down. Looking out, he sees his camp. He begins his morning prayer to Mother Earth and the great spirits above. He thanked them for keeping them safe. He thanks them for his wisdom and the wealth of the tribe. He thanks them for the buffalo that provides them with their food and shelter. When he is satisfied that his prayers are heard, he closes his prayer and reaches for his flute. Bringing it to his mouth, he glances out at the horizon and jumps to his feet in horror. He curses in his tongue as he races down the hill and into the camp.

He yells. "Blue Coats!"

He runs to every lodge, barking out orders and waking his men. Koawa is quick to jump to his feet when he sees his Chief barge in. Running Water grabs their blanket and covers their nudity before coming to their feet.

"Blue Coats coming in fast!" White Horse tells him.

Koawa races to dress as he hurries his wife and daughter out the door. Running Water is slow at putting on her clothes and orders Morning Dove to leave before her. She tells her to run to the caves and not look back. Koawa sees his daughter leave the tepee and assumes his wife is close behind, as he runs and jumps on his horse. White Horse wakes the last of his people before running to his own lodge, where his family lies. He throws open the flap, waking his sons.

"Blue Coats. Run!" He rushes to his wife, shaking her awake.

"Blue Coats on the horizon. Run!"

"Oh my God!" I jolted awake, hustling to put on my moccasins.

White Horse grabs any weapon in sight and holds the flap open.

"Come on, honey, hurry!" he rushes.

I then remember the bag that holds my personal and sentimental items that I do not want to lose. "My bag," I say, running to grab it from behind our pelt.

"There is no time. Come on!" White Horse yells, yanking my arm. I grab my bag tightly as I am rushed outside. I spot our men get on their horses and prepare for battle.

"Run to the hills," White Horse orders. "Hurry." He then jumps on his horse and is quickly off.

I make my run as the first shot is heard. My boys, where are my boys? I panicked. I continue to run as fast as I can. The shots are closer, right on my tail. White Fawn is old and slow on her run. I grab her hand and pull her along. I see Little Foot crying, frozen, scared. I scoop him up in my arms and run with them both. Kikimo, Minoke, Songbird, and Morning Dove are all within my sight. We are halfway up the first hill. White Fawn is extremely winded. I slow down for fear she will collapse. Kikimo turns to find me lagging behind.

"Go!" I yell at him as shots are heard all around.

He disobeys my order, running down to my side. He takes Little Foot out of my arms to lessen my load. He grabs his grandmother's hand, and together we continue up the hill. I dropped my bag with my precious belongings. I ran back down to grab it.

"Leave it, ma!" Kikimo yells, looking down from the top of the hill.

The shots are louder across the land. "Go Kikimo! Go to our place!" I yell.

"I won't leave you!" he shouts. Shots are heard only a few yards away.

"They are gaining on us," I yell in a panic.

I have never been so scared in my life. Our village is being destroyed as the Blue Coats come in. The smoke is high above the plains. I make it to the top of the hill, our secret hiding place underground close by. I abruptly stop again as I look down the hill.

"Running Water," I gasp.

She has been hit in the leg and is staggering to keep up. I order Kikimo to run and not to stop until he gets to safety. He is reluctant but takes his family and obeys. I ran, making my way down to Running Water, leaving my bag behind. Another shot is heard just a few feet away. With pain and fear in her eyes, she yells up at me, waving me on.

"Save yourself, run!" she yells in her tongue.

I refuse to just leave her. There is no way in hell. I ran the remainder of the way down the hill to her side. I wrap my arm around her waist and start to drag her up the hill. Another shot is heard, hitting Running Water in the back. She falls to the ground. I have little time to react as I hear the Blue Coats approaching. I lay down on the ground on my stomach next to Running Water. I took some of her blood, wiping it on me. I then played possum.

I quickly glance and see two Blue Coats advancing. "There are two more here," I hear one say.

"I knew I got one. Are they both dead?"

I hold my breath and fail to move. I can feel the hooves of one of the horses beside me. I know they are looking right down at me.

"Yeah, they are both dead," a soldier says. "Look at the hair on that one."

Oh, dear Lord, I pray, please don't turn me over.

"Hatford! Willis!" I hear from a distance.

"Over here, Lieutenant. We have two more."

"Leave them where they drop. We made our point." I hear a hideous laugh that curls my stomach.

"We got them Injuns good Frank. We killed them all."

My heart sank. I fight my tears as I lie motionless.

"Yeah, Horace, we did. Those dumb fucks didn't know what hit them."

I remain still until I hear the horses leave. I quickly make my way to Running Water, rolling her over. She is indeed dead.

"Oh, dear Lord," I cry.

I lift her head, putting it on my lap. I stroked her face.

"Oh, dear God, look what they have done." I begin to sob.

I can smell the burning of our lodges and the scent of death across the land. I remain still with Running Water's head on my lap.

"Damn you son of bitches!" I cry out. "Damn you!"

I look down at Running Water stroking her hair. "I promise you, my friend. I will honor your name. Morning Dove will be in my heart. I will make you proud, my dear friend. I will make you proud." I then kiss her cheek and rock her in my arms as I cry.

I have no idea who is alive. How crimson the land really is. I know I should leave to check, but I cannot leave my very best friend behind. I cannot allow any vultures to come and pick her away. I will not allow the wolves to drag her off. No, I will remain here. No matter what, I am not leaving her. If I must carry her with me and bury her beside the others, that is what I will do, because there is no way, no way in hell I am leaving her alone. Someone will find me, I tell myself. Not all can be lost. Oh, dear Lord, please tell me not all are lost.

Chapter Two

The Crimson Land

The Blue Coats have galloped off, leaving much bloodshed behind them. The Lieutenant cannot wait to see how proud his superior will be for leading such a great expedition and destroying the band of warriors that has allured them for so long. With the great American flag waving behind them, they carry smirks on their faces as they make their long ride back to the fort.

Kikimo comes out of hiding against Flying Hawk's orders. He is terribly worried for his mother and Aunt, who have not yet returned. He heard the shot just moments after he ran over the hill. He wanted to return then, but owed it to his brother and grandmother to get them to safety. He waited long enough. He is taking his chance and leaving the safety of the cave to search for them. He runs his way back down to the camp, abruptly stopping as he nearly vomits at the sight. He sees his friends, elders, and even horses slaughtered, swimming in their own blood. All their lodges burnt, many of them to the ground. He rushes over to where his lodge once stood proud. There is little remaining. He finds in the ashes his mother's hairbrush. It must have fallen out of her bag when she ran. He holds it to his heart and prays that she is still alive, but as he looks around, his stomach curls. How could she have survived this? Why wasn't he more adamant about staying behind with her, to help her up the hill? His sadness is interrupted when he hears the cry of a baby. He quickly rushes to the sound and slides down on his knees in front of the lifeless body of Little Doe, Blue Thunder's sister. He gently rolls her over to reveal the infant, three months old.

"Oh," he hushes it as he picks the child up in his arms.

"It's alright."

He comes to his feet, cradling the baby in his arms. "Shh," he consoles. "You are going to be alright."

He fights his tears as he remains strong. His optimism is running short as he fears the worst for his mother. He decides to take the infant back to the cave where the other women will care for it so he can continue his search for his mother and Aunt. He is quickly greeted by Minoke as he reaches the cave. She gently takes the infant from his arms. She does not need to ask, for she can see the sadness in her nephew's eyes. She rubs his cheek and faintly grins.

"I have to continue," he tells her in his tongue. "I have to find them."

"Just be careful. The Blue Coats may still be close," she warns him.

"I will."

He finds himself a surviving horse and heads further out to find his mother and Aunt. He must hurry, for soon the great circle in the sky will be down. Oh, why did he wait so long to adventure out? He wasted almost a whole day. He rides hard to the place where he saw her last.

I hum a tune, rocking my beloved friend. I curled her into my chest, so she wouldn't get cold. Her blood is draining all over my dress. I whimper a few words in between my tune. I must keep her company. I do not want her to feel alone. An eerie stillness fills the smoky air. The smell of death is all around. I think of my family and wonder if they are still alive. I worry terribly for White Horse. I know he must be frantic with worry, which is, if he is still alive. I must remain positive, for that is all I have left.

I know it will take time for me to be found. As no one will return until the area is clear of any Blue Coats. What if no one comes back? I think to myself, what if all has perished? What will I do? Where will I go? I remain there frozen with my best friend on my lap. I hum my tune. I stroked her hair. I talked to her all day. The great circle in the sky starts to set. Soon, I will have to adventure out carrying Running Water with me. Staying here will be dangerous, as the smell of blood across the land will attract predators, and I must protect Running Water. It could be days before any help arrives, especially if everyone is dead. It is up to me to get us out of here. I will do it. I will adventure out and see how bad it is.

Suddenly, I hear movement in the trees. Are the predators coming? Have the Blue Coats returned? Either way, I am protecting Running Water. I scoot her up on my lap and hold her tightly, as I gaze out into the woods. I hear it again as it moves in closer. I listen harder. A horse, I am sure of it. I listen again. No clicking. A horse without shoes. It is Indian. Oh, thank you, Jesus, I cry. I only pray it is a Lakota.

"They have come for us," I mumble to Running Water. "They have come for us."

Then I see the familiar horse through the trees. I sigh with relief. It is White Horse. "Over here," I call him.

I hear his tongue calling out to other warriors. "Over here," he says. "They are over here."

I then hear the trees move and spot the other riders. One of them is Koawa. I kiss Running Water's head.

"He made it. Your husband is alive."

Not all are dead. That means there is hope for more. Oh, dear Jesus, thank you! Then, as quickly as I am joyful, a flood of emotions fills my soul. Oh, dear Lord Koawa, poor Koawa, his precious Running Water is dead. Filled with relief and sorrow, I cannot help but cry again. Clinging onto Running Water, I rocked her in my arms. It is time to say goodbye.

White Horse is the first to jump off his horse. Koawa is quickly behind. Both men stop almost in unison when they see the lifeless body of Running Water on my lap. My tears grow harder as I watch Koawa's face go white. The moment of sinking in goes by as Koawa walks over to me, squatting down. He places his hand on his Running Water's face. He glances at me. I cannot watch his pain. I cannot see his eyes through my own tears. White Horse comes down to my side and puts his hand on my shoulder as I cry. Koawa lifts his wife off my lap and carries her away. White Horse takes me in his arms and allows me to weep.

"I tried to save her. I really did," I cry.

"I know, sweetheart," he consoles. "I know you did everything you could. It all happened so fast. There was very little anyone could do."

"The boys. Where are the boys?" I ask in a panic.

"They are both safe. They are with White Fawn."

White Horse helps me to my feet. He then sees my blood-stained dress.

"Oh, Carrie," he panics.

"It is not mine. By the grace of God, I was not hit."

I can see the relief in White Horse's face as he pulls me into his arms. "Kikimo told me he heard the shot just as he disappeared. Then he didn't see you or Running Water return. That is when he got concerned. We found him wandering around searching for you when we were returning to camp." "How bad is it?" I ask him, although I am not sure I want to know.

He pulls free from our embrace. His hollow eyes say it all. It is bad.

"There are many," he mumbles.

"Oh God," I cry.

"We are lucky we did not all die."

"White Horse, I am so sorry. I really am. This is awful."

He lowers his eyes and nods. This is a huge, huge loss for White Horse. My heart goes out to him.

"Come," he mumbles. "We must get to the others and move on."

Everyone who has survived is gathered in a ravine. Much sorrow is in everyone's eyes as the death toll increases. As of this moment, a band of one hundred and twenty men, women, and children, a total of sixty-seven of us, have lost our lives. Fifty-two of them are warriors. The rest were women and children. Six, we cannot find. We can only assume that they perished and lie somewhere on the plains or were burned in their lodges. Among the dead is Minoke's husband, Qutoh, of one year. He was one of the warriors who came here from another band after his camp was destroyed by Blue Coats. White Horse welcomed him with open arms. Qutoh was Minoke's life. She is devastated. Flying Hawk's wife, Blue Bird, is another one who was shot in the back as she ran to get away. Songbird's husband, Yellow Hawk, is among the missing. Blue Thunder lost his nephew and sister. There is not one here who has not lost someone they loved.

Many are praising White Horse for his quick action of spotting the Blue Coats before we were ambushed, as more lives would have been lost. White Horse is taking no glory. Every death is hitting him like a rock. He is a very strong-willed man of few emotions, but I know him well. He is a complete wreck.

Koawa has isolated himself from the rest. He sits under a tree with his back turned to mourn his wife in peace. He has wrapped Running Water in a blanket that is tied around her. He has her body under a tree by his horse. This is where he has remained since our arrival.

Morning Dove wants her father, but Koawa is too distraught to give her much mind. I have taken it upon myself to care for her. She has asked her mother several times. I do my best to console her and try to get her to understand that her mother is in a better place.

A fire is smoldering in the center of the ravine. We are extremely isolated and remote, hidden well in a canyon. It is very rocky and cold. Not the best place to set up a camp, but for safety reasons, until the Blue Coats tracks can be found, we will remain here with the hope of moving on sometime tomorrow. The younger warriors remaining, except for Koawa, are out hunting for food and tracking, concealing their emotions the best they know how. White Horse has returned from talking to Koawa, in hopes of helping him cope with his loss. Running Water's death is huge, even though she was a woman, she held great respect from many people, simply because Koawa is a superior warrior and next in line behind White Horse to be Chief. I worry for Koawa, as Running Water was truly a part of him, and a part of him has died too. White Horse finds a place next to me under a tree. The numbness of everyone is greatly seen. Occasional sobs are being heard throughout the hollow canyon walls.

White Horse appears in a trance and is very deep in thought. I have never seen him so down. I curled myself up, resting my head on his shoulder, staring out at all the sorrow. I see all the hurt, all the tears. I ask myself why? How could the people with whom I have grown up have so much hatred for another human being? How can these people call themselves Christians? How can one man have so much greed?

I look over at Koawa sitting all alone next to his dead wife. I have grown to admire him, see the side of him that only Running Water ever saw. She loved him so much, even when he was difficult and stubborn. She always brought a smile to his face, always showed him love. What a void he must be feeling. She wouldn't want this, I think. She would be finding something good in all this sadness. She would be bringing joy to the somber faces. I know she would. It is up to me. In the loving memory of my best friend, I will try to bring some peace to all the low faces. I lifted White Horse's hand, kissing it, and came to my feet. He comes out of his trance and reaches for my hand.

"Where are you going?" he softly asks.

"I am going to go talk to the women. I will be back shortly."

He faintly nods, relaxing my hand. He then continues back to his trance. I make my way over to where most of the women are congregated and kneel between Minoke and Fields of Flowers. I place an arm around each. Minoke tilts her head into my shoulder, and I hug her harder.

"I feel all your pains. Today is a day none of us will ever forget. Everyone has lost someone."

Songbird is the first to chime in, her teary eyes glaring up at me. "What have you lost? Your family is still one," she snaps.

"Have you forgotten, Running Water was my sister in-law, Minoke is Kikimo's aunt, and Qutoh was his uncle?" Songbird just lowers her eyes. "Women, we have all lost. We will all grieve for a very long time. But right now, we need to pull together as a group."

"But how?" Wings of a Bird asks. "Racing Buffalo was everything to me. How are my children and I supposed to move on without him?"

"With the courage he gave you," I answer her. "With the strength that he gave you that lies within you and your children."

I look around face-to-face. "Ladies, we are all our men have left. They need us to be strong for them."

I see the hesitation in many eyes, the disbelief of not wanting to care for anyone but themselves. "Ladies, do you not think, just because they are warriors, that they do not have feelings? Look at Koawa. Can you honestly tell me that he is not grieving? And what about Flying Hawk? Blue Bird and he have been together long before many of us have even been alive."

It is starting to sink in. My point is coming across.

"We need to stop our self-pity. Grieving is something that we will always do, but self-pity will destroy us. It is time we come together to rebuild what we have lost."

"But our children," Pink Blossom says, "I lost my boy, my only boy."

"I know Pink Blossom, and that is truly devastating, but we must move on. I know it is going to be hard, but we must try and keep our band going, because if we don't, then everyone died for nothing."

"So, we just forget the ones we lost, like it was nothing?" Songbird snaps.

"No, we will never forget the ones we lost, and we will grieve for a very long time. But we must be strong; we must be brave if we are going to survive."

"Prairie Dawn is right," Minoke says, wiping a tear from her eyes. "And if Qutoh were here, he would be telling me the same thing."

That I could believe, Qutoh was never short on words. Many times, he and White Horse would go round and round, but he was a magnificent warrior, and White Horse knew it.

"You have me," Minoke says.

Soon, all the other women have agreed, and a bond that we have never had before is formed. Running Water would be pleased.

The sun falls in the great canyon. We are in total darkness, with the reflection of the central fire being our only light. It appears as if even the moon and stars are grieving. Our bellies are full thanks to our hunters. I have just finished putting the boys to bed for the night. White Fawn took over Morning Dove, and they are asleep next to each other. I find a place next to White Horse under the tree that he has called his own for most of the evening. He left briefly with some of his warriors to scout the area and station his men for the night. He is now getting some well-deserved rest. Under the tree, away from the rest, he lies down beside me. He then leans over and gives me a kiss.

"Thank you," he says.

"For what?" I ask him.

"For getting the women together. I saw a few smiles."

"It is going to take time. I don't mean to sound so selfish, but I am so fortunate, although Running Water is very dear to me, it would have been worse if I had lost you or one of the boys."

"That is not selfish. I told myself the same thing. It is very hard not to think of yourself at a time like this."

"It has to be especially hard on you, my love," I tell him, stroking his cheek. "You have so many that count on you. I don't envy you right now."

I hear him deeply sigh. "This is true. My people need me now more than ever. I feel like I have failed them."

"Oh, White Horse, you have not failed anyone."

"Yes, I have, because I am stubborn. I refuse to back down."

"No love, you are standing up for what you believe in. Fighting for what rightfully belongs to us."

"Many say that the land belongs to the ones who can farm it."

"That is just an excuse; many cannot farm the land properly either. They just want it for its beauty. They do not understand how the land works." He faintly smiles over at me.

"You have always supported me in everything I do. You never question me why."

"You have given me no reason to. I trust you and so do your people."

"I wish I knew what to tell them to make their loss seem worth it." I lift my elbow, looking over at him. "You once told me that death is a circle of life. What is one's loss is another one's gain." He reaches up to stroke my hair.

"What gain do you see here?"

"Our freedom. You must not stop fighting for what you believe in."

"Go tell that to Koawa."

"Is he thinking about surrendering?" I wonder.

"No, Koawa is out for blood. He is thinking about joining the Dog Soldiers."

"I thought they were strictly Cheyenne?"

"No."

Dog Soldiers are a group of men who are the worst of the worst. They are a society of warriors who are not afraid to die or to kill. They fight brutally for what they believe in; any reasoning for peace is beyond their reach. They are feared by everyone, including their own. Once you join, you are a member until you die. To be a Dog Soldier is, in my opinion, signing a death wish.

"What about Morning Dove? Surely, he wouldn't leave her?" I ask.

"He knows that she will be taken care of. He feels that to avenge his wife's death, he must join."

"And you are going to allow it? I thought you didn't agree with the Dog Soldiers?"

"I agree with why they are fighting. I just do not always agree with the way they do it."

"So, you are going to do nothing and let him go?" I wonder.

"I do not like it. But I completely understand him wanting to avenge his wife's death."

I couldn't allow this. Running Water would be so angry if she knew he was considering this. I understand him wanting revenge. We all do, but joining the Dog Soldiers was not the way to do it. I had to talk to him. I had to at least try.

"Where is he now?" I ask White Horse.

"I am not sure. Why?" he asks. "I have to find him. I must talk to him."

"You are going nowhere tonight," he argues.

"But I must speak with him. I have to tell him something that Running Water told me."

"What," he wonders?

"It was a few months back," I tell him. "It is a promise I made to her. But I am sorry I cannot tell you, for she only wanted Koawa to know."

I am surprised White Horse doesn't push the matter. "That's alright," he nods. "You can tell him tomorrow when we are leaving."

"We are leaving tomorrow?" I questioned him.

"Yes, we are going to the sacred land that many speak of. It is a long journey, so you will need your rest." He rolls over on top of me and starts to nibble my ear. "First, my love. I need you." He then presses his lips onto mine. Although tonight our love making would have to wait, we remain with our lips locked and teasing of the ears, until we both decide to call it a night. It has been a long and emotional day, and sleep is welcome.

Chapter Three

Koawa's Greif

We awaken to the sound of horses heard on the rocks above the canyon. White Horse is quick at keeping everyone quiet and hidden, while several warriors leave to check it out. Fear enters everyone's mind from a replay of yesterday, but if that is the case, we are ready. All the women and children are covered with a circle of warriors around them. We are ready to run into the caves if need be. Eyes are tense. Hearts are pumping. Guns and arrows are drawn. Every man, including White Horse, is armed. The minutes tick away. All eyes are on the canyon above. I hear Blue Thunder speak his tongue to White Horse. All eyes look his way as he points, and guns go down.

"It is alright," White Horse says. "It is Running Bear."

Running Bear is White Horse's cousin and the Chief of a neighboring band. Ever since I have known White Horse, they have always helped each other out whenever needed. Running Bear is a very mysterious man and has many years on White Horse. But he is a good man whom I have grown to admire.

"What is he doing here?" I ask White Horse as I come to my feet.

"Most likely he saw the smoke and came," he answers.

White Horse, followed by several other warriors, walks through the ravine to meet our guest. One by one, Running Bear and his warriors are seen. Several are pulling travois behind them filled with our loved ones and whatever supplies that did not perish. What a wonderful sight it was to see him, but for Songbird, it was the greatest news of all. On one of the horses, injured but alive, is Yellow Hawk. I hear her gasp and then run to greet him. He is holding his side as he leaves his horse, an apparent victim of being shot. Songbird whisks her arms around him, showering him with affection. Eagle Scout runs up to him as well, so glad to see his father alive. White Horse greets him with an extended arm, followed by a masculine hug. You can see the joy all around on White Horse's face. Blue Thunder, Yellow Hawk's best friend, is just as happy to see him, and he too gave him a hug. Running Bear takes White Horse aside.

"We saw the smoke," he starts, "very high in the sky. I knew it was not good. We rode hard to get here. We found Yellow Hawk injured on the way. He told us what happened. We went back to your camp. We saw much destruction, but it appeared not all was lost. Yellow Hawk knew you would come here. So, we collected what we could. We have brought with us what bodies we were able."

"I thank you," White Horse says.

Running Bear puts his hand on White Horse's shoulder. "I know this is not easy for you. You have lost many. I feel your pain and anguish. Please do not let your pride get in the way of allowing me to help you. You will need hides, food, and horses. I can help you with all of this."

"It will be appreciated," White Horse thanks.

"Have you decided where you are going next?"

"Yes, I am moving to the sacred hills that many talk about."

"I think that is wise, and I, too, am moving my people to join in the hills."

White Horse glances over at Koawa. "Koawa's Running Water is among our dead."

Running Bear is obviously distraught, as Koawa is a cousin to him and knew Running Water very well.

"My Prairie Dawn was with her when she died," he concludes.

"You are very fortunate both did not perish," Running Bear adds. White Horse agrees. Running Bear looks over at Koawa under the tree.

"He has much healing to do. I will talk to him. He will listen." With that said, Running Bear leaves.

Our journey begins to our new home. Running Bear and his warriors will join us for part of the way. They will turn back at the end of today, only to join us again in the hills this fall. It will take us nearly three days to get there on foot. Only the warriors will ride to protect us, as there are not enough horses to go around for everyone.

Koawa has made his own travois where his Running Water lies, tucked tightly in a blanket. He looks so sad and remains to himself. Many of the warriors have tried to talk to him to cheer him up, to help him cope with his loss, but to no avail. Clearly, Koawa has taken her death to a remarkable toll on anyone else. It just breaks my heart to see him this way.

White Horse is stopping us frequently for water and rest. He does not want to chance any sickness due to the long walk and is being extra careful. Some of our breaks are very short, lasting only a few minutes, while others are longer, allowing us to sit down and rest.

The end of the first day arrives, and we set up a temporary camp just before sunset. Several warriors leave to hunt, while others remain behind to protect us. As I am helping Wings of a Bird in building a fire, I oversee Songbird fussing over Yellow

Hawk, not allowing him to do much and showering him with affection. Yellow Hawk is starting to get annoyed and spats off in his tongue to leave him be.

"Poor Songbird," I say in their tongue.

"I don't understand how she can put up with that man," Wings of a Bird says. "He always looks like he has his bow up his backside."

As mean as it was, I chuckled. Songbird walks away to come to join us when I see Minoke by all the other horses, kneeling down beside a travois that holds the body of Qutoh. She has been there since our arrival. I dust off my hands and make my way over to her.

"If you wish to be alone," I tell her in her tongue, "I will leave." She obviously has been crying, as I hear her sniff. She shakes her head no. In her hand, she is holding Qutoh's necklace. "Qutoh and I," she begins, "wanted to have children." I put my hand on her shoulder. "The great spirits never allowed it to happen. This is all I have left of his memory."

"I can remember when my father died," I tell her. "I had nothing as well, except for the necklace he gave me with the key on it. I have since lost the necklace, but I have not lost his memory."

"It is so hard," she cries, "to be strong."

"I know, but you must be for Qutoh, otherwise he died for nothing."

Minoke faintly grins, tilting her head into my shoulder. I put my arm around her. Our tender moment is brought to an abrupt end when Red Hawk rides up on his horse, stopping in front of us. Minoke is quick to leave as Red Hawk is a man that Qutoh warned her to stay away from. Can't say I blame him. He is ruthless. I, too, am intimidated by him.

He looks down at me from high on his horse, the deer he just killed lying across his lap. Around his neck, he is holding my par fleche that I lost at the attack. He removes my precious bag from around his neck and tosses it to me. I am taken aback a little, as it hits me in the chest. I look up at him, confused as to why he would care if I ever saw it again. In his native tongue, I thank him. He never flinches, does not even blink. Gives no knowledge that he even heard me. His eyes are completely swallowed in mine. He pushes the dead deer off his horse, allowing it to fall to the ground. He watches me briefly as I grab one of its legs and start to drag it. He then rides off as quickly as he came. Songbird grabs a leg, and together we drag the deer into camp.

The evening comes to a close. Bellies are full of deer meat and wild berries. I sit on the ground next to the other women, away from the men. I glanced over to see Koawa off by himself next to Running Water's body. I so much want to talk to him. To share with him what his wife told me, but White Horse has asked me to wait, to allow Koawa some time to be by himself. So, I have.

A sudden rush of warriors on horses comes into view. All eyes are on them and what they have behind them. I see both Running Bear and White Horse come to their feet. Quickly, the reason for the rush is seen. Blue Thunder and Night Owl just stole some horses. Neither Chief seems to mind; in fact, White Horse is rather pleased. At one time in my life, I would have totally been against this, and to a point, I still am, but out here, it is all about survival. We need these horses to survive. There is not one man here tonight who has not stolen at least one horse or another in their life, and that would include my dear beloved husband. The talk now around the campfire is how Blue Thunder got away with it.

We are in the middle of day two of our travels. My feet are so sore and my back aches, but no complaint is heard out of me, as I know I am not alone. During one of our longer breaks, I find a remote place where both little Morning Dove and I can void. We do our business, clean our hands in the stream, and head back to the others.

"Feel better, sunshine?" I tease.

She shakes her head yes. Smiling, I rub the top of her head. She is so sweet and cute, reminds me so much of her mother. Hand in hand we walk, making our way to the others. I suddenly stopped when I heard chanting. It is very faint, and if the wind hadn't hit just right, I probably would not have heard it. I motion for Morning Dove to be very quiet as I move in closer for a better look. The chanting became louder, deeper, and more pronounced. I push a few branches to the side to step further in. I abruptly stop when I see the back of Koawa's head. I look down to where he is kneeling, to find Running Water unwrapped from her blanket. He is chanting over her body. I quickly turn Morning Dove away. She does not need to see her mother in this state. I whisper down to her to go with the others and tell her Chief where I am. She quickly obeys.

I know the culture well enough to realize Koawa is performing a ceremony over Running Water. I watch for a few more minutes until his chanting stops, and then make my way in. I see Koawa wipe his eyes as he folds the blanket back over his wife. Koawa has a temper, which is known to snap out of the blue. I have to choose my words carefully, as I know he is ready to burst. I slowly make my way down to him. I stop when he notices me. His look is vague, so full of emptiness inside. He sniffs again and then looks away.

"You know better than to disturb someone during a ritual," he barks.

I stepped on the last rock and sat down beside him.

"I loved her too," I whisper.

Koawa looks down and starts to tie the blanket around her body.

"You were there when she died?" he finally asks.

"Yes, I was," I answer.

"Did she suffer?"

"No," I answer. I hear him sniff again.

"I want to know what happened," he says.

"I had just helped White Fawn up the last hill when I saw Running Water down below. She had been shot in the leg and was having trouble getting up the hill. She yelled at me to save myself, but I refused to leave her, so I ran back down the hill to help her. That is when she was shot in the back. I lay beside her until the Blue Coats left." He just nods his head as he sniffs. With his voice lowered, he then begins his story.

"We were together when the Blue Coats arrived. She hurried to get dressed. I left before her. When I was riding off, I saw Morning Dove leave our lodge. I just assumed she was right behind her." He shakes his head in disbelief. "I should have waited for her."

"Koawa, you had no choice. You cannot blame yourself."

"I do," he says, "It was my duty to protect her and our daughter." He lowers his head on his hands.

"How can I even look at Morning Dove? How do I tell her that her mother is gone?"

It is now my turn to tell him the conversation that I had with his wife just a few months back.

"Koawa, when the Cheyennes were attacked at Sand Creek, Running Water and I made a promise to each other." He looks up at me as I continue. "We both knew that the war was only going to get worse. We started talking about our husbands and our children. We made a promise to each other that if one of us should die before the other, the survivor was to help the other one out." Koawa just looked at me. "We both knew that if something happened to either one of us that our husbands would not handle it well. We promised that we would support and be there for each other. To keep our husbands alive at any cost, to help them fight for what is ours. I plan on keeping that promise for her." I reach inside my dress, pulling out a necklace. Koawa immediately recognizes it.

"That is hers," he says.

"Yes," I say. "She gave it to me to wear. I am to keep it around me until Morning Dove is old enough to wear it. That way, she has something of her mother's. If you look at her, she is wearing mine." Koawa just nods.

"She told me about the necklace, but never shared the reason why?"

"She loved you, Koawa, so much. If you are to join the Dog Soldiers, she would be so disappointed in you. You know I am right." By the nod of his head, he knew I was correct. "I beg you, Koawa, for her sake. Don't do it. Please don't do it."

"The Blue Coats will pay for killing my Running Water."

"She knew you would think that, as I know White Horse would, but she begged me not to let you do anything that would get you killed."

"I am not afraid to die."

"I know you are not, that is why she wants you to fight for what you believe in and not what cannot be changed. Koawa, joining the Dog Soldiers will not bring Running Water back. Morning Dove needs you. You are all she has left. Think of White Horse, think of the band. You're leaving, what is it solving? She is still gone. Don't let her death be meaningless. Stay here and fight alongside the people who care about you, who love you, who care about what happens to you. Koawa, you are a strong warrior who does not fall easily. What protection are you giving us if you leave? We need you, Koawa. Next to White Horse and my boys, you are all I have. Please don't leave us."

Something clicked. I am not sure if it was me or Running Water speaking to him from beyond, but I see his eyes watering up, and he is trying so hard not to cry.

"You know Koawa, being a warrior does not mean you are immune to feelings," I faintly grin," I promise, I won't tell anyone. Let it out."

I think Koawa was at his end and had it cooped up inside for far too long. He is a very stubborn and strong-willed man. More so than White Horse, but even the best of the warriors needs to cry. He lowers his head as I put my arm around him. He turns his head in and cries on my shoulder. As I console him, I see White Horse not far behind me. I am unsure how long he has been there or what he has heard. He walks over to the other side of Koawa and comes down, placing his hand on his shoulder. I hear him faintly speak his tongue. Koawa then turns his head away from me and leans into White Horse. I watch in silence as Koawa lets it all out in White Horse's arms.

Chapter Four

The Sacred Hills

I lay next to White Horse under a tree, just off from the rest. My aching feet and back are enjoying the relaxation, as another night comes to a close. Running Bear and his warriors have left us to do the rest of the journey ourselves. He will follow us into the hills come this fall. He has left us a few hides to start us out. White Horse is greatly appreciated and vows to return the favor as soon as possible.

Koawa seems to be doing better. He has put Running Water's body on the back of his travois, which is where she has remained during our travel. This in itself is an improvement, as he is no longer carrying her around. He is also finally eating something and is spending some well-deserved time with his daughter. Tonight, I have been told that it is our last night traveling, as tomorrow we will finally be home. I am filled with great anticipation, as is everyone else. This has been a long and exhausting trip, and everyone is eager to see it end. Many warriors are stationed several miles behind and in front of us as we sleep, guarding us for the night, as we rest in the unknown land.

The morning arrives, and great news finally comes our way. Blue Thunder spots a huge herd of buffalo not far away. We are all ecstatic, and after watching them roam, preparations are made for a hunt. This is, in my opinion, the most thrilling event imaginable. Kikimo is anxious about wanting to go along for the hunt. White Horse only agrees to allow Kikimo to watch it done from a safe distance, as this is extremely dangerous, and White Horse is reluctant to allow his son to participate in such a dangerous hunt until he is properly trained. For now, it will have to do, and Kikimo will have to watch on the sidelines along with Eagle Scout.

Killing a buffalo is a young man's skill, but every buffalo that can be killed is going to be needed, so every warrior will participate, even Flying Hawk, the oldest of them all, will join in the hunt. Kikimo and Eagle Scout watch in awe from on top of a hill, as one by one the buffalo fall to their death by Lakota arrows. The amazing skill of the warriors maneuvering their horses alongside the stampeding herd as their shots are made is breathtaking. In a matter of a few minutes, several dozen buffalo have fallen to their death. When the slaughtering is completed, it is then that the women step in and help prepare the buffalo for travel. This is truly the most disgusting thing I have ever done.

But I am aware of how important it is, and therefore I do not complain and do it.

Kikimo is watching his father as he removes the buffalo's liver. He then takes a big bite of it. This is something White Horse does routinely. However, today he shares it with his son. At first, Kikimo is not pleased with the taste, but if he wants to be a warrior like his father and uncle, he has to take a big bite. I personally think they are both nuts.

"You want a bite?" White Horse teases, putting it in front of my face.

"Get that nasty thing away," I say, pushing it away.

I hear him chuckle as the blood from the liver rolls down his chin. I continue skinning as Kikimo, who is just as ornery as his father, leans down pretending to give me a kiss with his bloody lips. Both men laugh when I slap Kikimo's hand away. Men, I chuckle, they are impossible. When all the buffalo are cleaned and ready for travel, much celebration is heard with the success of the hunt. Today's hunt will help us return to the way it was before our attack; however, many more kills will be necessary to survive the cold winter ahead.

White Horse keeps true to his word, and soon we find the place where we will call home. I quickly understand why this land is called sacred; it is everything you can imagine and then some. I am surrounded by rolling hills, deep canyons, cascading streams full of fish, clear, clean blue lakes, towering granite peaks, and pine and spruce trees that are mixed with patches of prairie grass that blanket the land. This place is truly amazing.

With a group effort from the women, lodges are put up with what we already have. With White Horse being Chief, he, of course, gets the best hides, not necessarily fair, but no one seems to care, as our lodge is the first to go up. In just a few hours, our camp is starting to look like home. With our bellies full and our backs aching, everyone sits around a campfire and enjoys our first night in our new home.

Tomorrow is being dedicated as a day of mourning. Tomorrow, all of our loved ones who died during the attack will be laid to rest. This is surely going to be an emotional time for everyone, especially for Koawa. The bright morning sun shines down on the scaffolds stationed not too far from camp. The burial ritual is underway. White Horse, who is on his horse, pays his respect individually to each and every scaffold. Many tears are again shed, and many faces are drawn low. Minoke places Qutoh's spear into the ground next to his scaffold. I gently squeeze her shoulder as I hear her sob. Wings of a Bird is consoled by her brother as she holds her children close to her side. White Fawn and White Horse stay close to Koawa, as he says his final goodbye to Running Water. We watch him as he cuts a strand of his hair and places it on top of her. He then kisses his fingers, and speaking his tongue for only her to hear, he places his fingers on her blanket. I then watched him ride to my side. I hand him Morning Dove, whom he places in front of him. He looks at me as I touch his leg and give him my regards. He squeezes my hand before riding off. It is a very hard and emotional day for all. Moving on is going to be difficult, as so much has been lost. But being a Lakota means moving on, and I am certain that although we never will forget the ones we lost, we will find the strength among us to carry on and rebuild our band.

Three months pass. The place where we call home has moved once, and we are now settled in our spring home. The fighting has not ceased, and more Indian lives around the nation are being lost. Retaliation is everywhere, as tension grows high with the Blue Coats.

White Horse has his scouts everywhere throughout, at all times of the day, keeping careful watch of the Blue Coats as their wagon trains get closer in. A few skirmishes have been made on the wagons, as White Horse attempts to back them away. He has involved himself in every raid alongside his warriors. He is home less often, sleeps little, and fights more. This, of course, has me worried, but what can I do? So far, we have lost no warriors but had a little scare when Blue Thunder was hit during a recent battle. Fortunately, it did not hit anything major, and he is expected to make a full recovery and will be out fighting again very soon.

White Fawn has fallen ill. Flying Hawk has tried everything he can think of and every herb he is familiar with, but still, she is not getting any better. I spend a great deal of my time taking care of her. Over the years, I have grown to love her and admire her strength and courage. She is a woman of great pride and self-esteem. Everything I know today, I have learned from her. She has made me the woman that I am. I think very highly of her and her knowledge. I only wish I had half of her strength and wisdom. I kneel beside her pelt, holding a tea that she needs to drink.

"Mother White Fawn," I say. "I have brought you more tea," I tell her in her tongue.

"Do not fuss over me," she says.

"It is no fuss." I leaned my head forward to help her drink. When I had finished helping her take a few sips, I lay her back down, tucking the blanket further into her. She reaches for my hand.

"You have been good to our people," she says in her tongue. "Good for my son. Your skin is white, but your soul is Lakota." I faintly grin. "You have made our people proud."

"Mother White Fawn, you need to rest. You are weak." She is adamant that she finish speaking. "Many white women do not have your strength, your fire. You are a warrior." I again grin.

"Promise me you will never lose to that strength. Fight for what you believe in." I can tell she is getting weak and growing very tired.

"Mother, you must rest," I tell her.

"Promise me, Prairie Dawn."

"I promise," I tell her as I tuck her in more. "Now, please rest. I will be back shortly to check on you."

I close the flap behind me and make my way to our lodge when I see riders coming in. I quickly realized that they are of a different Lakota band. I watch White Horse greet them and disappear into the smoke lodge, where they will remain for several hours.

Feeding White Fawn some soup, the flap opens, and White Horse comes in. I stop feeding her when he comes down on his knees, taking her hand into his. I watch him lift it up to his lips and gently kiss it.

"How are you feeling, mother?" he asks.

"I am feeling better," she says in a raspy voice.

Both White Horse and I know she is lying. He kisses her hand again.

"Rest, mother," he then comes to his feet. I follow him out, closing the flap behind me.

"I am really worried for her, White Horse."

"Her time is near," he says.

"No, White Horse, you must not think that way."

"Sweetheart, mother has had a good life. She has seen much. The spirits will call her soon." He kisses my cheek. "Now I must call council, for there is much to discuss."

I normally do not involve myself in White Horse's business. That is strictly for the men, but I can see the concern on his face. "Is everything alright?" I ask him.

"Those men were from the big Chief's camp. I have been asked if I would be interested in a treaty signing with the Blue Coats."

"And are you?" I wonder.

"I agreed to meet with the Chief and discuss it."

"This is good news, right?"

"It is a start," he comments.

"I know how much bringing peace to us is important to you."

"Yes, it is all lately that I can think of."

"When are you leaving?" I ask.

"Tomorrow morning. I will meet with the council now to discuss the details."

This is huge. Our head Chief of the entire nation is a very powerful and respected man, whom White Horse idolizes. He has known him for years. I personally have only met him once at Sundance. I am certain White Horse is not only honored to be asked, but very eager to oblige.

As the night dwindles away, White Horse has made all arrangements and will be leaving first thing in the morning. The estimated round trip is to take him roughly ten days. He has selected a few of his warriors to ride along with him. Koawa is not among them. White Horse knows he is upset, but states he needs him here to look after everyone. Reluctantly, Koawa agrees. With the night at its end, White Horse and I unite on our pelt. This will be our last night together for over a week. Before he turns in for the night, he goes to his mother's lodge to tell her that he is leaving. He comes down on his knees, taking her hands into his.

"My son," she weakly smiles.

"I have come to tell you that I will be leaving tomorrow for our head chief's camp to discuss matters of peace," he says.

"I am so proud of you," she says. "You are a good leader."

"Koawa will remain here."

"I think that is wise," she says.

When White Horse hears her cough and struggle for air, he knows she has had enough. He kisses her hand and gets ready to stand. White Fawn takes her frail hand and squeezes his.

"What is it, mother?" he asks.

"Prairie Dawn," she coughs again.

"She has turned in for the night with the rest," he answers her.

"Must keep her near," she coughs.

White Horse sees that his mother is in need of rest. He kisses her hand.

"Mother, you need your rest," he says.

She struggles to move as she grabs White Horse's hand, preventing him from standing up.

"No," she rasps.

White Horse leans over her as she motions for him to come closer to her lips. She faintly whispers. "Listen, my son," she continues. "My spirits have spoken to me. Keep Prairie Dawn close, for if not, great danger awaits her."

White Horse respects his mother, but knows she is gravely ill, and her mind is slipping away. He kisses her forehead before standing up, ignoring the warning.

At first light, White Horse and his select few are ready to leave. I walk up to his side and hand him his pouch of pemmican, dry meat, to take along with him on his trip. I watch him tie it around his waist.

"Be careful," I whisper to him.

He faintly grins my way as his warriors jump on their horses. This is the first time since we have been married that we have ever been apart for this long. I am going to miss him so much.

"You too," he smiles.

I watch him as he jumps on his horse. He looks down at me, remembering his mother's words.

"Carrie," he huskily says. I look up at him. He hesitates for a moment and decides to say nothing. "Give the boys a hug for me."

"I will," I smile.

I watch him as he orders his men in his tongue that it is time to leave. I stand there and watch until he is only a speck in the dust. Lord be with him, I pray to myself, as I walk back to our lodge.

Chapter Five

A Mother's Warning

Two days pass. I am making my way to White Fawn's tepee to give her some soup when I am stopped by Kikimo just outside the flap.

"Ma," he smiles slightly winded from his run to catch up to me." May I leave the camp?"

"What for?" I ask him.

"Eagle Scout and Yellow Hawk tracked a buck yesterday but lost its tracks just a few miles from here, and I want to go find them and get the buck for myself," he states.

"Kikimo," I huff. "I am disappointed in you. The land is full of bucks; you don't need to steal someone else's."

"I know, ma, and I wouldn't, but Eagle Scout has already found two, and that is only because Yellow Hawk was helping him."

"Do I sense a little bit of jealousy in your voice?" I tease.

"I'm not jealous," he retorts. "I am just tired of Eagle Scout smearing my face in it every time he gets something better than me."

"Why don't you ask Blue Thunder or Koawa to help you?"

"I did ask Blue Thunder. He picked up the track this morning, but he has to leave and patrol and can't help me anymore, and Koawa is busy." He puts his hands together and begs me, Please.

"I don't know, son. I don't like the idea of you out there alone. Just yesterday, our men tracked Blue Coats not far from here."

"I know, Blue Thunder told me, but he also said they led them the other direction, and they are keeping an eye on them to make sure they don't turn around. I will be fine, Ma. Our warriors are all around. Besides, I have father's instincts, remember?" he grins.

"Alright," I sigh. "But I want you back well before sundown, and you stay within the patrol area, understand?" Kikimo smiles and gives me a kiss on my cheek.

"Thanks, ma." he then runs off.

I sit beside an ailing White Fawn. She is growing weaker by the day, and I am very concerned about her. Flying Hawk has given up on any hope for a recovery and is only attempting to make her comfortable. Koawa has come in several times to sit with her, but makes his visits short as he has been busy keeping the camp running.

Today, as I am feeding her one of her meals, she pushes the spoon away and motions for me to come to her ear.

"White Horse," she whispers.

"Mother White Fawn, he is not here," I answer her.

"White Horse," she repeats. She is clearly getting agitated.

"Mother, he has left to go to the head Chief's camp, remember?"

She shook her head. "No, must see." She tries to get up.

"Mother, no!" I say, gently pushing her down.

"Must see White Horse."

She is so agitated and uncooperative that I leave to go get Koawa. He comes down to his mother's ear, softly speaking in his tongue.

"What is the matter, mother?" he asks.

"White Horse," she raspy says.

"Mother, he is not here. What do you need?"

"Danger." Koawa just looks puzzled at his mother.

"Mother, is White Horse in danger?" he finally asks.

Koawa is aware of the special gift his mother has in receiving visions, which is very rare for a woman to have as many as she does. She quickly shakes her head no.

"No, must tell him, must make him understand."

"Mother, why don't you tell me, and I will tell him."

"No," she argues.

Koawa is getting nowhere, and clearly, the more he speaks to her, the more agitated she becomes. He leans in and kisses her forehead before rising to his feet. The concern is clearly written on Koawa's face. I follow him as we leave her lodge.

"Why does she want to see White Horse?" I ask him after we are outside.

"I believe she had a vision. She is nearing her time and wants to see him before she dies."

"Are you going to go get him?" I ask.

"White Horse is too far ahead, and I cannot allow any more warriors to leave unnecessarily, as we are already down. I am certain he is alright," he reassures.

"Her mind is no good anymore; she is talking nonsense." Koawa gets ready to leave. I grab his arm.

"You have to do something. Clearly, she wants to see White Horse before she dies," I beg.

"I am afraid there is nothing I can do."

"So, you are just going to let her die?"

"It is not up to me to decide when our spirits come to take her."

"Koawa, she wants to see her son before she dies. I do not think that is unrealistic."

"White Horse was aware that she may not be here when he returned. That is why I stayed, so at least one of her sons is here when she dies."

"Isn't there something Flying Hawk can give her to keep her here until he returns?" I ask.

"We do not stop our forefathers from taking what is theirs," he argues. "Her circle is nearly completed. There is nothing I can do." He turns to walk away.

"Then I will do it myself," I snap.

He stops abruptly in his tracks and looks at me. "And just what are you planning on doing?" he arrogantly asks.

"I know of a medicine that Roger would use on his patients when they grew ill like this. It is not a cure, but it may give her enough strength until White Horse returns." Koawa is slightly amused.

"And how are you planning on getting this white man's medicine?"

"It is not hard to find. I am sure a soldier train would have it." Koawa instantly grows angry. "You need your head examined! Did your brother have medicine for that, too?" he snaps.

He starts walking away and then turns around. "You are not a God. You will stop thinking such foolishness." He then turns and walks away.

I chase after him. "I can do it, Koawa. I am one of them."

"You are not one of them!" he roars. "Was it not you who was there when they came into our camp and killed my Running Water? Do you think they would not have thought twice about killing you?"

"I can look less Indian. I still have one of my old dresses from all those years ago. All I have to do…"

"No!" he yells, "I forbid it."

He comes straight up to my face, looking me square in the eyes. Koawa is not a man you want to anger. Chiefs' wife or no Chiefs' wife. Koawa demands respect.

"You will not leave this camp. If you try, I will personally tie you to your lodge until your husband returns. Now go make yourself useful, woman."

I glare at him as he walks away. The nerve of him, that arrogant, pompous fool. I will show him. I rush back to my lodge and pull out the old dress from the parfleche that is behind our pelt. I am determined to help White Fawn and grant her wish to see White Horse before she dies. I will get that medicine, and there is no way anyone is going to stop me.

"Vision," I huff. "She isn't having any vision. If she wants to see her son one last time before she passes on, then she will. I may not be able to cure her, but I will be able to get her to hold on for a few more days, and I don't care what Koawa says. I will go."

I spend a great deal of time inside the lodge repairing my old dress that has seen better days over the years and thinking about my escape route. I begin to think out loud as I stitch. I was hesitating to allow Kikimo to leave the camp alone because Blue Coats were spotted not too far from here. He told me that Blue Thunder led them in the opposite direction, and our warriors are keeping an eye on them should they turn around. This could cause me a problem if they spot me as they are scouting. I will just have to ride most of the way at night when our warriors are less likely to be scouting, and I have less opportunity of being seen.

"Yes," I assured myself. "This will work."

I hold the dress up to me. "I knew one day this would come in handy," I say to myself. Making the last few adjustments, my dress is done. No sooner had I finished when the flap opened and Blue Thunder walked in. This is a complete surprise to me, as Blue Thunder is not usually this rude about barging into people's lodges. I can see the anger in his eyes, again a rare sight for a man who is usually very passive.

I have known Blue Thunder for years, and he and I are pretty close. Next to Koawa, Blue Thunder is really the only other warrior that I communicate with on a routine basis. I consider him part of my immediate family, as he and White Horse are very close.

"Koawa, tell Blue Thunder your crazy plan," he says. "I come to tell you I agree with Koawa. If you leave, I will hunt you down. I will drag you by your sunny hair back to your lodge, where I will tie you up. I will give you no food and no protection. There you will remain until my Chief gets home." He towers over me. "Do you understand Blue Thunder?"

What can I say? I am in total amazement. I have never seen this side of Blue Thunder. I nearly dropped my teeth as I saw the warrior side of him emerge.

"Yes," I tell him. "I understand."

"Good," he says. "And just to be certain that you do not get a crazy thought on leaving again, I will be watching your lodge outside." With that said, he leaves. I deeply sigh, as now I must come up with another idea for my escape.

Koawa returns to check in on his mother. He helps her with her drink and puts her head back down to rest. She motions for him to come down to her mouth. He comes down to her head as she attempts to speak.

"Prairie Dawn," she says.

"She is in her lodge, mother. Do you wish for me to get her?"

"Keep her close," she whispers.

Koawa is somewhat confused by his mother's words. Did Prairie Dawn tell her about her ridiculous plan before he had put a stop to it? He assumes that is the reason.

"Mother, Prairie Dawn is not going anywhere. You need to rest now."

The words of Koawa, that Prairie Dawn is not going anywhere, seem to calm her down enough to rest.

The sun falls on the sacred land. Kikimo returns frustrated as he has lost the tracks of his prized buck. Koawa reminds him of the patience that is needed in order to make the proper kill. He advises his nephew to get another buck as the woods are full of them, but Kikimo, like his father, is being stubborn and wants that one. Koawa just chuckles to himself as he listens to Kikimo whine.

I walk into White Fawn's lodge to check on her before she turns in for the night.

"Prairie Dawn," she rasps. "Yes, Mother, it is me. I have come to give you more soup and tuck you in for the night."

"No," she pushes the soup away.

"Are you cold, Mother White Fawn? I can make your fire warmer."

"No." She motions for me to come down to her. "White Horse," she whispers.

"Mother, please save your strength. I do not want you to worry about White Horse, I will take care of everything."

I sit back up to tuck her in. She reaches for my hand.

"No, Prairie Dawn, danger!"

Odd comment, I think. Had Koawa told her about my plan? Clearly, it is understandable why she would feel it was dangerous, but I have everything under control. This time tomorrow, I will have the medicine for White Fawn to make her stronger. She will be here when White Horse returns, and all will be well. Koawa and Blue Thunder will be angry with me, but in the long run, they will see I was right.

"Mother, it is late," I say, tucking the blanket in over her. "Sleep. I will be back tomorrow to check on you." I see a faint smile on her face as I come to my feet.

White Horse is lying under the stars as his warriors sleep. It has been a very long day of riding, and his body is tired, but sleep is the furthest thing from his mind. He hears his mother's warning over and over again. "Keep Prairie Dawn close," she said, "or she will be in great danger." His mother is a woman of great supernatural power. Perhaps he was too quick to shrug it off. But what danger could she be talking about? He knows Prairie Dawn is aware of the dangers of leaving the safety of the camp unprotected. There are bears, cougars, wolves, and, if nothing else, Blue Coats. He knows how to get around the men in blue. How to track their ponies, but she has never been shown. She is so vulnerable and so naive. Then there is Koawa, perhaps he should have told him what their mother said. No, he thinks. He trusts Koawa; he knows he will watch his Prairie Dawn and keep her safe. He needs to sleep, to clear his mind. Tomorrow he will be at the Head Chief's camp. There will be a talk about peace for the next two days. Talk about a treaty. He needs a clear mind. He needs to be refreshed. He closes his eyes and puts his trust in Koawa.

The camp is in slumber. It is time for my escape. As the children sleep, I put on my old dress and an old pair of shoes that I traded for years back. I pin up my hair and make my escape under the flap, at the back of the lodge. Over the years, I have been taught how to run on the prairie grass without being heard, keeping light on my feet. I put it to the test and came to the side of the lodge. I see Blue Thunder holding true to his word, sitting in front of a fire with his back turned next to our lodge. I creep by and make my way to the corral. I get to my horse, who is eager to greet me. I rub his nose to keep him quiet and jump on. Riding through the camp is rather easy; getting past White Horse's sentries will be another story. It is a good thing that there is only a quarter moon out tonight.

Since our latest attack, White Horse has put his sentries around the clock to watch for any danger. They are usually our young men who haven't yet mastered the skill of being a good warrior. The sentries are rotated and will vary depending on who White Horse assigns. Tonight, my luck, one of our best warriors is guarding, and that is Night Owl. He got his name for a reason. He has eyes like an owl at night and is very light on his feet.

I am soon near the first lookout. I get off my horse to make it easier to slip by. I see Night Owl standing high on top of a ridge. Fortunately for me, he is looking away from the camp and not at it. Many years ago, when White Horse and I first got married, he taught me how to sneak past an enemy. I put his lessons to the test, coming into darkness. I press up against the rocks, keep it low, get light on my feet, and sneak by. One down and one more to go.

I continue walking with my horse behind me, remaining as quiet as I can be. The last and final sentry is only a few yards away. I am passing the clearing by the lake, when I hear some movement near the water. I stop dead in my tracks and look around. I quickly realize that our second sentry, Yellow Hawk, is preoccupied with drinking water, making my escape easy. Some guard, you are, I think to myself as I go by.

I am in partial darkness, as I gallop across the land. It is going to take me all night and part of the morning to reach the soldier wagons. I am going to ride nonstop or until my horse needs to rest. I have one more obstacle that I am going to have to face rather soon. I will be riding within a few miles of Running Bear's camp before the sun is up. He, too, has sentries. I only hope I can get by.

I have no fear of Running Bear. I have known him and his warriors for many years. Red Hawk is the one I worry about. He is to Running Bear what Koawa is to White Horse, with the exception that Koawa has a heart. Red Hawk has a nasty disposition, especially with women. He is mean, heartless, and rude, a perfect example of what a white man would call a savage. He is known for many ruthless killings on wagons and homesteads. He is a thief and a liar, and on a number of occasions has kidnapped white women for ransom.

69

Although White Horse swears, he has never violated these women, I for one would not put it past him. This could be a challenge if he is on duty. I bring my horse down to a slow trot when I come near Running Bear's camp. I glance around for any sign of any sentries above on the ridges or in the trees, but it is so dark that I can hardly see a thing. I can feel the hair standing up on the back of my neck. I have a feeling I am being watched.

Chapter Six

The Medicine

Creeping through the night, a chill goes up my spine. I indeed know I am being watched. Somewhere amongst these trees is at least one Lakota warrior. I know I do not look like the Prairie Dawn they are familiar with, so I put my Lakota language to use.

"Hello," I call out. I keep creeping by on my horse, looking around into complete darkness.

"I know you are out there. It's Prairie Dawn, Chief White Horse's wife."

Whoever is out there is playing with me. Making me sweat, getting their thrills on watching my heart pound in my throat. I ride further into a clearing, and that is when I see the one named Red Hawk, and he is not alone. He comes up right in front of me. The other warriors are on each side of me. I am completely surrounded. He speaks his tongue.

"You say you are a Chief's wife. A one named Prairie Dawn. But your dress is that of an ugly white woman. Red Hawk demands to know why?"

Demands, I think. No one demands of me. Calm down, Carrie, I tell myself, don't make him angry if you wish to get by.

"White Fawn has fallen gravely ill. I am on my way to get medicine from the soldier wagon that will help her."

"White man medicine?" he questions. "The Chief never mentioned to me that his wife had the mind of a pig," he smarts off. The other warriors laugh.

"I resent that. I have not come here to be insulted by a fool," I snap.

Red Hawk's eyes immediately turn cold. Oh crap. I thought. Now he is pissed. He comes closer to me with eyes of ice that penetrate my soul.

"You are lucky you are who you are, or I would drop you in your spot. Now go back from where you came from, before I change my mind."

"I have come too far to turn around now. I will pass," I boldly say.

"You dare tell Red Hawk what you will do," he roars.

"You so much as lay one finger on me and the Chief will have your neck," I snap.

"Does your mighty Chief know you are here disrespecting me?"

"You are aware that my husband is at the head of the Chief's village, so do not insult the intelligence that you clearly do not have. Now I must leave, and I would kindly appreciate it if you would get out of my way." Red Hawk holds his ground.

"You left like a coward in the night. Koawa will be very angry with you when you arrive. Your mighty Chief will punish you severely. I cannot wait to see this. I will let you go." Oh, he is so infuriating. I huff. He steps aside, allowing me to advance.

The morning sun rises on our Lakota camp. Koawa enters his mother's lodge, only to discover she passed on during the night. He lowers his head down and kisses her forehead.

"Rest in peace, mother," he mumbles and then raises her blanket over her head. He then leaves to go find Flying Hawk. Kikimo runs up to his uncle. He is unaware of his grandmother's passing. Koawa places his hand on Kikimo's shoulder.

"Your grandmother passed on last night," he tells him. Kikimo is upset, but was prepared before his father left that her time was getting near and that her death should not upset him, as her circle of life had been completed.

"I am saddened by this, but father told me before he left that soon her spirits would take her away, that she had fulfilled her life, and I should not be sad, but rejoice as grandmother brought great things to us."

"Your father is correct," Koawa assures. "Still, I am sorry, Koawa." He then gives his uncle a hug.

"Everything will be alright. It is your mother who I am afraid will not take it well," Koawa says.

"That is why I have come for you. Mother did not sleep on her pelt last night."

"Are you sure?" Koawa asks.

"Yes, she was there when my brother Little Foot and I went to sleep, but when we woke up this morning, she was gone. I have looked everywhere for her." Just then, Blue Thunder walks up.

"Prairie Dawn's pony is gone. Our Chief taught her well, as she slipped by all of us."

Koawa is certain he knows where she is. He tells Kikimo to tell Flying Hawk about his grandmother. He then hurries and goes into his brother's lodge. He finds Prairie Dawn's parfleche, in which she keeps her personal belongings behind their pelt. His insides burn when he sees her prairie dress gone. He gathers Blue Thunder and a few of his men, and they quickly leave the camp to make their way to the soldier's wagon.

The wagon is within my sight. I am quickly spotted when I get to the top of the hill. Several men rise to their feet and look my way as I trot down.

"It is a woman," one soldier says. I bring my horse to a slow walk as I make my way to the wagons. I notice just to the right of me two soldiers wringing some clothes out at the watering hole. They both stop when they see me coming in. I briefly glance their way out of the corner of my eye. I notice one as being quite large around the waist with little hair. He really stuck out as a misfit from the others. The man standing alongside him just gave me the creeps. He has bright red hair like fire, and the evilest smirk. They both appear, by their uniforms, to be the lowest in rank. I am met by a man who is very well-groomed and appears to be in charge. I bring my horse to a stop in front of him.

"Hello there, madam," he greets me. I glance around at all the eyes on me.

"Hello there. I need to speak to the gentleman in charge," I say.

"Well, I guess that would be me," he smiles.

"Is there a doctor here?" I ask.

Another man comes up alongside him. "This gentleman here claims to be a doctor."

I look over at him. He is an older man in need of a shave and doesn't look like a man who would know anything about medicine. He is quite large in size, but not overweight. He is very well built, like a lumberjack with a grizzly effect. A total and complete opposite of what my brother Roger would look like even in his worst attire.

"Please, if you would, doctor. My husband has fallen very ill with a fever. I have been trying on my own to lower it to no avail. I am wondering if you perhaps would have any Quinine."

"Quinine, you say?"

"Yes, I would not need much," I reassure, "just a few days' worth."

A skeptical look appears across his face as he looks me over.

"And where is your husband right now?" he asks.

"At our homestead, not far from here," I answer.

"Well, I will tell you what," he begins. "I will be more than happy to see your husband and give him any medical attention he may need. Just let me get my bag."

"No!" I snap as the doctor turns around. "I mean, I would not want to be a bother, and besides, my husband is a doctor himself. You see, we just moved here from out East, and he has yet to find any work, and he has fallen ill, and we have no medicine. We were just hoping you would be able to help us out."

"I see. Well, in that case, I will get you some. Let me get it out of the wagon."

I sigh in relief when I see the doctor and the other man go out of my view behind the wagon. I sit there on my horse, as I try to remain calm. I feel many eyes on me. I hear snickers and crude jesters behind me from the watering hole. My skin begins to crawl as I become very uneasy, especially with the two behind me. Suddenly, I see the red-haired man from the watering hole stand more erect. He is now really starting to stare me down. I am becoming extremely uneasy. I see the doctor and the other man with the bottle of medicine. Thank you, Jesus, I mumble to myself. The doctor walks over to my horse. He gets ready to hand me the medicine.

"Tell your husband I can help him find work when he is better. I know of a town that is in need of a good doctor."

"I will tell him," I say to him. "Perhaps you have heard of it," he states as he looks deeply up into my eyes. "Willow Creek."

I grow very still upon hearing the name Willow Creek. I look down at the doctor, trying to remember if I have seen him before. Did he somehow know Roger from my past? How ironic is it to mention Willow Creek, which is nearly a month's ride from here? This is making me extremely nervous, and I desperately want to get out of here.

"I have never heard of it," I tell him.

"Umm, I see. It is a nice town. I doctored there for several years after their doctor moved away." He stops for a moment, as if he is thinking. "What was his name again? Oh yes, Doctor Briggs, a Doctor Roger Briggs."

I momentarily am frozen stiff. He knows Roger, but to me, he is a complete stranger. How does he know Roger? What did Roger tell him about me? I am so nervous and need to get out of here, fast.

"Thank you for the medicine, doctor. I must be leaving." I reach for the medicine. He holds on to the bottle, looking up at me.

"What did you say your husband's name is again?" he asks.

"I didn't." I then take the medicine out of his hand and turn my horse around. I kick his ribs, and without looking back, I get the hell out of there.

"What do you make of it?" the doctor says to the Lieutenant, as they watch me ride over the hill.

"I believe she is lying. There are no homesteads around here for at least a hundred miles."

"I know that she is lying. I have seen her face before," the doctor says.

"Who is she?" he asks.

Before the doctor could respond, the red-haired man approached his Lieutenant.

"Sir," he salutes.

"At ease. Hatford."

"That woman, Lieutenant," he excitedly says. "I believe she is the one that Willis and I saw when we attacked that Sioux village, sir."

"I thought you told me you killed them both."

"Yes, sir, but her hair, Sir. I remember her hair. And that horse she was riding, the blanket, sir, is Indian."

"Lieutenant," the doctor says. "When I worked in Willow Creek, the doctor I replaced told me about a sister that he had. He had a picture of her on his mantle. He said she got married and moved away. After he left, I was told another story, of a Chief taking a white bride that lived there."

"Yes, I do recall that now. A bunch of renegade Indians attacked a small town. A Sioux Chief came to their rescue and took off with the preacher's daughter for payment."

"Did you see the way she looked at me when I mentioned Willow Creek and the doctor?"

"Yes, I did."

"And that necklace she had tucked under her blouse. That was Indian."

"Yes, I did notice that."

"You don't suppose that could be her, do you?" the doctor asks.

"It would be a shame if she were. She definitely was nice on the eyes."

They both snicker as they agree.

"What do you want to do?" The doctor asks.

"Hatford!"

"Yes, sir?" he salutes.

"I want you to take Willis with you and follow her. Only see where she goes."

"Yes, sir, right away, sir."

Chapter Seven

Deep within the Canyon Walls

I have never been more relieved than when I entered the canyon walls. I am certain that somehow, that doctor knew me from my past. But how? To me, he was a complete stranger. He said that he practiced in Willow Creek for several years, perhaps the connection is with Roger, and not me? What did Roger tell him? It does not matter now. I am a good distance away from the wagon and feel safe. I made it. I accomplished what I set out to do. By nightfall, I will be home. Shortly, I will be at the Running Bears camp. I cannot wait to rub this medicine in Red Hawk's face.

I bring my horse for a casual walk. No need to hurry. The canyon will keep me safe. I need to let my horse rest as we still have a little way to go. I am sure my absence is known to Koawa by now, and he is probably on his way to Running Bear's camp. I am certain I am going to hear it from both Koawa and Blue Thunder, and probably be reprimanded severely when I return. But I do not care, this is so worth it.

Koawa and his warriors arrive at his cousin's camp. He is greeted by Red Hawk and several other warriors on horseback. He asks if any of them saw Prairie Dawn pass by? Red Hawk tells him that he saw her last night. A brief conversation ends with Red Hawk agreeing to take a few of his men and helping Koawa bring Prairie Dawn home. Red Hawk, for one, cannot wait to see Koawa physically drag her home by her golden hair. He finds Prairie Dawn disrespectful and feels that Chief White Horse is blinded by her beauty, but nonetheless, he is a Chief, so he will do it.

My horse and I stop briefly to take a drink of water in a stream before continuing on our way. Getting my fill of the water, I come back up on my horse as he continues to drink. I lean down to pet his neck.

"You are such a good boy," I tell him. Just then, I hear a rustle in the trees. I look up, and it stops. This canyon is filled with wildlife, both small and large. Fortunately, I have a knife tucked in my boot in the event one gets close enough to me to use it. Assuming that is what it is, I look away. My horse starts to graze on some low-line trees.

"Sorry, boy," I say. "You are going to have to wait until later to eat. We need to head home."

I grab my reins just as I hear the rustle again, this time it is closer. I look up across the stream. "Oh my God!" I gasp, as I see before me just a few yards away, the two men from the soldiers' wagons that gave me the creeps. The red-haired man has the most God awful smirk, and the heavy-set man's eyes are big with lust.

"Run, boy, run!" I tell my horse, and off we run down a rocky ravine.

My horse is picking his way down as quickly as he can. The soldiers are fast on my tail. The loose gravel tosses stones behind me, as my horse's hooves kick up the dust. The once secluded canyon walls open up, as the chase is on. My horse is snorting to keep up with the run. I am gaining speed and pulling ahead. Just then, a shot echoes through the canyon walls, and my horse is hit. He whinnies in pain and rears up. Before I can control him, I am roped and dragged to the ground. Another shot is heard, and my horse is killed. I fight to get up by pulling the rope free, only to be dragged a few more feet. I lay stunned, bleeding from my lip, when both soldiers stop in front of me and get off. I roll over to catch my breath and make a run for it, crawling up the side of the ravine. My leg is pulled by the red-haired man, sliding me down to the rocks below. He tosses me over onto my back. He has eyes of ice glaring down at me. The man with the big waist gives out a cackle.

"You got her, Frank. You got her!"

"Shut up!" he roars. The one named Frank holds me down by my wrist.

"Where are they?" he roars. "Where are the Indians?"

"I don't know what you are talking about?" I lied.

"You lie," he yells, smacking me hard across the face.

The hatred is heavy in his eyes; he firmly grasps me by my arms and shakes me.

"I know you are one of them, now where are they!" I glare up at him and spit in his eye. He wipes it clean and smacks me again.

"You filthy whore, you filthy Indian whore!" he yells, as I receive another hard smack across the face.

"I will make you talk," he barks.

I then see him free his hand and begin unbuckling his belt. It is then that I start to panic. I start to wrestle to wiggle free. He pushes my wrist further into the ground. It is then that I kick him in the groin. He releases his grip, bellowing in pain, allowing me time to free myself and reach for my knife. I know I cannot kill him, as his rage has given him remarkable strength. I have to do the next best thing. I have to injure him enough so I can get away. I am a strong runner and know I can outrun the man with the large waist. I only have to injure the one named Frank and get his gun. I make my move and lunge my knife at his stomach. The knife makes contact with his skin. I see him go to the ground, grabbing his side. I reach for his gun in the holster and nearly have it out when he grabs my arm and tosses me to the ground.

"You bitch!" he yells, as he tries to come to his feet. Forget the gun, Carrie, I tell myself. Get up and run. I stumble to my feet and make a run. The man with the big waist starts to run after me. I am soon amazed at how fast his fat little body can run. I clearly underestimate him and am soon captured. He has me around my waist. I look up at him with horror. The amount of lust in his eyes is nauseating. His yellow and missing front teeth shining down at me gave me chills.

"I like them feisty," he cackles.

I kick him in the knee as hard as I can and break free. I run away again down the ravine. I am brought to the ground when I am hit from behind with a belt. I let out a piercing cry in pain. I stagger to my feet, terrified of being killed. I attempt to run again. Another smack is heard opening up my skin and stopping me dead in my tracks. I am now in tears as I try to catch my breath. Another smack is given. In between my screams, I receive two more. I lay there paralyzed, with tears rolling down my face. The one named Frank then kicks me in my ribs. I feel several of my ribs crack as I cry in agony with pain. Blood is seeping from his stomach. I see him hold onto his side as he catches his breath. He glares down at me.

"This is the last time I will ask you. Where are they?" he yells.

My eyes are full of pain. I am at his mercy at his feet, but I am not giving in. They will have to kill me before I reveal our location.

"Go to hell," I spat. This brings him a tremendous amount of rage. I watch him remove his glove as he kicks me again in the side. I attempt to catch my breath.

"Get the rope," he tells the other man. He comes down on his knees and shoves the glove in my mouth. I try to kick him off and let out a muffled scream. The other man returns with the rope.

"What are you going to do with her, Frank?" he asks.

"Scar the bitch up enough that they will not want her either," he said, taking the rope from his friend. He then takes my wrists, tying them together. The man with the big waist lets out this hideous, most gruesome laugh. I watch the man, through tearful eyes, come to his feet. Then, full of frenzy, he pulls me by my tied hands to the edge of the ravine. I feel every stone and every rock cut up the back of my legs. He then kicks me over and repeats the same again, this time cutting up the front of my legs. I then watched him remove his shirt. I hear the man with the big waist stutter.

"She sure is purty," he says, as he gets his excitement from my dress being torn from my shoulders in the scuffle.

"I wanna do her man. I wanna do her," he cackles.

My eyes grow huge. I start to squirm to break free. The man named Frank straddles me, holding me down by my wrist. I hear that hideous laugh again.

"Do it!" I hear Frank yell at him. I start to wrestle, trying to break free, when I am punched on the side of the head, knocking me out cold.

I come to with heavy jerking from below. I feel the man inside me pushing hard with his arousal. I hear his heavy breathing from his enjoyment. I know I am in a bad way, and the damage is already being done. I turn my head to the side, seeing the man named Frank looking down at me. The blood from where I stabbed him is at a slow trickle. He seems in very little pain and unfazed by any of it. My eyes are blank; the tears are heavy. I am pleading for him to stop. I know it is not going to happen anytime soon, when I notice he is naked from the waist down. His manhood is fully erect. Is he waiting for his turn? Was he going in again? I am not sure, as I do not know how long I have been out. I look away to receive yet another punch.

I awake again just as Frank comes to his feet. The man with the big waist inserts again. I watch Frank pull on his pants and light a smoke. He speaks not a word, as he looks down at me and smirks. I turn away, there is nothing I can do. I want them to stop. I want them to go away. My insides burn, my thighs ache. I close my eyes and pray. I think of White Horse, the love of my life. The man I would give my life for. I think back on our lives, on our love. I think of my children. Will I ever see them again? Will I ever see the Lakotas again? Is this my last memory before I die? A blue shirt is tied around my head, and I am dragged across the rocky ravine again and tossed into some bushes. It is there that I am left to die.

"Let's go, Horace," Frank says.

"Back to camp?" he asks. "Hell no! We can't go back. Not after what we just did."

"Do you think she is dead?"

"Yeah, this time we got her, she ain't breathing."

"Do you think she is the same one?"

"Don't reckon I have seen too many Indians with that color hair. Yeah, she is the same one. This time we killed her."

"They are going to be looking for her," Horace says in a panic.

"When they see her all scarred, they will not want her anymore. They will leave her here to die. Let's go."

Koawa and Red Hawk bring their warriors to a stop when they spot tracks. They have already been to the soldier wagons, as far as they can safely go. They see her tracks going in and leaving. They became alarmed when they spotted heavier tracks from shod horses following behind her. Koawa squats down, touching the grass.

"They went into the canyon," he tells Red Hawk.

"That canyon goes on for many miles," Red Hawk tells him.

"There are many ways to get to the end."

"She would take the direct route. I am certain of it."

"If she took the direct route, we would have run into her on our way here."

Koawa knows Red Hawk is right. The extra two horses that they have tracked
are what is making both men very nervous.

"We will go back the way of the canyon," Koawa says. "Then we will split. We will meet at the end." Red Hawk agrees and takes his men and splits when they get to the canyon's entrance.

The sun is nearing the time to fall. The men have been looking for hours. They know their time is running out, as soon the sky will be in darkness, hindering any efforts of finding anything. His warriors have been looking everywhere. He is growing more and more concerned. He hears his mother's words over and over again, warning him to keep Prairie Dawn close. Why didn't he listen to her? Why didn't he see this coming? He knew what she was planning. Why was he so quick to think she would listen? She never listens; he huffs to himself. Why should this time be any different? He has to find her. He has to find her fast. As he continues searching, he begins to think about how, over the years, he has grown quite fond of Prairie Dawn. More so than he should. He thinks his Running Water was correct in her thinking that he is falling in love with Prairie Dawn. He, of course, denies this. She belongs to his brother, and he will respect that, but he must admit he sure likes her fire, her spunk, her strength, but most of all her heart. Oh, where is she? he asks himself, agitated. Why has she not surfaced? Is she hurt? Did she fall off the edge and lie somewhere below? He is so concerned. He has to find her. Just then, he spots some tracks leading down into the ravine. He calls his warriors, and they turn their horses and head down to the rocky incline.

Red Hawk is ready to give up and meet Koawa at the other end. He then spots something off in the distance. It is a swarm of vultures circling above. He points to them as his other warriors look out.

"To have that many, whatever is dead is fresh," he says.

"That is down at the bottom of the ravine," one warrior says. "We'd better check it out." The men turn their horses around and head down the steep ravine to the ground below.

Chapter Eight

The Cave

Dusk hits the walls of the canyon. Red Hawk and his warriors make their way down to the ravine. The vultures fly off when they hear the Lakota horses approaching. A chill came over Red Hawk when he saw Prairie Dawn's horse lying dead on the rocky ground. He is quickly off his horse, as are the rest of the warriors. He ran up to the horse to see that it had been recently shot. He looks around. He knows something really bad has happened. He spreads his warriors out to search the ravine. An exhaustive search is done. One of his warriors finds the bottle of Quinine on the ground, along with a piece of Prairie Dawn's dress. He runs over to Red Hawk to show him what he found.

"Spread around, she has to be close," he says in his tongue.

I awoke from unconsciousness to hear movement in the gravel. Oh, dear God, I cry to myself, they have come back for more. My hands are still tied. My mouth is still gagged. I lie in complete darkness as the shirt is still over my head. Every ounce of my body is screaming in pain. I then hear voices. A language I know. It is Lakota. Oh God, they are here. They have found me. I hear the voice of Red Hawk. Oh, how happy I am to hear that arrogant voice. I try to scream, but it is only a muffled sound. I started to cry out of frustration. I cannot think I am in so much pain. I am exhausted, but I have to do something. I have to make them look in the bushes. But how? My hands are bound. My mouth is gagged. As much as it hurts, I have to get up. I have to move. I bellow in pain as I try to crawl out. I feel around with my feet to find the opening of the bushes. When I find it, I try to back out. The pain is excruciating. Darkness starts to fill my head as I feel as if I am going to pass out. I feel the breeze on my legs. I am out. I am out of the bushes. I lay my head down on the rocky ground, exhausted, and I weep. It is not long after that when I hear a voice say, Over here. I hear rustling of the rocks. I feel someone come down in front of me. The shirt is removed, and I am rolled over. I look up with tearful eyes to Red Hawk. I cry with joy. He speaks his tongue as he removes his knife and unties my hands.

"What have they done to you?" he says.

My gag is removed from my mouth. It is then that I whimper. Red Hawk lifts up my head as he orders one of his warriors to get the blanket off his horse. He looks down at me.

"You are going to be alright, Prairie Dawn. You are safe now."

The blanket arrives. Red Hawk lays it across his knees and then lifts me up. I scream out in pain when his hands touch my welts, when he moves my legs, or when I try to breathe.

"I know you hurt Prairie Dawn. Red Hawk will make you better," he softly says, as he wraps the blanket around me. I hear him tell one of the warriors to ride ahead and find Koawa. He then comes to his feet with me in his arms. Just the pain of him lifting me up is so intense that I pass out, limp in his arms. Darkness lies thick across the great canyon. I faintly awake in a whimper, curled up on Red Hawk's lap on top of his horse. He hears me whimper in pain.

"We are almost their Prairie Dawn," he says in his tongue. "Stay with me."

I am not sure exactly how badly I am hurt, but I know by his tone of voice and how awful I feel, it must be really bad. I feel him bring his horse to a stop and speak his tongue.

"We found her in the ravine about a mile from here. They tied her up, gagged her so she couldn't scream, and covered her face so she couldn't see. They killed her pony. She has been beaten and who knows what else." I then feel a hand touch my hair with another voice. It is Koawa.

"Prairie Dawn," he says. All I can do is whimper.

"She is weak," Red Hawk says.

"Your camp is closer," Koawa states.

"She does not have the strength to take the long ride. I know of a cave not far from here. We can take her there."

On arrival at the cave, Blue Thunder runs inside to make sure it is all clear of wildlife. Koawa jumps off his horse and comes to Red Hawk's side. I am then passed down into Koawa's arms, where I lie limp. Getting word that the cave is clear, Koawa carries me into the cave and lays me down. A fire is being started by Blue Thunder. Red Hawk comes down beside Koawa. Koawa begins to examine all the damage that has been done. He is quickly angered.

"I cannot understand why anyone would do this to their own kind?"

"She is not one of them," Red Hawk says. "She is one of us."

"Revenge will be severe. I promise you that," Koawa growls.

"Yes, my hands as well will have their blood on them." Blue Thunder chimes in. He then squats down in front of me, taking my hand.

"Prairie Dawn, this is why Blue Thunder was so harsh on keeping you in the safety of the camp, for it is very dangerous out here for a woman. I could not help you stay safe, but I will find the ones who hurt you." I faintly whimper at him. "Prairie Dawn, I need to know who did this to you?"

"Blue Coats," I mumble.

There is instant rage throughout as the cave is filled with many warriors, but Blue Thunder remains calm.

"How many?"

"Two."

"I will start tracking them, and I promise you, I will find them."

He then stands up to leave. Koawa looks up at him, the rage in his eyes and the depth of his voice are clearly seen. Koawa is furious.

"Take two of the best and go. When you find them, you bring them to me, alive." Blue Thunder nods his head and leaves.

"What about Chief White Horse?" Red Hawk asks. "He would want to be here. We ride hard and through the night, we can be there by this time tomorrow."

Koawa thinks for a moment. "No. He has already been gone for three days. Let him finish his journey."

"And Prairie Dawn?" Red Hawk wonders.

"I will do whatever I have to do. White Horse cannot lose her."

The men work together as a team to keep me alive. Red Hawk finds some water and tears off a piece of my dress to use as a cloth. He then starts to clean off my face and arms. I flinch with every dab he applies. He speaks very softly to me, saying many kind words, not at all like the monster I have always thought he was. I cannot respond, although I try, as every time I open my mouth, all I can do is whimper in pain or cry. When he finishes what he has to do, he takes my hand and squeezes it. I then watch him stand up and go to the fire. Koawa then comes down beside me as Red Hawk returns with a burning stick.

"Let me see, sweetheart," Koawa says, as he gently rolls me over on my stomach, being careful of my broken ribs. I then feel him finish ripping the back of my dress, revealing my welts. Instant rage fills him again. He has to take a moment to calm himself down before tending to the bleeding. Red Hawk comes down in front of me, cupping my hands into his. I see him hand the stick to Koawa. I know what is coming.

"I am sorry, sweet one," I hear Koawa say. "This is going to hurt."

And Koawa is not bluffing. I feel the hot flame on my back. I hear the sizzle, as it clots the blood that is seeping from the welts. I scream in agony. Red Hawk squeezes my hand, holding me down as I arch to get up. One by one, Koawa applies the burning flame to my welts, cleaning them and clotting the blood. The amount of pain is excruciating. Red Hawk keeps talking to me, keeping me focused, keeping me awake. I look up at him with tearful, painful eyes. His eyes look deep into mine, revealing the kindness, the caring, the concern, something I never thought he was capable of having. I bury my head into his palms as Koawa continues on the last few welts. I fight the pain. I fight my tears. I feel Red Hawk lower his head near mine. He speaks his tongue.

"You can squeeze my hand. Red Hawk will not mind."

Don't mind if I do, I thought to myself. I squeeze his hand harder as Koawa continues. When Koawa finishes, I am carefully rolled back over.

"I need to get this dress off of you," Koawa softly says. "It is all torn and dirty. I do not want it on your wounds, because they are clean."

I understand and am too weak and too exhausted to care. He keeps the blanket over me to hide what he can, to give me what privacy he thinks I deserve. He remains a gentleman by making Red Hawk turn around, as he cuts the remainder of what is left of my dress off of me. He turns his head as he adjusts the blanket when certain parts become exposed. He binds my broken ribs and cleans the rest of my body. He then tucks the blanket around me and lays me back down. He then removes my moccasins as Red Hawk is allowed to turn around.

Red Hawk notices under all her scratches and bruises the curviness of her legs, the smallness of her feet, and the cute, delicate toes at the end. He now understands why the Chief had fallen for her. He has seen her strength, her fire, her will to survive, how tenacious she really is, and all of this within a beautiful body and face. Yes, now he understands, and he vows quietly to himself that from this day forward, he will protect Prairie Dawn. He will make these men pay. He will make all the Blue Coats pay for what they did to her. He does not care if she was disrespectful to him in the past. All this is forgotten. He lives for the moment, and in this moment, all he cares about is her and his revenge. He watches as Koawa comes down alongside her and lifts her head.

"I need you to drink this," he tells her.

Red Hawk watches him as he raises the drink to her swollen lips. He watches as she drinks it slowly down. He sees how delicate and fragile she is. He watches Koawa as he slowly puts her head down and tucks her in. He watches as he speaks softly to her, wishing he understood. He then sees Koawa stand up and Prairie Dawn close her eyes. The men are sitting at the entrance of the cave as I sleep. Koawa's mind is racing.

He is uncertain if he has made the right decision on not getting White Horse. He is certain that White Horse will not take this well and is concerned about what will become of him if his Prairie Dawn dies. He then thinks of the Blue Coats and what they have done to Prairie Dawn. He worries for her when the reality sinks in. He knows she is strong-willed and a good fighter, but is she strong enough to deal with this? He is certain she has been raped and can only hope that the baby tea that he made and gave her is strong enough, as he is certain she was raped more than once. His insides are on fire with rage as he thinks about what these two soldiers did to a defenseless woman who went to them for help. He thinks of his brother, who has left to find peace with the people who have destroyed his wife. How hard is he going to take this, as his Prairie Dawn is his life? He holds himself responsible and wishes he had kept a closer eye on her. He knew her plan and knew how tenacious she could be when her mind was made up.

"She is strong," Red Hawk says to him, breaking the silence.

"I know, but I worry if she is strong enough." "She will be alright. She is a fighter," Red Hawk says.

"Yes, she is, and by the looks of it, she fought hard."

"The Chief's revenge will be severe," Red Hawk says.

"This is what concerns me."

"I do not understand."

"When White Horse finds out about this, he will declare his own war. No one will be safe from his wrath. Prairie Dawn will not like this. She will fight him to the bone."

"She is only one woman. What harm can she do?" Koawa snickers.

"You don't know Prairie Dawn like I do," he says.

Just then, both men hear a blood-curdling scream. They both jump to their feet and run inside. Koawa slides down in front of Prairie Dawn. He finds her in a cold sweat, trembling and in tears.

"It's alright, sweet one," he softly says, as he starts to stroke her cheek.

"Don't let them hurt me," I sob.

"Shh," he says, as he consoles. "No one will hurt you, sweet one, I will not allow it."

"I'm so scared."

"I know, sweet one. I know you are, but I promise you, no one will ever hurt you again."

Koawa's reassurance that I am alright is holding little toll on me as I can clearly see my attacker's faces in my mind. I smell their scents. I can hear their voices. I am absolutely terrified that they will return. Koawa starts to wipe my tears away, when I look down at my trembling hands.

"Oh my God!" I cry out. What has happened to me is finally sinking in. Hysteria and fear overpower me.

"Oh my God." I look at my blue marks around my wrist. I remember being tied and held down. I feel my face and the swelling around my eyes and lips. I remember being punched. I look at my arms and legs, remembering being dragged. I feel the stinging on my back and remember being whipped. I look up at Koawa with vacant eyes full of tears. I remember being raped.

"Oh my God!" I whimper.

Koawa has nothing to say. He knows that I remember. He slides himself in closer and opens his arms, pulling me into his embrace. I then sob uncontrollably as Red Hawk watches on.

Later that evening, I lay next to the fire feeling numb and depressed. Koawa squats down holding a cup of tea.

"You need to drink this," he says.

He helps me with the painful task of sitting up, and I take the cup. He sits down beside me as I take a sip. I see Red Hawk sitting against the cave wall, across the fire, watching on. I feel Koawa's eyes upon me.

"What am I going to tell White Horse?" I mumble to him.

"The truth," he answers. I shake my head no.

"I can't tell him."

"Prairie Dawn," he cautions. "You have to tell him."

"No!" I argue by snapping my head in his direction. "It would ruin everything if I told him."

"What do you mean?" he asks.

"Any chance of peace with the Blue Coats will be gone. White Horse will want revenge, and he will not stop with only the two who hurt me. Everyone in his path will suffer."

"Do you blame him?" he asks.

"Koawa, all White Horse has been wanting for the last several years is for the fighting to stop with the Blue Coats, and now we have the chance for some peace. If he knows what happened to me, any chance of peace for us is gone." I shake my head.

"I cannot live with myself if I am the one to blame for more lives to be shed."

I hear Red Hawk chime in, asking Koawa what is wrong. Koawa tells him my concern. Red Hawk just shakes his head. I hear him mumble in his tongue.

"She is not to blame," he says.

"Yes, I am," I argue. " I was the one who chose to defy your orders and leave. You tried to warn me."

I look over at Red Hawk. "You even tried to warn me, but my pigheadedness didn't listen." Red Hawk looks at Koawa, wanting translation.

"Tell him," I say to Koawa. "Tell him it is my fault that he is here." Koawa just looks at me. "Tell him!" I say adamantly.

Although I am capable of doing it myself, Koawa takes the honors and translates. Red Hawk looks over at me from across the fire. He then speaks his tongue.

"Red Hawk is here because he wants to be here. It is true because you did not listen, you took the chance of getting hurt, but you went on with a good heart. They were the ones who ripped it out. The fault lies with them, not with you." I just lowered my head.

"Prairie Dawn," Koawa begins. "White Horse must be told. It is not fair that he does not know what his wife has endured."

"Koawa."

"No!" he snaps. "He will be told," he says. "I will not keep this from him."

The fear of knowing White Horse is going to be told and there is nothing I can do about it, put me into tears. I look up at Koawa with tearful, pleading eyes.

"Let me tell him, please. He will take it better coming from me." Koawa nods.

"Alright, I will allow it," he says.

"Thank you," I say. Just then, I remembered the medicine. "The medicine," I gasp. "We must get it to White Fawn." Koawa grabs onto my shoulder and gives it a squeeze. I see the sadness in his eyes. I am too late. White Fawn is already gone. I lean my head back and lie back down.

"No." I wail. She is gone. Everything I have been through. All I have endured, I did it for White Horse, I did it for her. The thought of failure to both my husband and White Fawn is breaking my heart. I pull the blanket over my head and cry. I feel Koawa's hand on my shoulder, consoling me as I weep.

Chapter Nine

The Lie

The first light of a new day is among us. Red Hawk left before the sun was up to help Blue Thunder and the others in locating the two soldiers. Koawa remained by Prairie Dawn's side all through the night. She tossed and turned and woke up several times, crying. There is little he can do to ease her pain that is so deep inside. How he wishes his brother were here. He feels that it is White Horse's arms that she really needs and not his. He debated all night on whether to get him, but still feels he made the right choice. He will just continue to comfort her the best he can until White Horse gets home. He leaves for a nearby stream to catch their breakfast, as Prairie Dawn sleeps. His brother weighs heavily on his mind. He starts to think back to the first time his brother laid eyes on Prairie Dawn, how she literally swept him off his feet. He knows his love is strong for her, and he would be devastated if something happened to her.

This is why Koawa is concerned about what he will do when he finds out how his wife was violated. He is certain that his revenge will be catastrophic, which he completely understands, but Koawa is more concerned about what the emotional stress will do to him. He knows White Horse is strong when it comes to his Prairie Dawn. He is certain he will take this hard. He thinks about the warriors that are out there right now tracking the area for the soldiers. He wants to join them, but feels he cannot leave her alone and has to trust that Blue Thunder and Red Hawk will find them. His thoughts are interrupted when he hears her scream. He quickly grabs his few fish and runs inside.

"Koawa!" she yells. He races down to her side.

"I am right here," he says.

"I woke, and you both were gone. I got scared."

"Red Hawk left to join Blue Thunder. I went to get us some food." He holds up the fish. I sigh, feeling stupid, as I know Koawa would never leave me. I watch him as he goes to the fire to prepare our fish. I painfully sit up, tossing the lower part of the blanket off my legs. I get the first good look at all the damage that has been done. The deep cuts and scratches, the beginning of the hideous black and blue bruises, and the swelling of my legs and thighs.

"I look awful," I mumble.

"No," he smiles, "you look pretty."

My stomach does a circle. My insides go numb. I cover myself back up. "That is what one of the soldiers said." He looks up from the fire. "He said she sure is purty." I can feel my eyes well up. "I always took great pride when White Horse told me that I was beautiful. But now I am ugly. What if he does not want me anymore?"

"Hey," Koawa says, "I do not want to hear you talk like that. White Horse loves you. It is clearly seen all over his face every time he talks about you. Every time you walk past him. He is a man who still desires you. Trust me, Carrie, I know the man better than you."

"That was before. I am different now."

"How are you different?" he questions.

"I have been with someone else," I answer.

Koawa comes to his feet and kneels down beside me. "Let us get one thing straight," he tells me. "Those men took it from you. You did not give it to them at will." My tears are harder.

"Why Koawa? Why did they do it?"

He brings me into his embrace. "I don't know, sweet one. I don't know."

White Horse sits around a full council next to the man he has idolized for years. He feels honored to be here. He feels proud to share the pipe with this magnificent man, but his mind is elsewhere. He had a dream last night that put the chills down his spine. He feels his mother's departure and is certain she has passed on, but that is not what is weighing on his mind. He saw his Prairie Dawn lying in a pit of fire, screaming for help. In his dream, he reached out for her, and she got further away. He has had enough dreams in his life to know what he saw was a vision. He fears that his Prairie Dawn is in danger. His thoughts are interrupted when a warrior speaks his name. White Horse, feeling sheepish, smiles and pays more attention.

After spending another day in the cave, Koawa feels that I am strong enough for the ride home. He lifts me up on his horse, placing another blanket around my shoulders. He then jumps on himself. He curls me onto his lap and we head home. The trip will take us all day. With the threat of Blue Coats still high and Koawa being my only protection, he decides to take the longer way home, over the hills, until he reaches Running Bear's camp, where our warriors will meet up with us and take us home. Koawa is easing across the plains at a slow walk, as any sudden jerk will give me breathtaking pain. He stops several times to bring me water and carry me to a bush, so I can relieve myself. He turns his back while I do my business. The pain in squatting and voiding is nauseating. I am so uncomfortable that it is making me sick. He hears me moaning as I am voiding.

"Are you alright?" he asks. "This just hurts," I whine.

"I know, honey. I know it hurts," he consoles.

How he wishes he could do more to help her pain. How completely helpless he feels at this particular moment. His heart is going out to her.

"I'm done," I tell him after a few seconds of finishing up. He steps into the bushes, gently lifting me up, and carries me to his horse and jumps on.

"I'm cold," I whine. Koawa curls me further onto his lap, pulling more of the blanket over me.

"If this is too uncomfortable for you, we can stay at Running Bear's camp for the night. We will be there very soon," he suggests.

"I thought he went with White Horse?"

"He did. He left Red Hawk in charge, and I know he will not mind. So, if you feel you need to stop, I will." I am feeling very sore and growing incredibly tired, but the fewer people who know what happened to me, the better.

"No," I say, "just take me home."

I curl the blanket more over my shoulders. "I feel like sleeping."

"Sleep, sweet one," he says. "I will wake you when we get there."

White Horse is invited into the smoke house by the head Chief. A smoke is exchanged between them before the great Chief speaks.

"I feel some apprehension in your voice, my friend. Your mind is heavy?" White Horse faintly smiles. "You are a wise man, my Chief. I am afraid my mind has been off."

"Tell me what makes your heart so hollow."

"I feel my mother has moved on into the other world. This brings me great sadness, but that is not what bothers me. I had a vision about my Prairie Dawn. I fear she is in danger." The Chief nods in understanding of White Horse's concern.

"What did you see?" he asks.

"I see her lying in a fire pit, screaming for help. I reach for her, and she sinks further into the pit."

The great Chief nods. "You need to go to her," he says. "For what you saw is not good." White Horse agrees with the great Chief, but knows he has a big responsibility that lies outside of his Prairie Dawn. He cannot allow himself to be so selfish at a time when the people he is responsible for and loves need him the most.

"I have a responsibility to our people. We have suffered many losses. I owe it to them to bring peace," White Horse says.

"Soon we will sign the white man's paper, bringing peace to our nation again. Until then, my friend, you need to go to your wife." White Horse just nods his head. How he admires this man.

"My cousin Chief Running Bear will remain, but I believe you are correct and I must go." The great Chief reaches for the pipe. "Let's smoke," he says, and the pipe is passed again.

I awoke to the noise of many horses alongside us. I can only assume that we have made it to our scouts, and they have come to ride with us the remainder of the way home. I do not want my face to be seen, so I lower it into Koawa's chest and put the blanket over my head.

"Prairie Dawn, do not hide yourself," Koawa says.

"I do not want anyone to see me or know what happened."

"Next to Blue Thunder, they don't. I told them you had an accident on your pony. Until our Chief is told the truth, that is what everyone believes."

I know that lying is terribly difficult for Koawa, as he is always extremely honest with the other warriors and White Horse. For him to lie like this means a great deal to me.

"Thank you," I mumble.

"I will lie to them, but I will not lie to White Horse," he snaps. "You will tell him quickly." I gave no argument to Koawa. I know I have no leg to stand on.

White Horse has to be told, but dear Lord, how on earth am I going to do it. After a very long day of travel, we enter the camp. All eyes turn to us.

A small crowd begins to wander our way. Blue Thunder and Night Owl pull ahead, ordering everyone to step back, allowing Koawa a clear path to the lodge. I hear the voice of Minoke with a tug on the blanket, as she is running alongside Koawa's horse. Koawa pushes her hand away.

"I want to see her," she snaps.

"She does not want to be seen. Now leave." She steps back as Koawa forces his way by. I hear her yell out.

"I love you, Prairie Dawn!" Koawa stops in front of the lodge. Flying Hawk quickly comes to his side and starts to remove the blanket from my face.

"Leave her be," Koawa barks.

"If the Chief's wife is hurt, then I need to help her," he argues. Koawa slides off his horse, taking me with him. "She has all the help she needs," he snaps.

Before Flying Hawk can argue any further, Koawa whisks me inside. Blue Thunder and Night Owl quickly keep guard of the flap, allowing no one in. I am gently placed on the pelt that I share with my husband. It is such a relief to finally be able to lie down. I cannot remember being in so much pain, especially through my ribs. Koawa squats down in front of me, pulling the blanket over my legs.

"Carrie," he begins, "I fear you may have broken some ribs. Flying Hawk can help you with this."

"No," I argue. "He takes one look at me and he will realize I did not fall off a horse."

"And you do not think White Horse will see that?" he declares.

"He will not be home for several days. By then, the swelling will go down, and I will be strong enough to walk. I just need to rest." I know I am testing Koawa's patience, but I am adamant. I do not want anyone in here. I am refusing to be seen until the swelling in my face goes down. I am not going to chance anyone going to White Horse before I do. Before he returns, I am determined to be on my feet and among everyone else as normal. Koawa deeply sighs and grants my wish.

White Horse and his warriors are quickly on their way home. He runs his faithful horse, Fly like the Wind, rapidly through the prairie grass. He is so grateful that he decided to choose this horse over the several other ones he has. The eagerness of his horse to please his owner has given White Horse the opportunity to open his horse up and live up to his name.

Koawa leaves, allowing Prairie Dawn to sleep. He orders Night Owl to continue guarding the lodge and gives him strict orders that no one is to go in. That is not saying that no one has tried. Kikimo attempted several times to see his mother, even bringing Little Foot with him, but he is no match for the beast Night Owl. Flying Hawk is insisting on knowing the reason why he cannot go in and is very upset with Koawa for standing his ground. Minoke tries to sweet-talk her way past Night Owl. She is a beautiful woman and very hard to resist, but Night Owl doesn't back down.

"You beast," she snaps as she storms off.

A few hours later, she tries again. Gathering all the women together, they form a pack and corner Night Owl. Night Owl is our meanest warrior. He is a brute who is very loyal to his Chief and the one in charge. If Koawa says no one gets in, then no one gets in. End of story. Soon, the ladies realize this, and an argument brews. Koawa comes up to silence it down.

"Quiet! Prairie Dawn is finally sleeping," he barks.

"We want to see her," Minoke insists.

"She wishes no visitors."

"We are not visiting," she snaps. "We are here to help her. We know better how to tend to her needs as we are women, and you are a warrior."

"There is truth in what you say," Koawa admits. "But I am sorry, this is her wish, not mine."

"What is wrong with her?" Songbird asks.

"She was severely injured, and that is all I will tell you until our Chief arrives. It is then up to him what he tells you."

"Chief White Horse will not be happy that his Prairie Dawn is hurt," Songbird says.

"That is why women, you must not say a word. Prairie Dawn will tell him."

"Lie to our Chief?" Minoke questions.

"You are not lying if you are not asked. You owe it to Prairie Dawn to grant her her wish. Let them have their privacy." The women just look at each other. Finally, Minoke speaks up.

"Prairie Dawn is family, not only to me but to all of us. She was there for us when we lost so much and helped us whenever we needed her. When my Qutoh died, she consoled me. She consoled all of us. For this reason, I will honor her wish." The other women finally agree that Minoke is right and will honor Prairie Dawn her wish

"Thank you, women," Koawa grins. "Please tell her we are here for her when she is ready. And if you need anything, Koawa, please tell me."

"I will," he grins.

The day dwindles down. Koawa returns, bringing me some food.

"How did you sleep?" he asks, putting it down next to me.

"I didn't," I answer.

"Is it the pain?" he asks me.

Unbeknownst to us, Kikimo found a spot outside the back of the lodge to crawl under and hide. He puts his ear near the flap and listens in.

"No, not the physical pain, at least," I say.

Koawa kneels down beside me. "You want to talk about it?" he asks.

I wipe a tear from my eyes. "Those men," I start. "They had so much hatred for me, so much hostility for a human life. They didn't care that I was a woman. All they saw was the Indian I have become." I sniff and dry another tear. "This is why I do not want to tell White Horse the truth, because it scares me about what it will do to us when he finds out it was Blue Coats." Kikimo silently gasped.

"I understand your concern, and you are correct, White Horse's revenge will be brutal, but Carrie, is it really fair not to tell him?"

"I guess not." I sigh deeply. "How am I going to tell him?" I cry. "How can I make him understand why he should not seek his revenge?"

"I know, sweet one, but you have to tell him."

"How?" I wail. "How can I bring this shame on him?"

"Oh Carrie," Koawa says, stroking my cheek. "You have brought no shame to anyone."

"Yes, I have, because of me, more Blue Coats will come."

"No. I will not allow any more Blue Coats to hurt you."

"Not just me, everyone."

"I do not want you to think like that."

"How can I not? How can you be so sure no Blue Coats will ever come here again? I wail. "How can we be so certain that no one else will get hurt because of his need and thirst for revenge? You know as well as I do that White Horse will not settle for peace when he hears what happened to me. How can I live with that? How can I live with the guilt of all the lives that will be destroyed by Army guns because of me and his will to find justice?"

Koawa deeply sighs as he takes me into his arms, allowing me to cry. He knows I am right. All hell is about ready to break loose, and it is because of me. Kikimo had heard enough. He is not really sure what to make out of it all, but one thing he knows for certain is that if Blue Coats are involved, it cannot be good. He gets up on his elbows and begins his crawl backwards out of his hole. He abruptly stops when he backs right into Blue Thunder's leg. He looks up at a very cross Blue Thunder. Blue Thunder is irate at Kikimo for his deception and grabs his leg, pulling him the remainder of the way out, bringing him to his feet.

"You were told not to come!" Blue Thunder roars in his tongue.

"No one will tell me what is wrong with my mother, so I came to find out myself," he boldly says.

"What is going on with your mother is none of your affair. You defy your uncle by going in, for that you will be tied down until you learn to listen."

"You cannot keep me away!" Kikimo yells. "I will tell my father that you threatened harm to his son. He will punish you severely." Blue Thunder huffs.

"You, a mere boy, dare threaten Blue Thunder?"

"You don't scare me," he lies.

"Your uncle is in charge. Go make your threats to him."

Kikimo is bold, but not that bold. He knows better than to be curt with his Uncle Koawa. Koawa, hearing the ruckus, quickly rushes outside so as not to wake Prairie Dawn.

"Silence!" he scolds as he comes around the back of the lodge.

"I caught him with his ear to the hide," Blue Thunder tells. Koawa glares over at Kikimo. "I told you to stay away," he snaps.

"I want to see my mother," he argues.

"I finally got your mother asleep. You will leave her be."

"I overheard you two talking. Mother did not fall off her horse. You lied." Koawa towers over Kikimo to shut him up.

"You snoop around again, and I will personally take my bow and hit it on your backside. Do you understand me?"

Kikimo knows better than to argue any further. He knows his uncle very well and knows he will do it. He glares up at him and runs off. The two warriors watch him leave.

"He wants to be like you," Blue Thunder says.

"He has too much of his father in him to ever be like me."

"That is good," Blue Thunder teases. "I would hate to have another one of you around." When it sinks in what Blue Thunder said, Koawa playfully kicks him in the behind, leaving them both in a chuckle

Chapter Ten

Like Father, Like Son

I sat up from a sound sleep. I see a figure step inside from the flap. I focus on getting a better look.

"White Horse," I greet with open arms. "Darling."

"Hello, Beautiful," he smiles. I smile widely as I watch him come down beside me.

I reach up to give him a hug. That is when I see the face of the red-haired man. I jolt awake with a scream. Koawa is sleeping on Little Foot's pelt. He races to my side, putting me into his arms. I am trembling in fear.

"It is alright, Prairie Dawn. It is alright."

"I saw White Horse. I reached out for him, but it was the soldier's face. They are coming back. He came to get me."

"There is no one here," he whispers.

"I saw them," I cry.

"It was just a dream, sweet one."

"I felt him. I smelled his breath. He was here."

"No, sweet one, he is not here. You were just dreaming."

"I am so scared they will return and hurt me again." I cry.

"Shh, I will not let them hurt you anymore, I promise. No more."

Koawa then scoops me up on his lap to calm me down, consoling my tears and keeping me safe. He will remain here with me curled in beside him until I fall asleep. When morning light appears, Koawa leaves me to sleep and heads down to the lake.

White Horse and his men have been riding all night. They stop briefly for water before heading back on their way. Their home is less than a day away. White Horse is pleased with the time they are making. Soon he will be home to his Prairie Dawn, where he will hold her and put this gnawing feeling that something is wrong behind him. An abrupt stop is made by all three warriors when they get on top of the next hill. Over the horizon, not far away, is a group of soldiers. White Horse sizes them up.

"They were not here when we came," Grey Wolf states.

"They are on the move," White Horse says in his tongue. "My guess is they are going to the fort."

"What do you want to do, Chief?"

White Horse is still a few moments as he thinks and sizes up the situation. There are not enough warriors for them to fight their way through, and none of them is carrying a rifle. He is left with no other choice.

"We are going to have to turn back and go around and come up behind them."

"We cannot run. They may see the dust," Grey Wolf cautions him.

"I have trained you well," White Horse smiles at the young warrior. "We will remain at a walk until we are around them."

It is not what White Horse wants to do, as this will delay his trip home to his Prairie Dawn by almost a whole day. He is gaining little from leaving early, but there is nothing he can do. He is of no help to his wife or people if he is dead, so slow and steady is his only option.

Kikimo opens up his aunt's flap. He takes a peek outside and, seeing that the coast is clear, he makes a mad dash to his lodge. He pushes open the flap to find his mother asleep on her pelt. He does not want to disturb her as she sleeps, but has to see for himself that his mother is alright. He sees her golden hair spread out on the pelt, her face away from him. He steps in closer for a better look when she stirs. He stops short and stands still. He sees her move her leg free from her blanket. He gasps when he sees all her bruises and cuts. It is then that his mother wakes up.

"Ma!" he calls out, rushing down on his knees to her side. He sees part of her face still swollen and black and blue.

"Oh, ma!" he whines.

Although Kikimo has never fallen from a horse, he knows that her injuries are not the result of a horse. He then remembers what he overheard about the Blue Coats and puts two and two together. He immediately became irate. He slams his fist down on the pelt next to his mother.

"These Blue Coats will die a long, painful death for what they did to you."

"Kikimo!" Koawa yells as he steps back into the lodge.

Kikimo comes to his feet. His eyes turn nervous. He cowers, backing up as Koawa steps further in. "You disobeyed me," Koawa growls.

"I just wanted to see my mother," he nervously argues.

"What did I say I was going to do if I caught you snooping here again?"

Kikimo's eyes grow huge. He remembers his uncle's warning about taking his bow across his backside. He remembers when his best friend, Eagle Scout, disobeyed his father, Yellow Hawk, and he received several lashes on his back from his father's bow. He remembers Eagle Scout could not sit for two days. He does not want the same fate as his friend. Kikimo backs up a little more towards the flap.

"You don't scare me," he lies.

Koawa lunges forward in peer intimidation, and Kikimo runs to the flap. Koawa has him trapped. Kikimo squirms to break free.

"Leave him be," I mumble.

Both of them stopped their squirming and looked over at me. Koawa gives Kikimo a blatant stare and releases his grip with a shove. For the moment, Kikimo is safe.

"Come here, son," I say, holding out my hand.

He rushes over to me, putting his hand into mine.

"You are right. I did not fall from my horse," I state.

"Ma, what happened?" I look up at Koawa, who is standing behind Kikimo.

"Your mother ran into some problems when she left to get the medicine." Kikimo glares up at him.

"Stop treating me as a child!" he snaps. "This is not a little problem."

Koawa and I just both grin. I admire Kikimo's tenacity and ability to stand up to his uncle. He is so much like his father in so many ways. Koawa squats down next to him.

"You are right," he says, rubbing the top of his head. "How soon I forget how much you are like your father, much wiser beyond your years." Kikimo grins. "Your mother was a victim of a vicious attack by two Blue Coats on her way back from getting the medicine for your grandmother."

"Is she going to be alright?"

"I am going to be fine, son," I reassure him. Kikimo shakes his head.

"Father is going to be very angry when he hears this."

Angry, I am asking myself? Angry is not the word that I would use to describe White Horse when he hears how his Prairie Dawn was violated. It would be more like barbaric.

"Son," I say. "You have to make me a promise."

"Sure, ma, anything."

"You are not to tell your father what has happened."

"But ma." I held my finger up.

"Kikimo, you must not tell him. I must be the one to do it." He thinks for a moment.

"Alright, ma, I promise," he finally says.

"And son," I continue. "What is said in this lodge stays in this lodge. Am I clear?" I warn.

"Sure, ma. I won't say a word." He then leans in and starts to give me a hug.

"Careful," Koawa cautions. "Watch her ribs."

Kikimo gently wraps his arms around me, and we embrace. Kikimo holds true to his word and keeps his mouth quiet to anyone who asks. The rest of the morning, he is waiting on me hand and foot, bringing me my food, brushing my hair, and keeping everyone away. He is acting just like his father and not backing down to anyone. By the afternoon, I really want to take a bath and get some clothes on. Except for the one time when I had to find a bush and then Koawa carried me, I have not yet been on my feet. Kikimo leaves to go find Koawa to help me up. Koawa is willing to carry me down there, but I insist on walking and do not care how bad it hurts. Kikimo grabs what I will need to bathe and follows Koawa and me down to the lake. Night Owl and Blue Thunder are riding on their horses alongside us, sheltering me in like a box so I am not being seen by the others. I quickly realized I am weaker than I thought, only making it part of the way through camp. Blue Thunder offers to ride me down there, but instead Koawa lifts me up, blanket and all, and carries me the rest of the way to the remote area of the lake. Koawa turns to walk away after putting me down.

"Come on, Kikimo," he says.

"I want to help her," he argues.

"Kikimo, I can manage," I say.

"Ma, you can hardly walk," he argues.

"Son, I am just bathing. I will be fine."

"What if you slip? You cannot swim."

"Koawa will be close if I need help. Now go." I say, as I swish him away with my hands. Kikimo is skeptical and does not want to leave me alone.

"No, I'd better stay," he says.

"Kikimo," Koawa grins. "I understand your need to help your mother, but your mother needs her privacy."

"What for?" he questions. "Your mother has areas that are different than ours."

"So," he argues. "I see Morning Dove all the time when she bathes." Koawa is trying so hard not to laugh.

"That is different. Morning Dove is just a little girl," he finally says through his chuckles.

"How come," he wonders?

Clearly, when White Horse had the talk with his son, certain things were missed. Koawa smiles over at me as he puts his hand on Kikimo's shoulder.

"I will explain it to you while we are waiting in the trees."

Kikimo just shrugs. "Ok."

Amused at what has just transpired, I chuckle to myself as I start to disrobe, grab my bathing supplies, and make my way to the water.

Minoke is certain that something serious is wrong with me. She noticed how I was walking slowly to the lake. My head was lowered and completely covered by the blanket. She thought it odd how Blue Thunder and Night Owl shielded me from being seen. Why so much secrecy for just falling off a horse? she thought. "What are they hiding?" She noticed today when she walked past the corral that my horse is missing. What happened to it? She wonders if it got lost and ran away? Or if something more serious is going on? She has noticed how unusually quiet Koawa has been, and she is certain he is hiding something. But what? Koawa is never short on words and never speaks with a forked tongue. This can only mean that something serious has happened that only her Chief can be aware of.

She remembers the night that she kept Prairie Dawn's children in her lodge. She awoke when she heard Prairie Dawn scream. She was ready to check it out when she saw Koawa through the hides, cradling her as she wept. What had Prairie Dawn so upset? Why is she refusing her help? She remembers back when she first met Prairie Dawn, how much she despised her for taking the Chief away from her. She fought fiercely with her knife. She was amazed that day by her strength and courage. She has since learned to see the good in Prairie Dawn. The kind and loving heart she has for the Sioux. Her strength and courage to stand up to their Chief and warriors, of which very few ever do. She made a promise to Prairie Dawn back when her Qutoh had died. She formed a bond with her. It was Prairie Dawn and her words that helped her move on after his death. She felt compelled to be there for Prairie Dawn, as she was for her.

She quietly makes her way through the trees overlooking the other side of the lake. She sees Koawa and Kikimo under a tree with their backs turned, talking to each other. She finds me bathing as she crouches down. Nothing unusual, she thinks, as she watches me wash my hair. She gazes on for several minutes, watching me finish my bath. She perks up. "What's this?" she wonders. She squints for a better look as she sees my back to her as I am drying off. She gasps when she sees the welts. Slouching down, she silently creeps further in for a closer look. She gasps again. Now she is certain I did not fall from any horse. She is certain I have been beaten. But who would do such a thing? She remembers me being gone from camp for several days, as well as Koawa. Where was she? She then sees me go back into the water. Odd, she thought. She has bathed many times with me, and she has never seen me use such unusual bathing patterns.

She watches me as I violently start to rub my skin with the soap. She does this several times. She notices the distress on my face as I frantically try to get clean. She watches me rinse off and repeat it yet again. Minoke is puzzled at the unusual behavior and is ready to make sure I am alright when she sees me exit the water. Her face became puzzled again when she saw me pick up the knife and go back into the water. She then watches me in horror when I flick the blade of the knife and start scratching myself with it. She runs out from the trees, looking over at Koawa and Kikimo, who are still involved in their discussion.

"Prairie Dawn, stop!" she yells.

The holler aroused Koawa's attention to his feet. He comes clear of the trees just as he sees Minoke dive into the water from the other side of the lake. He looks over at Prairie Dawn and quickly realizes what the commotion is all about. He, too, then runs into the water. Minoke surfaces and is making the short swim to Prairie Dawn. Kikimo runs to the shore to grab a blanket and rushes out into the water to join the others. Minoke approaches Prairie Dawn and reaches for the knife, just as Prairie Dawn changes hands. "Leave me alone," I tell her.

"Give me the knife, Prairie Dawn!" she yells and tries to reach for it again.

I take the knife, pointing the blade out at her. "Get away from me!" I yell.

Minoke steps back when she sees Koawa coming up behind me. He grabs me around my waist. I raise the knife over my head as I try to fight Koawa off.

"Leave me alone!" I yell. "I'm dirty!"

Koawa is incredibly strong, and I know I am fighting a hopeless battle. I am nothing to him, and I am quickly overpowered, and the knife is out of my hand. He turns me around to look at him. "What are you thinking?" he snaps. "I am dirty. I only want to get clean." Koawa just sighs. He can see the terror in my eyes through my many tears. It is at that moment that he realizes my wounds go much deeper than what is seen on the surface. He reaches for the blanket that Kikimo has run out to give him. He wraps it around me and curls his arm around my waist to exit the water. He watches Minoke put her arm around my shoulder, speaking softly in her tongue for only me to hear. Together, they walk a very fragile Prairie Dawn out of the water and back to her lodge. Inside the lodge, Minoke will help me get dressed and brush my beautiful, long hair as I slip into a very dark and deep sadness.

Chapter Eleven

The Homecoming

Koawa is refusing to leave me alone in the lodge. He feels I am too fragile and unpredictable about what I will do; therefore, Minoke, who graciously volunteered, is sitting with me. Koawa did not tell her what is going on, and she has never asked me, but I am certain it is written all over my face. She has been very good to me, consoling me when my tears occasionally fall now and then. As I sit in front of the fire, I slip into my own dark world. There is very little she can do to snap me out of it. Darkness hits the land, and both my boys insist on sleeping in their own lodge. Minoke offers as well, but I refuse, feeling she has already done so much. After watching my boys play a game of dice, we call it a night and fall asleep. I stir as I dream.

"She sure is purty."

"It's a shame ain't it?"

"I wanna do her."

CRACK!!!CRACK!!!!!!CRACK!!!!! Goes the belt. I stir some more as I hear the hideous, repulsive laughter and the sound of the rocks as I am dragged across the ravine ground. I hear echoing gun shots and my horse falling to its death. I awoke with a scream, shaking, short of breath, and in tears. The boys woke with a start. Kikimo rushes to my side. He notices my white, sweaty face, hears the heavy breathing, and sees me trembling. He is unsure what to do or what to think.

"Little Foot, go get Koawa!" he yells. Little Foot is eager to help and runs to get his uncle.

"Ma," Kikimo softly says, touching my arm. He quickly removes his hand when he sees me jump.

Koawa pushes open the flap, racing to my side. Minoke, hearing my scream, is shortly behind him. A frightened Little Foot is quick to rush to Minoke's side, tightly wrapping his arms around her waist, where he cowers.

"She won't stop shaking!" Kikimo says.

Koawa comes between us, slowly touching my face.

"Carrie," he says. I shake him off and whimper. He tries again.

"It's alright, sweet one."

He starts to stroke my hair and caress my cheek. Over and over, he is convincing me that I am alright. I am safe and nothing is going to hurt me. Slowly, I start to calm down and realize it is him. I rush into his arms, needing the security around me. Minoke is just beside herself as she watches me in tears, as she cuddles Little Foot beside her. Koawa remains with me, stroking my hair gently with his thumb while I sleep on his lap, a routine he is getting used to.

As Koawa sits there rocking me back and forth, he starts to think about his brother, who is due home any day now. He worries that she will not be able to handle his arrival very well. She is a very strong woman who has always brought their band incredible luck. Some say it is the color of her hair. Others believe she is spoken to from beyond, but he fears she has met her match and is too fragile to handle much more. He can only hope, as he rocks her back and forth, that White Horse can turn her around.

I awoke in the morning from a very restless sleep. I roll over to see Kikimo lying beside me, sound asleep. Poor guy, I think. I must have given him a scare, and he felt obligated to stay beside me after Koawa left. He is more and more like his father every day.

I painfully come to my feet, putting on my leggings. The swelling in my face is virtually gone. The bruise around my temple has turned a yellowish tinge. The welts on my back are only painful to the touch, but my ribs are still raw and very sore. I am beginning to think that Koawa is right and that I have indeed broken some. I know White Horse is due home any day, and I must get up and pull myself together if I am going to pull this off.

I step outside to see where my youngest has run off to, when I am stopped by Koawa.

"Does this look familiar?" he asks me as he shows me a glove.

"Yes. I was gagged by one that looks very similar to that. Where did you find it?"

"Southeast of here. Blue Thunder found it yesterday evening just before dark behind some bushes, along with Blue Coat's clothes."

"What does that mean?" I ask him.

"It means they changed their clothes. They are running scared."

I shake my head. "It has been nearly a week. I am sure they are in the next town by now." Koawa disagrees.

"No. Red Hawk picked up their tracks yesterday, not more than a day from here."

"If they are indeed running, then that also means they left their post. That could bring some major problems our way when the Army goes looking for them."

"You need to stop thinking like that."

"I can't help it, Koawa. This whole thing just doesn't sit right with me. I really think you should let it go."

"After what they did to you?" he argues. "No, these men will be found, and they will succumb to Sioux justice. This I promise you."

I only sigh as I know there is no changing his mind, and I am going to have to learn to accept it.

"Koawa, I want to thank you for everything you have done for me, and I want you to know that I have pulled myself together and you don't need to worry about me anymore."

"Prairie Dawn, you are far from being alright, and White Horse will see it."

I lower my eyes as I know Koawa is right. "White Horse loves you, and that love is what you need right now."

As it has been for the last few days, I start to cry, upon seeing my tears starting to form, Koawa rubs my shoulders.

"Prairie Dawn, do not underestimate White Horse. He is a very strong man."

"This is going to devastate him," I interrupt.

"Yes, he will take it hard, but he will survive because you are alive."

"I just do not want to hurt him."

"Sweetheart, the only one who is hurting is you."

My tears are heavier, and our conversation is brought to a stop when Blue Thunder walks up. He, of course, upon seeing that I am crying, gently rubs my shoulder as he hands me my necklace. I completely forgot I even had it on. Was that what gave me away?

"Where did you find it?" I ask him.

"About a half a mile from the Blue Coat's clothes, hanging off a bush."

"I bet that is what gave me away…Damit."

"It does not matter what gave you away. What matters is that we find them, and I promise you, Prairie Dawn, I will find them."

Except for Koawa, who is my brother-in-law, I do not usually give hugs to any of the warriors, but today, Blue Thunder was going to get one for everything that he is doing. He returns the embrace before leaving.

Later on in the morning, when I am in our lodge, Minoke walks in. She kneels down next to me by the fire. "I want you to have this," she says. She puts a small, black, smooth stone in my hand.

"What is it?" I ask her.

"It is a rare stone that Qutoh found one day when he was hunting. He told me that when you rub it with your thumb, it will take your evil thoughts away." I faintly smile.

"Thank you," I say and give her a hug.

"I have not told any of the women what I saw at the lake," she says. I lower my eyes. "Thank you."

"You need not worry. Our Chief will make you smile again. He will fix everything."

"I think this is something that not even White Horse can fix, but thank you."

She faintly smiles, stands, and walks out. My lodge has become my sanctuary, the only place where I feel safe and able to remain in the deep black hole that is growing deeper by the minute. My desire to escape my sadness is too great for me to deal with. Facing the demons that are swallowing me up inside is too terrifying to face. I feel alone and isolated. Lost in my sadness, I fail to hear Koawa walk in and squat down beside me. I feel him put his hand on my shoulder, and it is then that I look up at him.

"White Horse has been spotted a few miles from here," he says.

"He is a little early," I say.

"A little," he agrees. "I am going to ride out and meet him. I can get another horse if you want to come with me."

"No," I utter softly. "I will wait for him at the bottom of the hill."

"Prairie Dawn, it is a good walk. Are you sure you can handle it?"

"I do not have a choice. I am not going to tell him until tonight when we are alone in our lodge, until then I have to go on as if nothing happened."

"Sweetheart, he is going to see the bruise on your face and immediately know something is wrong."

"I can handle it. Please, Koawa, I will be alright."

"Alright," he says.

I then watch him as he stands up and walks out of the flap. Kikimo nearly knocks Koawa over as he comes running in.

"Ma, father is here," he says excitedly. "May I run out with Eagle Scout and catch up with him?" he asks.

"Yes," I answer. "Take Little Foot with you." I can tell by his look that it is not what he wants to hear, but nevertheless, he obeys.

"Alright," he says. "Do you want me to get you a pony, Ma?"

"No son, I will walk."

"Are you sure?"

"Yes, Kikimo, I am sure."

"Alright," he says and heads out the flap.

I only have a few minutes to pull myself together, as the walk there to the bottom of the hill is going to take me some time. I stand up and change into a dress that covers me more and is longer to the ground. I take my hair down and curl the sides of it with my thumb to cover the fading bruises as much as possible. There is little I can do about my slow pace, as I can only move as fast as my body will allow. I can only hope White Horse does not notice it.

Walking through camp, I am greeted by Minoke and Songbird, who start walking with me. No conversation is made. No questions are asked. I can feel it in my heart that they are only here for moral support, and I love them for it. How I wish I could tell them what has really happened, but until White Horse is told, I feel this is the best way.

Koawa and several other warriors catch up to White Horse and his men.

"You are home a little early, brother," Koawa says.

"I would have been home earlier if we hadn't met up with Blue Coats and had to go around," White Horse answers.

"I am glad you are home," he says.

"How is Prairie Dawn?" White Horse asks.

Koawa just looks at him, uncertain whether he should say anything. He then remembers his promise to her and feels he has to at least give her the chance to tell him.

"She will meet you at the bottom of the hill," he finally answers.

White Horse seems relieved that his Prairie Dawn, whom he loves more than life, is alright.

"Hello, father," Kikimo greets as he finally catches up to his father.

"Hello, my sons," he greets back.

White Horse sees his youngest son riding behind Kikimo. He reaches across, lifting him off the horse and sits him down in front of him. He then rubs the top of his head and watches his son give him a little smile. Little Foot has always been a shy boy, so unlike Kikimo at his age. White Horse feels he needs to protect himself more. Guide him into not being so scared of his own shadow. He sees so much of Prairie Dawn in him despite the skin of his father and the way he carries himself. The kindness and love he has for everyone are so much like his Prairie Dawn in every way. Perhaps that is why he treats him differently from Kikimo, who is more like him.

The view of the camp is seen over the horizon. White Horse gives his horse a little kick in the ribs and gallops the rest of the way in. Little Foot is loving it. The others are following him, and they all gallop across the prairie together. White Horse sees his Prairie Dawn leaving the other women and walking down the hill. He smiles at her beauty as he brings his horse down to a walk, stopping just a few feet from her. He jumps down, handing his horse's lead to Kikimo, who, in return, walks off with Little Foot holding on.

Our eyes meet. I bite my lower lip so as not to cry when he reaches and takes my hand.

"I have missed you, my Prairie Dawn," he smiles.

I can see the deep love he has for me in his eyes. The sincerity in his voice when he speaks my name. My anxiety grows as White Horse pulls me into his arms. I realize how much I missed him. How much I love him. How hard is it going to be to tell him? I hold my embrace, paying no mind to my pain in the ribs. I need to hold him. I need him near. I swallow back my tears as he pulls free from our embrace. Then arm in arm we walk up the hill with him keeping pace with me as we talk.

"There will be many who will be just as happy to see you as I am," I tell him.

"Yes. I imagine the big lodge will be full tonight with many stories." I lean my head into his side as he puts his arm around me.

"I reckon you have a lot to talk about in the smoke house."

"Yes, I do," but first, before we enter the camp, he turns me around behind a tree and passionately kisses me. He releases his lips from mine, stroking my hair. It is then that he sees the bruises.

"What happened, love?" he asks.

I should not be surprised he caught it so quickly. I have never met a person more observant than him.

"It is rather silly," I lie. "I fell off my horse."

"Oh, honey, you must be more careful," he warns. "You could have really been hurt."

I hate lying to him, but now is not the time to tell him.

"I will. I'm sorry."

"As long as you are alright, that is all I care about," he grins.

We finish our short walk into camp when he is quickly greeted and whisked away. I sigh deeply. One lie I tell myself. How many more am I going to have to tell him until I have enough courage to tell him the truth?

White Horse remains in the smoke house for several hours, allowing me time to get myself together. When he returns, he finds his usual spot under his tree by the lodge and watches me as I prepare our meal. This is a normal routine at this time of day, which usually involves a conversation that will last through the meal, but tonight, despite my feverish attempt, I am more into my sadness and less into talking.

Deep in thought, White Horse is no fool and quickly picks up that his wife is not acting right. He watches her every move.

He looks deep into her thoughts. He sees much sadness. She is quiet and holding her eyes down as if she is hiding something. She appears to be lost in another world. Not her outgoing self at all. Something is bothering her. Something heavy is on her mind. He does not like the way she is moving. She appears to be in a great deal of pain and almost in tears. She is a tough woman, one of the many qualities he loves about her. But her strength seems to be gone. Her confidence was destroyed. He is good at reading people, especially ones as easy as his Prairie Dawn. He decides not to say a word; he will just watch her and see what she does.

Kikimo and Little Foot run up and join us just as our dinner is ready to be served. Little Foot runs up to his father and sits on his lap. Kikimo comes up to me as I am coming to my feet. He is holding a flower in his hand. He kisses my cheek as he places it in my hair. I grin at him and hand him his plate. I then go to White Horse to hand him his. He fixes his eyes on mine before removing the plate from my hand. I then kneel down to serve Little Foot.

"Ma," Kikimo softly says. "You need to eat."

"Later, son," I say, as I slowly stand back up, holding my ribs. I glance over at White Horse, who is watching my every move.

"You feeling alright, honey?" he asks me.

"Yes," I lie. "I'm fine."

I walk over to the big tree by our lodge and lean up against it. I look out at the land around us, shutting out everything else. I vaguely hear Kikimo start a conversation with his father. I quickly tune it out, returning to my sadness. White Horse is definitely hungry and paying little attention to his son as he thinks and watches his wife while he chews. He observes the sadness in her eyes and the blank look on her face. He has never seen her so down, he thinks. He cannot help but wonder what can be so heavy on her mind. He is certain he saw her wipe a few tears from her eyes, then deeply sigh as she closes them back inside. He has seen enough. He looks over at his boys, who have finished their meals.

"Kikimo, my horse needs to be washed," he says.

"Yes, Father."

"Take Little Foot with you."

He watches his boys leave as he comes to his feet. Lost in my sorrow, I fail to hear White Horse come up beside me. I jump, becoming startled when I turn my head and see him standing there. His eyes are thick on mine.

"You are very quiet, my love," he starts. "What is wrong?"

"I guess I am just thinking of White Fawn." He faintly nods.

"Yes, I, too, miss her."

"I am so sorry, White Horse." A lonely tear finds its way. White Horse grabs it with his thumb, wiping it free.

"She lived a good life with no regrets, but I cannot help thinking something else is making you sad."

I choke back the tears, giving a pat on his beautiful, well-formed chest, and step away. I take the sluggish steps to the plates, slowly leaning down to pick them up. I feel White Horse's eyes following me.

"You didn't answer me," he finally says as he walks my way.

"I am fine, White Horse," I again lie.

I know by his look he does not believe me, but ignores it.

"I did not see your horse in the corral when I arrived. Where is it?" he questions.

"He tripped in a hole, which is why I fell off of him. He broke his leg. Koawa had to shoot him." Again, I know he does not believe me.

"I see,"

"I need to check on Morning Dove," I tell him as I quickly turn away. He grabs my arm as I am ready to escape. His eyes deeply penetrate mine.

"Carrie, what is wrong?" he asks.

By the grace of God, I am rescued when Blue Thunder and Night Owl come up to White Horse and coax him away. I sigh in relief, at least for now, I am safe.

Chapter Twelve

The Dark Lady

Darkness falls across the great hills. Everyone gathers in the big lodge for storytelling and laughter. White Horse always enjoys this time when he can gather all his people together for a night of laughter, but tonight his heart is not into it.

Flying Hawk is telling a story about a cow that has been going on for quite some time. He will occasionally give a grin or a chuckle, as he is only halfway listening to the story. His eyes and concentration are more on his Prairie Dawn, who is sitting across the lodge from him. He has been watching her for over an hour. She seems very uncomfortable and absorbed in a different thought. Her sadness is very apparent, and White Horse is very concerned. He remembers his dream, the reason he came home early. He saw his Prairie Dawn in a pit of fire, falling to her death. He could not reach her; he could not help her. Is there some truth to his dream? He watches her flinch and holds her ribs as she slowly comes to her feet. He sees his son Kikimo give her a hand as she rises. Chuckling as the punch line has been received, he watches her sneak out the lodge door. He glances over at Koawa and observes a quick look exchanged by him and Prairie Dawn before she leaves.

A beautiful reflection of the moonlight shines down on the lake. I find myself in deep thought, gazing out at the rippling water. I think of my father. How I wish he was here. What magical words would he have to make my sorrow disappear? I think of Running Water, who could always make me smile, and of White Fawn, how I wish I had her strength and courage. I look up to the heavens where my three little angels lie, praying to my God to take my pain away. I feel nothing anymore. I am all numb inside. I have no meaning in life; my fight is gone. I am dead. My sadness surfaces quietly, and I start to cry. My hopes and dreams seem so far away. My strength and fire have disappeared, leaving an empty hole inside. I wipe a tear as another one comes. There just doesn't seem to be any end to my river inside. I wipe several more when I feel White Horse's arms come around me from behind. He plants a gentle kiss on my wet cheek.

"It is a beautiful night, is it not?" he says.

"Yes, it is," I agree.

"Then why are you so sad?" he asks. I shrug my shoulders.

"I am just thinking of my father," I finally say.

White Horse turns me around, lifting my chin.

"Your eyes are telling me a different story," he mumbles. "They have lost their shine, their color." He sets his eyes heavily into mine. "Something has made them look lost and empty. Something deep and painful." He strokes my cheek as the last tear falls before I suck them in. "Something is very heavy in the heart of my Prairie Dawn. Something has her lost."

I turn my face away, looking out towards the lake. If I do not look at him, my sadness will not escape. "I am fine, White Horse," I mumble.

He shakes his head. "No," he turns my face to him. "I know you and you are not fine."

I turn away as I can feel the tears coming again.

"White Horse, stop, please." I plead as I shrug him away.

He comes up behind me, turning me around, finding me in tears.

"Oh, sweetheart, why are you doing this to me?" he moans. "Let me help you. Let me take your tears of sadness and turn them into a beautiful rainbow."

There is no holding them back. I can feel them getting harder, and I cannot stop them from flowing. This is my chance, the perfect opportunity to tell him, but instead, I shake my head as I just cannot do it. I cannot tell him what happened. I cannot hurt him. I just can't do it. As painful as it is, I briskly walk away into the lodge, leaving White Horse behind.

White Horse came close to chasing Prairie Dawn down. He was going to insist she tell him what was going on. He was not going to take no for an answer. He would badger her until she broke, and he didn't care if it took all night. But she is so upset and appears so fragile. He has never seen her in this state. He just doesn't have the heart to push her anymore. He has another idea. He saw the look that Koawa gave her when she left the big lodge. Of course, why didn't he think of it earlier? Koawa has to know what is going on. He will get it from him. He finds Koawa as he is walking to his lodge with Morning Dove in his arms.

"We need to talk," he sternly says.

Koawa puts Morning Dove down and tells her to meet him inside. White Horse watches as she runs off.

"What is on your mind?" Koawa asks him.

"Prairie Dawn," he answers. Koawa stiffens.

He saw them together earlier by the lake. He had watched her run off in tears. He is pretty sure that White Horse must not know the reason behind her tears, because if he did, he would not be so calm at this moment. He promised Prairie Dawn that he would not tell him, only because he agrees that it should come from her. He has every intention of keeping his word, at least for now.

"What about her?" he finally asks.

"Did anything happen to her when I was gone?"

Koawa did not want to lie, so he plays dumb.

"Ask her," he says as he leans down to open the flap. White Horse grabs his arm, glaring over at him.

"You know better than to try to make a fool of me," he growls.

"I would never dream of it, White Horse, but if your wife can not talk to you, that is not my problem," he snaps as he opens the flap to his lodge.

"Koawa, please," White Horse pleads.

Koawa can see the desperation on his brother's face and the deep, heavy pleading in his eyes for answers. He stands back up to face him.

"Alright," he says. "Yes, something happened to Prairie Dawn when you were gone. I promised her I would not tell you as she wants to do it herself."

"But she won't tell me. Every time I try to get it out of her, she starts crying." Koawa puts his hand on White Horse's shoulder.

"You need to trust me on this, brother. You do not want to upset her any more than she already is."

"If my Prairie Dawn is in danger, I need to know."

"She is not," Koawa reassures.

White Horse is frustrated. He has never known Koawa to keep anything from him. Koawa and he are extremely tight. He knows for his brother not to tell him; it has to be huge. He is trying to keep his cool, but is quickly losing it. He starts to pace a little to calm himself down. He hates looking like a fool, and right now he feels like one. He gives Koawa a push that just barely moves him.

"Why won't you tell me!" he yells in frustration.

Koawa pats White Horse on the shoulder. "You need to stay calm, my brother. Prairie Dawn cannot handle you losing control. You must remain patient with her and keep her close. She needs you. Do not push the matter anymore tonight. Allow me to talk to her tomorrow, together we will tell you."

White Horse sees the compassion in his brother's eyes. He can see the love and concern for the situation. White Horse knows Koawa would never steer him wrong. He has to trust him on this. He has to do this for his Prairie Dawn. He lowers his head and evidently agrees. Koawa pats him on the shoulder again.

"Go to her White Horse and keep her in your arms." He then turns and walks into his lodge.

When White Horse enters the lodge, he finds his Prairie Dawn kneeling in front of the fire and his boys playing dice. He finds his seat across from her and sits down, his eyes penetrating her every move as he tries to get inside her thoughts. His mind is in circles. He notices how she has the blanket tucked around her like a cocoon. He finds this odd as the lodge is quite warm. White Horse watches on.

"Father," Kikimo begins as he rolls the dice. "Remember that buck that Eagle Scout and I lost track of before you left?"

"Yes," he answers.

"I picked up its trail yesterday. Remember, you told me if I found the trail, you would help me bring it in."

"Yes, I remember."

"Can we go tomorrow morning? I want to go before Eagle Scout takes Yellow Hawk and gets it before me."

"Yes, we can go."

"I want to go too, Father," Little Foot chimes in. "I want to show you my rabbit trap."

"Sure, son. You can go to."

"You promise?" he asks.

"Yes, son. I promise." Both boys show their excitement. It is now Little Foot's turn to roll the dice.

"I won again," Kikimo says as his brother rolls a small number.

"You always win," he huffs.

"No, I don't. I never beat my father." Kikimo looks over at his father, who is looking at his mother. "I have never beaten you. Have I father?"

"No, son, you have not."

"I want to see you beat him, father, please," Little Foot begs.

White Horse accepts the challenge and takes the dice from his son. He rolls, and it lands right in front of me. He watches me blink. I snap out of my trance when the dice land in front of me. I look over at White Horse and then down at the dice. He rolled snake eyes, or in my mind, two soldiers who are snakes on the ground. My eyes welled up in fear. Kikimo is quick to my rescue.

"Ma," Kikimo says. I glance over at him. "Did you hear Father? He promised to take us hunting tomorrow morning."

"That is wonderful, son," I faintly smile.

"Me too, Mama," Little Foot says. "I am going too." I smile over at him.

"Then I reckon you better get some sleep," I say.

"Alright," he whines. Little Foot crawls over to me, giving me a big hug.

"Night, mama," he says.

"Good night, honey," I say back.

He then goes to his father, repeating the same action. I glance over at White Horse as he scoops his son up in his arms and gets on his feet. I follow him with my eyes and see him playfully lift Little Foot over his head, plopping him down on his pelt. Little Foot is laughing. I believe White Horse did this to put a smile on my face, and it worked. Kikimo is the next to say goodnight with a kiss on my cheek. I faintly hear him whisper in my ear. "I am right here, ma, if you need me." I faintly smile as he makes his way back to his pelt. It is now my turn to get up and get to our pelt. White Horse sees me struggle. He wraps his arm under my shoulders and lifts me to my feet. We come eye to eye. His look deepens, absorbing my vacant eyes. Suddenly, he pulls me in and kisses me hard. Before releasing his grip from around my waist, he takes one final look into my eyes. I watch him as he then walks to his pelt and lies down.

Chapter Thirteen

The Shattered Queen

Rain clouds appear in the dark skies, opening up to a waterfall across the prairie grass. The thunder rolls over the hills. The lightning strikes, brightening up the darkness of the land. The flap waves back and forth with the wind, as yet another monstrous dream fills my soul. I start to stir as I relive my attack. I hear the gunshots and my horse falling to its death, the rush of my body as I am dragged across the land. I hear the cracking of the belt opening up my flesh and the sudden jerking of being raped. I hear my screams, my pleading for help. I see their faces and smell their breath. I feel the kick and the breaking of my ribs, the hideous laughter as I struggle to get away. The lightning cracks. The thunder roars. I wake up with a scream.

White Horse jolts awake to find me trembling and in tears. He rushes to console me, as I sit in a trance.

"Carrie," he says, grabbing my wrists.

He quickly dodges away when I let out another scream and start to swing. White Horse grabs my wrists again in an attempt to calm me down. He sees me kick and frantically fight him off.

"Father!" he hears from behind. "Don't hold her down!" Kikimo yells as he comes between us, pushing his father's hand away.

"Ma," Kikimo softly says as he attempts to touch my face. He quickly moves his hand away when his mother gives a sudden jerk. He tries again. "Ma," he says as he tries to stroke my hair.

"No!" I yell. "Leave me alone."

He watches me as I cower in the corner of the pelt. I curl my legs up in a ball and start to shake. It is then that White Horse sees my bruised legs. His eyes grow huge.

"Kikimo, what happened to her?" he demanded.

Kikimo ignores him as he concentrates on his shattered mother.

"Ma," he starts to plead. "Do not be frightened. You are safe now. No one can hurt you." He watches me tremble, shaking with fear, my face white, drowning in tears. He slowly starts to stroke my hair.

"No," I cry. "Don't let them hurt me. Please don't hurt me."

"Ma, I will not allow anyone to ever hurt you again. I promise you."

"I am so scared," I say.

"I know, ma, I know you are, but you are safe now. I promise."

White Horse is full of rage. He has heard everything his son and Prairie Dawn have said. His insides boil just thinking that someone dared hurt his precious wife.

"Kikimo, who hurt her?" he growls.

"Father give me your hand," Kikimo calmly says as he reaches out to grab his father's hand.

"Answer me, who hurt her?" White Horse yells.

"Father!" Kikimo snaps. "Ma needs you. Give me your hand."

White Horse can see the pleading in Kikimo's eyes. He remembers his brother's words only a few hours before. He looks over at his wife, all shattered and torn. His heart aches. His soul burns, but his Prairie Dawn needs him, so he gives Kikimo his hand as he slides in closer to her.

"Ma," Kikimo softly says as he slowly places his father's hand on his mother's cheek. White Horse is quick at caressing it.

"It's alright, Ma. Father is here now."

I feel White Horse's palm on my cheek. The soft, gentle stroking of his thumb. I reach up and hold his arm.

"White Horse," I say.

"Yes, Love, it is I."

I finally snap out of my trance to see that White Horse is in front of me. I quickly rush into his arms.

"Oh, White Horse," I sob.

White Horse holds onto his shattering wife. He showered her with love and affection, holding her tight in his arms as she wept.

Morning light hits the opening at the top of the lodge. Kikimo and Little Foot are ordered to leave by their father and tend to their morning chores. White Horse has been up for hours, stroking his wife's hair as she sleeps. Last night's events are strong on his mind. He has so many questions, so many concerns. He remembers the fear in his Prairie Dawn's eyes, her desperate pleading to Kikimo not to let them hurt her. He saw the deep bruises and scratches on her legs. He remembers how she was walking. He is certain she has been beaten, but wonders by whom? Who would hurt her? He is certain none of his warriors ever would, for there is not a one who would not give their life to protect her. So where did she get them? And where were they? He is certain she did not fall off her horse. Why would she lie? What is she afraid of? And why is everyone afraid to tell him? He remembers his mother's warning the day that he left. He remembers his dream and how he couldn't save her. He remembers Koawa telling him to remain calm. He is certain this is huge? What can be so big that not even Koawa can tell him? He will remain patient. He will remain calm, keeping his temper under control. He will get to the truth. Today he will know. He sees her stir; she is nearly awake. Patience, White Horse, he tells himself, I will get her to tell me.

I open my eyes to White Horse looking down at me. I feel his gentle stroke on my hair and his loving eyes staring into mine. I am sure last night's events are strong on his mind. I am feeling weak today and emotionally drained. I do not know what has come over me, why I cannot get out of my depression. It is so unlike me. I am beginning to think Koawa is right, and telling White Horse is going to be hard for me. I only hope I am able to stand up to him and his interrogation that I know is coming. I slowly come to my feet, taking the blanket with me to shield my legs. He quickly reaches forward, whisking it off me. I watch him toss it to the side.

"I have already seen them," he huskily says.

"Oh," I mumble. I cannot remember what was said last evening or even what he saw. I only pray I can remain strong. I turn to walk to the other side of the lodge, avoiding his eyes. As long as I do not have to look at him, I know I will be alright.

"Who gave them to you?" I hear him ask. I stop at Kikimo's pelt to fold his blanket.

"I told you I fell off my horse," I answer. I hear him come to his feet.

"You never have been a good liar," he says. He comes up behind me, putting his hands on my shoulders. "Now, I am going to ask you again, and this time I want the truth. Who gave them to you?"

"It doesn't matter anymore," I mumble.

"It matters to me."

"Just drop it, White Horse."

White Horse is not taking no for an answer. He reaches around me, pulling the blanket out of my hand and whisking me around to face him. I turn my face to avoid his eyes.

"What are you afraid of?" I avoid the question and cower my face. "Look at me," he commands.

I refuse to look up at him as I know if I do, I will break down. He gently shakes me. "Look at me!" he barks.

I shake my head back and forth to avoid his eyes, but White Horse is persistent in making me obey. He grabs my chin, forcing it up so I have to look at him.

"Who hurt you?" he growls.

I want to tell him. I truly do, but I cannot do it. I cannot tell him what happened to the woman that he loves more than life. I know it will destroy him, and I cannot bear any more suffering for the ones I love. I know White Horse's revenge will be severe, and that is what scares me. I love every person in this camp, and I will not allow any more blood to be shed because of my carelessness in leaving the camp unprotected. I push his hands free and step away. I can hear White Horse deeply sigh, and for a few moments, the room is still as White Horse tries to calm himself down. Finally, the silence is broken.

"I can remember a time," he starts, "when you were never afraid to tell me exactly what was on your mind. You had no fear of how I would react. Your fire and your strength would stand up to the fieriest warrior. Something has shattered your strength, has extinguished your fire. Carrie, I want to help you, but I cannot if you will not tell me."

"I do not need your help. I am fine," I spat.

"No, sweetheart, you are not." He comes up behind me, gently placing his hands on my shoulders. "Last night, you were terrified. You pleaded with Kikimo not to let them hurt you anymore. Sweetheart, who hurt you?"

As hard as I was trying, I could feel myself getting emotionally weak and the tears coming. White Horse hears me sniff and turns me around.

"What are you afraid of, Love?" he coaxes, stroking my cheek. "Hmm? What are you afraid of?"

"You," I finally admit. White Horse is taken back a moment.

"Sweetheart, I would never hurt you. You know that."

"Not me," I cry.

Finally, White Horse feels he may be getting somewhere.

"Ok," he nods. "It is not me you fear, it is what you know I will do to the one who hurt you that you fear?"

"Yes."

"Is it one of my warriors?"

"No," I gasp. "Never would they hurt me."

"If it is not one of my warriors and they were not there to protect you, then who is it and where were they?"

I now clam up. I have already said too much. White Horse is no fool, and if I say much more, he will figure it out. I turn and step away to a nearby pelt, reaching down to grab the blanket, when I do, the pain in my ribs takes my breath away.

"Ah. Ouch!" I bellow in pain. White Horse races over to help me. "Just leave me alone!" I yell.

"Honey, you are hurt and I fear you are hurt bad."

I catch my breath and glare up at him, unfortunately, my tears are unstoppable. White Horse is growing more and more concerned with me. He knows me very well and has never seen me so fragile and in so much pain.

"Sweetheart, please do not do this to me. Do not shut me out. Carrie, I love you. Please let me help you. Tell me what happened."

"I can't, because of that love. I can't tell you. I'm sorry."

"We have never had secrets from each other. We have always been honest with each other, no matter what. Why, why now?"

"It is for the best?"

"The best for whom?" he questions.

"White Horse, please don't make me do this."

He comes forward, taking me into his arms. He gently pecks my cheek as I go in.

"Sweetheart, I am not trying to be mean, I just want to help you." He looks down at me, caressing my hair. "Don't shut me out. Let me help you."

Just as I am nearing my breaking point, Little Foot steps in from the flap.

"Not now, son," White Horse says.

"But you promised," he says.

"Not now!" White Horse yells.

Shy and timid Little Foot jumps when his father yells. He looks as if he is about ready to cry. My tearful eyes meet White Horse's.

"Go," I plead.

"No," he argues. "I will not leave you like this."

"White Horse, go, please!"

His eyes are thick on me. His heart aches to see me in tears, to see me so fragile and ready to break. He sees me close up inside, shutting in all my demons. He knows he will have to start all over and allow me time to calm down. He was so close to getting me to talk, he thinks. He deeply sighs.

"Little Foot, go get your brother," he says to his youngest.

He watches his son as he excitedly runs out of the flap. He looks back down at me as I dry my tears. He briefly embraces me.

"I will not be gone long," he says before leaning in and kissing my cheek. I watch him briefly stop, as he picks up his hunting gear before exiting the lodge, and looks back at me, still not sure if he wants to leave.

Chapter Fourteen

The Innocent Truth

White Horse takes his boys to an area in the woods that is abundant with rabbits and deer. His mind is clearly distracted by his wife, whom he left behind, and he wants to make his trip short so he can hurry and get back to her. He quickly finds a place for his youngest to set up his trap, and after feeling confident that it meets his standards, he finds him a spot to wait under some shrubs.

"Now you wait quietly here and very soon your trap will be filled," he tells him.

Little Foot is eager to obey and crouches down on his stomach, peeking out of the shrubs where he will wait. When White Horse is confident that Little Foot is safe, he then leaves with his oldest.

"Over here, father," Kikimo says. "I found it yesterday just over here."

Just then, White Horse stops and squats down. Kikimo follows suit.

"Deer droppings," Kikimo says.

"Yes, and they are fresh," White Horse adds.

He then looks out at the ground. "It appears, son, that your buck has found a new home and has not moved much, assuming it is the same one."

"I am sure it is Father. He probably found a female."

"That could very well be. Let us go find it."

They follow the tracks for a little distance before White Horse finds a place where they can sit down and wait.

"We will wait here," he says. They both sit down on the ground. White Horse leans back against a tree and thinks of his Prairie Dawn.

"Father," Kikimo says.

"Son, the buck will not come your way if you are not still," he warns.

Kikimo just smiles. He knows his father is right and is certain that is why he has not caught it yet, as sitting still and remaining patient is definitely one thing that he dislikes the most, but he wants this buck before his friend Eagle Scout gets it. He has to prove to his mouthy friend who the better hunter is. He rests his chin on his fist and quietly waits.

White Horse is far from being patient and is very anxious to get home. He sees before him his Prairie Dawn crying, shattered beyond words. His mind is racing. His thoughts are going wild. Who would hurt his wife? Where were his warriors when she was attacked? Who would come into camp and hurt his wife, and no one comes to her aid? Something did not add up. He thinks of her horse, whom she babied all the time. What happened to it? Was she out riding when this all happened? But he knows Prairie Dawn would only ride if it was safe and she always stayed close to camp where his sentries could keep an eye on her. He is so confused. So much of this does not make any sense. Why can't he figure it out? Why won't anyone tell him? Then it hits him. Kikimo, he is certain he will know what is going on. He will get it from him. He knows Kikimo will tell.

"Son," he says.

"Shh," Kikimo says, placing his finger over his lips.

White Horse lifts his brow, taken aback a little by his sons' rude behavior.

"Kikimo," he repeats.

"Shh, Quiet!" Kikimo snaps. "You said to be still, now be still."

White Horse is not amused. "Kikimo, forget the deer. I need to talk to you."

"I have been following this deer for weeks. I am not forgetting it."

"I will track you another deer."

"But I want this deer," he argues as he remains still again.

White Horse is in no mood to deal with an unruly boy. He rolls his eyes at his son, asking himself why he had to be so much like him. He picks up his bow, smacking it on Kikimo's knee to get his attention.

"Ouch!" he yells, rubbing his knee. "What did you do that for?"

"I told you to forget the deer. I need to talk to you."

"What about?" Kikimo asks, annoyed.

"Your mother."

"What about her?" he whines, still rubbing his painful knee.

"What happened to her?"

"I cannot tell you."

"Why not!" White Horse barks.

"Because I promised her I wouldn't."

"Son..." Kikimo stops his father's thought by waving his finger in his face. "You always told me never to break a promise. You told me."

"I know what I told you, son, but this is different."

"In what way?" he argues.

"Son," White Horse calmly starts, "sometimes you have to break a promise to help the ones you love. I cannot help your mother if I do not know what is going on."

"If I tell you, ma will be sad, and I do not want to see her sad anymore."

"That is why you need to tell me, son, so I can help her."

"I don't think you can, father. Ma is pretty messed up."

"Son, I have to try. I cannot sit back and do nothing and watch it destroy your mother."

Kikimo grows still as he looks out at the landscape before him. White Horse watches the effect it is making on his son's face. He can see how strong Kikimo is trying to be.

"I never should have promised her father. I knew it was wrong." Kikimo looks over at him. "But she is so scared."

"What happened to her son?"

Before Kikimo could respond, they heard Little Foot running up. They both come to their feet as Little Foot stops in front of his father, carrying a dead rabbit by its hind legs.

"I did it, Father. I did it," he excitedly smiles.

"I am proud of you, son."

"You think Mama will like it?"

"Oh, I am sure she will."

"May I give her a rabbit foot, Father, may I?"

"She would like that," White Horse smiles.

"I am going to make her a necklace and put it on her, then maybe she will smile." White Horse rubs the top of his head.

"That is very kind of you, son."

"I have to do something because she has been so sad since the Blue Coats attacked her." White Horse's eyes grow huge.

"Little Foot!" Kikimo scolds.

Little Foot lowers his eyes; he knows he was not supposed to tell. White Horse comes down to his son's level.

"Little Foot, were the Blue Coats here?" he asked.

Little Foot just shakes his head no.

"Little Foot, you promised," Kikimo snaps.

White Horse glares up at Kikimo. "Quiet!" he barks.

Kikimo knows better than to disobey. White Horse looks back across at his youngest boy. "Son, how did your mother meet up with the Blue Coats?"

"When she left at night to get White Man's medicine for Grandmother White Fawn at the soldier wagons."

White Horse's insides explode; he curses in his tongue before coming to a stand. He glares down at Kikimo, who knows he is in trouble.

"Little Foot, go wait for your brother at the creek."

"Yes, father." Kikimo cowers in place as he feels his father's eyes piercing him. "How could you keep this from me?" White Horse spats to his son.

"She was crying so hard, and she was so scared. I didn't know what to do."

White Horse can see the sadness in his son's eyes. His loyalty and love for his mother are admirable. He calms himself down by taking a deep breath before he speaks. "Tell me what happened, son," he calmly says.

"All I know is that Mother left in the middle of the night to get medicine for Grandmother. When she never returned, Koawa went looking for her. They didn't return for several days. When they came back, he was carrying her in his arms. She was wrapped all in a blanket. He allowed no one in to see her. I crawled behind the lodge and overheard her and Koawa talking. She was really crying. I have never heard her cry so much. Koawa was consoling her. They started talking about you. Ma was so afraid to tell you because she knew you would want revenge, and she was afraid that more Blue Coats would come and we would all die. Koawa told her that you needed to know, which made her cry more. Koawa held ma like she was a baby while she cried. That night, I heard her scream when I was sleeping at Aunt Minoke's lodge. I wanted to come to her, but Minoke wouldn't let me go; she said Koawa was there and that he could take care of her. The next morning, I snuck into the lodge when she was sleeping and I saw her legs. I knew then for sure she did not fall from her horse. She was crying and pleaded with me not to tell you because she was going to do it herself, and I told her I would."

White Horse could see his son was getting very upset. "They messed her up real bad, Father, really bad." Kikimo is trying not to cry, fighting the tears as hard as he can. "She was all black and blue, and she could barely walk. I helped her go out to the lake because she wanted to bathe. Koawa and I left her. We heard Minoke scream, and we ran. Ma was in the water with a knife, trying to hurt herself. She said she was dirty. Koawa took the knife from her." Kikimo takes a deep breath to close in his tears. "It was terrible, Father; I have never seen her like that."

"It's alright to cry, son."

"No," he sniffs. "A warrior doesn't cry."

"Kikimo, just because you are a warrior does not mean you don't have feelings. Learning to cry is a skill that all good warriors have."

"You have never cried!"

"That is where you are wrong, my son. For even I have mastered that skill."

Kikimo lets it all out, running into his father's embrace. "I hate them, Father. I hate them for what they did to her."

"Me too, son, me too."

"What are you going to do?"

"First, I want you to take your brother back to camp and do not tell your mother our conversation. I will do it myself, but first I have to talk to Koawa."

"Do not be too angry with him, Father. He treated her well."

White Horse had no doubt about this; in fact, there were times when he felt Koawa treated her too well. "You go on," he orders, handing Kikimo his hunting gear to take back with him.

Kikimo catches up with Little Foot by the creek. He rushes past him and hurries back to camp.

"Wait for me," Little Foot whines.

Kikimo, annoyed, stops in his tracks. "Hurry up," he retorts.

"Stop going so fast."

"It is not my fault you have the feet of a snail," Kikimo barks.

"Why are you so angry?"

"The only reason I told you about mother was to close your mouth from bellyaching. You made me a promise and you broke it and because of that Eagle Scout will get my buck and you will get Koawa's bow on your backside for telling."

Little Foot gasps with the thought of his Uncle Koawa hitting him with his bow. "Now come on."

175

Chapter Fifteen

A Chief's Rage

White Horse takes a different route into camp, dodging trees and bushes as he runs. So many thoughts are racing through his mind, so many questions that he needs answers for. Why would anyone let his Prairie Dawn leave? Why wasn't she watched like they were instructed to do? How did she get past his sentries? He knew someone had a lot of explaining to do. His rage is high with both the Blue Coats and Koawa. How could he keep something of this magnitude from him? What was he thinking? He thinks of his poor Prairie Dawn and what she must be going through. His heart goes out for her and now he understands why she was afraid to tell him. He slows down his run to a brisk walk when he sees his brother behind his lodge painting a hide. Patience is the last thing on his mind. He is fuming. He comes up behind Koawa, kicking his leg with his foot. Koawa tumbles over. Catching his balance from such an unexpected blow, Koawa rushes to his feet and pushes White Horse back.

"What is your problem!" he shouts.

"You son of a bitch," White Horse growls. Giving Koawa another push. "I trusted you!"

Koawa backs up a little. He sees the rage on White Horse's face. He is certain he knows the truth. He knows his brother well and knows his temper. White Horse is out for blood. He considers himself a very strong man that backs down to no one, but this kind of rage from the mightiest warrior he has ever known, is even more than he can take on.

"It is not going to do Prairie Dawn any good by taking your anger out on me," he says. White Horse is too angry for any reasoning.

"How could you do this to me Koawa?" he growls. "I put all my trust in you and this is how you treat me, like a fool?"

"It is not like that White Horse."

"You are nothing but a coward." White Horse is grinding his teeth. His rage is near explosion. "You didn't tell me because you knew if anything happened to her on your watch I would rip your head off." He pushes Koawa again. "You knew that if Prairie Dawn got hurt, I would never forgive you."

"No, White Horse that is not true."

"You have managed to make a mockery out of me in front of everyone. You have made me look like a fool in front of my people. You call yourself a warrior, but yet you can't stand up in my face and tell me the truth. My six-year-old son was the only one who had the courage to tell me."

Oh course, Koawa thinks. Little Foot, he should have guessed.

"White Horse I can explain," Koawa says holding his hands up to avoid another push.

"You can explain to your death. My Prairie Dawn was attacked and it is your fault."

Koawa is losing his patience. He refuses to take the blame for Prairie Dawn's attack. "My fault," he argues. "You weren't here. How would you know? You weren't here when she stole away in the night and slithered past your sentries. You weren't there when she went to the soldier's camp and got the medicine to keep our mother alive until you got home, so you could see her before she died. You weren't there when her body was left to be eaten by vultures. You didn't carry her lifeless body into a cold, dark cave because you were afraid she may not make the journey home alive. You didn't have to hear her scream when her welts were cleansed with a burning stick from when she was whipped raw by a belt. You weren't there to hold her trembling body in your arms. You weren't there to wipe down her swollen black and blue face. You weren't there my brother, to see the fear in her eyes and wash away her tears when she realized she had been raped." White Horse grows very still as an angry Koawa continues on. "You can blame me all you wish my brother."

Koawa gives him a push with every syllable. "But you weren't there."

Koawa watches as White Horse comes to terms with what has happened to his Prairie Dawn. He watches his brother come down on his knees and bury his face to his hands, for several moments Koawa remains there watching his brother start to tear up. Koawa comes down on the ground beside him, putting his hand on his shoulder.

"What have I done?" White Horse asks. "Mother warned me but I didn't listen. She saw great danger for Prairie Dawn but I ignored it. My wife left because of me. I allowed her to get hurt. I failed to protect her by not warning her. I know how stubborn Carrie can be. I never should have left."

White Horse is beating himself up. He vowed to her father all those years ago on their wedding day that he would always protect her and never allow any harm to come her. He feels as if not only has he failed his wife, but her father as well. White Horse grabs Koawa's shoulder giving it a squeeze.

"My brother I was so foolish to blame you," White Horse cries.

"White Horse, mother warned me as well. I tried to stop her. I too know how stubborn your wife is, but I never thought she would be that naïve too leave. Brother, we can sit here all day and point fingers at each other, but that will not help Prairie Dawn." White Horse wipes his eyes and agrees. "She is very fragile White Horse. She is not well in her mind."

"I cannot imagine the amount of pain she must be dealing with."

"She is a very strong woman," Koawa states. "But I do not believe she can handle this on her own. Those men were very brutal and she is left with many scars."

White Horse shook his head as his rage starts coming back. "These men will meet their fate with my bare hands," he snarls. Koawa agrees.

"That is what she is afraid of. She knows how much you want us all to have peace and stop the fighting. She knows you will start war."

"War was started when they violated my Prairie Dawn," White Horse growls.

Just then White Horse sees Little Foot come running up to him. He frantically pulls on his father's hand trying to get him to come.

"What is it son?" White Horse asks.

"Mama," he rushes out pointing to the lodge.

White Horse is quickly on his feet followed by Koawa. Both men are in a dead run to his lodge. He is greeted by Songbird outside by the flap. A loud ruckus is heard from within.

"Kikimo went to check on her." Songbird anxiously says. "Oh dear."

White Horse steps in to see Minoke and Kikimo wrestling a knife away from Prairie Dawn. White Horse becomes alert of the situation and races in. Koawa pushes Minoke out of the way, just as the knife accidentally cuts her. Prairie Dawn is heard screaming as White Horse dives on the ground to get the knife out of her hand. After the knife is removed, he watches her as she quickly curls up into a corner, lowering her head to sob. He immediately is at her side.

"I didn't mean it," I cry, "I just want the pain to go away."

I touch White Horse's heart. He cradles me in his arms, sliding back on a pelt where he allows me to cry. He exhales deeply as he realizes how close he almost came to losing his wife again. White Horse remains with his Prairie Dawn cradled in his arms. He allows her to sob, as he strokes her hair and rocks her back and forth. She is like a child resting in his lap, burying her head in his chest. It is not until her tears stop that White Horse speaks a word.

"My beautiful Love, how you have suffered," he whispers caressing me. "You will suffer no more."

"I am scared White Horse."

"I understand and I will take that fear away."

"I feel they are still here, that they will return for me," I sob.

"No, they will not. I will not allow any more pain and suffering to come to you."

"This is all my fault."

"No Love, it is not."

"I left. I brought this on myself," I argue.

"Carrie, you left because you thought they could help you. They in return, helped themselves. I do not put you at fault."

White Horse hears me sniff and dry my tears. "Sweetheart, I know this is very painful, but I have to understand everything that happened."

He is grateful I gave him no dispute and agree to talk. I sit up out of his lap and start my story.

"White Fawn," I begin, "was getting worse. I had remembered a medicine that my brother Roger would use. So, I asked Koawa if I could go to the soldier camp and get it. He was angry that I even suggested it. He threatened to tie me to the lodge if I attempted to go. Even Blue Thunder threatened me if I would leave." That gave White Horse some relief knowing that Koawa did try. "I just wanted her to still be alive when you got home. She kept asking for you. I just assumed she wanted you here. I had to try."

White Horse took my hand as I continued on. "I found an old dress from my other life in my bag of personal needs and the old pair of shoes that I traded for last fall, the ones you were not happy that I got." He just nods as he remembers how upset he was when I traded for them and not for something he thought they could use more, like flour. "I made myself up and left in the middle of the night. I crawled out of the back of the lodge, because Blue Thunder was guarding the front. I got past your scouts just like you taught me and rode all night. I met up with Red Hawk. He was not going to let me pass. I was so mean to him. I told him he had to let me pass, because if he tried to stop me I would tell you and you would go after him. I abused being your wife to get my way." He wasn't surprised because it was not the first time I had done it.

"I got to the soldier's wagons early that morning. I made up a story of a sick husband, so I could get the medicine and it worked but something gave me away. I knew they were on to me when the doctor mentioned Willow Creek and my brother. I did not recognize him, but I think he did me somehow. There were these two soldiers when I first came in that kept looking at me. They were making rude jesters and comments to themselves, but I was sure they were talking about me. One was really making me nervous. I was so glad when I got out of there. I ran hard until I got to the canyon. I stopped for water. That is when I saw the same two soldiers from when I first went in. I ran and I ran my horse hard. I almost got away until my horse was shot. I fell to the ground and when I got up to run, I was roped and drug a few feet. That is when the other man killed my horse."

White Horse could see that his Prairie Dawn was getting upset again. He cannot allow her to close back up. He is so close to hearing the truth. He repositions to better console her, as she continues on. "The one who roped me held me down. He demanded to know our location. When I refused to tell him, he started beating me. I fought him hard. I was able to get my knife out, stab him, and make a run for it. The other soldier caught up to me. My escape made the other man even more furious. He started hitting me again, dragging me across the rocks. I fought him some more, and when I got up to run, that is when I was hit by his belt. He hit so many times, and it hurt so bad. He hit over and over and over. He wouldn't stop."

White Horse watches as I stop a moment, my tears starting to fall again. He rubs my shoulder and squeezes my hand until I pull myself together and am able to continue. "After he stopped, I was rolled over and my hands were tied, and a glove shoved in my mouth. The other man, who just watched everything, told the other soldier that I was pretty and he wanted to do me. I didn't know what to do. I tried to stop them, but I couldn't. I couldn't do it."

I am extremely upset. It is taking everything White Horse has to calm me down enough to continue on. After a few moments and several deep breaths, I am able to go on. "I was punched and it knocked me out. When I came too, he was on me, and the other one was waiting for his turn. I am punched again. I don't know how many times White Horse. I don't know."

He takes me in his arms, consoling my pain and tears. White Horse has heard enough and is not going to allow me to continue on. He holds me tight as I shake and cry.

"You do not need to be afraid anymore, my love. I will take care of this."

"No, White Horse," I beg. "That is what scares me."

He breaks free of our embrace, lifting my chin to his eyes. "Koawa told me your fear, and I love you even more. But, sweetheart, you must understand what I have to do. I will not allow these men to get away with what they have done to you. Soldiers or no soldiers, these men will pay the Lakota price for violating you."

I know there is no changing his mind. White Horse will do what he feels he needs to do, and there is nothing I can do about it. I can only pray that his revenge will stop with the soldiers and not start his own war with the Blue Coats. Several hours pass. White Horse takes his fragile Prairie Dawn under a tree just outside the smoke house. He asks Minoke and Songbird to remain with me until he returns. Minoke takes a very sad and fragile Prairie Dawn by the tree and sits her down. She asks nothing, as Prairie Dawn sits in her sadness.

White Horse steps into the smokehouse. All his faithful warriors are already there, gathered around in a circle, waiting for his arrival. All eyes turn to him as they watch their somber Chief sit down. Koawa hands White Horse the pipe. He takes a smoke and then passes it on. He remains there emotionless, as the pipe circles around. Many eyes from his warriors are on him. All of them can tell by his drawn face that today's meeting is very personal to their Chief. Koawa is the last to take the smoke before handing it to White Horse. He places it down beside him and quickly gets to the meaning of the meeting. He speaks his tongue.

"Men, I do not have much time, as I need to get back to Prairie Dawn, so I will get to the point. It has come to my attention a matter that will affect us all. When I was gone, my Prairie Dawn took it upon herself to leave the protection of the camp in pursuit of medicine for White Fawn. She went to a Blue Coat camp. On her return, she meets up with two soldiers who were looking for us. When my Prairie Dawn would not reveal our location, she was then beaten, whipped, and raped."

There are many boisterous gasps heard throughout. White Horse puts up his hand to silence them. "I went to the head Chief's camp to speak to him regarding a treaty for peace with the Blue Coats. I have decided not to sign the treaty. I will not make peace with the White Men, and mostly with the Blue Coats. This will most likely cause war and more death. I have appointed Koawa and Blue Thunder to aid in the search for the two soldiers who attacked my Prairie Dawn. These men will be found and brought back here to meet my wrath. I will not be leading this search, as my Prairie Dawn is not well and I need to be with her. I need two volunteers to go and start a new search further to the east."

Night Owl is quick to stand. "I was here when Prairie Dawn was brought in. I see with my own eyes her pain. I will go."

White Horse faintly grins. It is now Yellow Hawks' turn. "Prairie Dawn has proven her loyalty more than once to all of us. She has the skin of a white woman, but the strength of a warrior. I will fight right alongside our Chief, and I will fight for Prairie Dawn. I will go as well."

White Horse is so proud of his warriors. "I thank you, my men, for your loyalty. Koawa will fill you all in on the search. Each of you takes two of your choosing to go along with you. The rest of you will remain with me and do a local search. I feel these men are close and still within Sioux territory. No rock will be left unturned. No cave will be left untouched. I want these men, and I want them alive. I do not care what you do to whomever is in your way, but these men will be brought back to me in one piece."

There is not one warrior here who does not feel or see the rage in their Chief. White Horse is out for blood, and he does not care who gets in his way. He is not going to rest until these men are caught. There is not one warrior here who complains, for they all know if it were their wife, he would do the same. He feels he got his point across and wants to get back to his Prairie Dawn. He allows Koawa to finish off and comes to his feet.

"Now, if you will all excuse me, I need to get back to my wife."

He is ready to leave when Koawa stops him. "It will not take much to find two snakes cowering in the grass; however, Prairie Dawn could make it easier if she could tell us what they looked like in case they went back to the fort."

"I will allow it; however, I will not upset her any further. If she becomes distressed in any way, we will find them on our own without her help. I will go get her."

White Horse finds me where he left me under the tree beside Minoke and Songbird, helping them stretch a hide. I slowly get to my feet when I see him coming. "You need to be careful what you are doing, Love. I understand you want to carry your weight, but until those ribs are healed, I want you to rest," he tells me.

"I have to do something," I argue, "or my mind does circles."

"Then do something that is not too heavy," he strokes my cheek. "For me," he smiles.

"Alright," I agree.

"Thank you. Now I need you to come with me."

"In there?" I question.

The many years I have lived with the Lakota, never once has a woman been allowed in the smokehouse. I am clearly skeptical of the change.

"Yes," White Horse answers. "The men would like to speak with you."

"Is that not forbidden for a woman to go in there?" I ask.

"It is highly unusual but not forbidden."

White Horse sees my apprehension. "As your Chief, I give you permission to enter."

"Are they clothed?" I ask

"It is not like a sweat lodge, dear. They are clothed." He takes my hand. "Come, Love, you must not keep them waiting."

White Horse walks me to the smokehouse and opens the flap. I briefly hesitate before stepping in. I feel all eyes turn on me as White Horse closes the flap behind us. There is not one warrior here that I do not personally know. I know all their wives and all their children. They are like family to me, like brothers, but right now I am feeling very intimidated. This is their domain, and I clearly feel like I am intruding.

"Sit down, honey," White Horse says.

Except for Koawa, none of these warriors speaks any English, so White Horse can speak to me at will without being understood. I found a place close to the flap between White Horse and Koawa. I feel Koawa grab my wrist as I struggle to come down. When I am down, it is then that I look across and see Blue Thunder. To the left of him is Yellow Hawk, and next to him is Night Owl. Night Owl is our fiercest warrior. He reminds me a great deal of Red Hawk. After seeing his fierce face, I saw no more. I put my eyes down and look away. I know White Horse feels me becoming uneasy.

"It is alright, honey. These men want to help you."

"Because I am your wife?" I wonder.

"No, because you are Lakota," he answers. I faintly grin.

"When I get nervous, my Lakota tongue is really bad."

"We will help you," White Horse says.

I deeply sigh, my anxiety of not wanting to be here is great, but after a few breaths, I finally agree. Koawa speaks in my tongue.

"Prairie Dawn, you told me you saw the two men when you went to the soldier camp."

"Yes," I answer.

"Do you remember what they look like to help us find them?"

"How could I forget, every time I close my eyes, they are there?"

White Horse grabs my finger around his to calm me down, as he can see I am becoming tense. "You do not have to do this," he says.

"No, I can do it," I argue.

I look across at Blue Thunder, next to Koawa, he is the one I feel the most comfortable with. I stay focused on him and begin in my mind what these men look like. White Horse translates.

"There were two of them. The leader of the two had hair like fire that was wavy and untrimmed, was a heavy smoker, lean, and tall. The other man was thick around the waist, with little to no hair, and missing two front teeth. He looked like he didn't belong with the others, real dirty looking."

Suddenly, White Horse sat straight up he looked over at Blue Thunder and spoke in his tongue.

"Did you say you found those clothes Southeast of here?"

"Yes," he answers.

He looks over at Koawa. "I know where they are at!"

"You do?" I say, confused.

"Yes, on our way home, we had to take a different route because of Blue Coat's. We came up to a mine. There were two men there. When one of the men saw us coming, I overheard him say I told you they would find us. He was thick-waisted and took off running like a coward. The other man just watched us as we rode by. I didn't think anything of it until now."

"That has to be them," I confirm.

"I am certain of it." White Horse addresses Koawa. "I want you to take Grey Wolf with you. He can take you to the mine."

"How far away is it?" Koawa asks.

"One day at the most. You ride hard; you will be there by morning." White Horse says nothing more and comes to his feet, helping me to get to mine. I hear Blue Thunder call my name. I turn to look at him.

"When you lie in that cave, I made you a promise, and I intend on keeping it. We will find them. I promise you," he says in his tongue.

I faintly smile and thank them all. Koawa is quick and soon has everyone briefed, and they are ready to leave.

As White Horse and I are standing by the corral, Kikimo comes running up to his father.

"I want to go with Koawa," he tells his father.

"Do you think you are ready?" White Horse asks.

"Yes," he answers.

"I will be riding hard," Koawa warns.

"I do not care. I want to go."

"Alright," White Horse says. "I will allow it, but you listen to everything Koawa tells you to do. No matter what he tells you, you do it."

"I will, Father. I promise. May I go?"

"It is up to your uncle." Kikimo looks over at Koawa.

"Hurry and go get your horse," Koawa says. Kikimo was happy and rushed off to get ready to go.

White Horse and I watch as the warriors leave. Koawa rides up beside me and looks down at me. "I will not stop searching until they are found," he says.

"Just be careful," I say, squeezing both Kikimo and Koawa's hands.

"Kikimo, you mind?" I warn him.

"I will, Ma. Please do not worry, I will be fine."

"I will watch him," Koawa assures. He nods over to White Horse and turns to ride off with Kikimo right by his side.

Chapter Sixteen

Confessions

I have been getting very little freedom from White Horse. It appears my episode with the knife gave him quite a startle, although I have promised him that I would never do anything that foolish again, he is taking no chances and watching me like a hawk. He convinced me to have Flying Hawk look at me, and he gave me some medicine to help the discomfort in my ribs, as well as re-wrapping them. White Horse is adamant in not allowing me to do much around the camp until my ribs are completely healed, leaving me way too much time to think and worry.

Today, the women are at the lake doing some chores. I take Morning Dove and Little Foot along and make my way to join them when I see my husband.

"Where are you going, Love?" he wonders.

"I am on my way to talk to the women. After our recent attack, we formed a bond, and I have decided it is not fair to them to continue leaving them in the dark, so I am going to tell them what happened."

"I think that is wise. I will join you."

"Sweetheart, I am sure you have better things to do than watch a bunch of women doing chores."

"Yes, I do," he agrees, "but you are the reason I remain here and did not lead my men on their quest."

"I will not be alone," I tell him.

My love for this man is beyond words, but sometimes I wish he were not so protective of me.

"Please go do what you need to do. I will be fine," I reassure.

He cocks his eyebrow up as he thinks. "Alright, but I will not be gone long."

I reach up and kiss his cheek. "Neither will I."

I take the children's hands and make my short walk to the lake. The conversations stop when I am spotted. I sit down on a log as all eyes turn to me.

"Women," I begin in their tongue. "I am afraid I owe you all an apology. It is my fault that your men are gone. I did not fall from my horse like I said."

Everyone's ears perk up, and all chores stop. "I left in the middle of the night to get White Men's medicine for White Fawn at the soldier camp. My disguise did not work, and I was discovered and later chased by two soldiers. When I refused to give them any information on our whereabouts, they shot my horse and then I was beaten and raped."

Everyone gasps. Songbird and Minoke rush to my side, both with their arms around me. "You should have told us," Minoke says.

"I was embarrassed and I did not want anyone to know until our Chief could be told."

I looked at each woman, and there was not one who did not have a look of remorse on their face. "I am so sorry I did not want to lie to you all, but I had no choice. I had to keep the secret until my husband could be told. Will you all ever forgive me?" The love that I am shown by everyone is an indication that I was forgiven.

From the entrance of the smoke house, White Horse can see his Prairie Dawn sitting on a log. He watches the women as they gather around her. He sees the hugs and the tender words that are most likely being spoken. He watches as his Prairie Dawn wipes a tear, and Minoke gives another hug. She will be alright, he tells himself, for now, everyone knows the truth.

He lies beside his Prairie Dawn on their pelt as the evening is brought to a close. Little Foot and Morning Dove are already asleep. He can tell that I am deep in my thoughts. He curls me up in his arms, placing a kiss on my forehead.

"What is keeping you so quiet?" he asks me.

"I am just thinking of the women."

"Did they say something to you to upset you?"

"No, when they heard the truth, they could not have been better."

"Then what is the problem?"

"Their men are out there for me. Their men could die, and it is because of me."

White Horse comes up on his elbow to look down at me. "We have been through this already. These men, our men, are doing this because it is the Lakota thing to do. It is not because I am their Chief and you are my wife. It is because you are a Lakota woman and there is not one warrior or brave here that would not protect any woman or child in this camp."

"I know, I just cannot help but feel guilty. It has been over a week since I was attacked. These men are most likely either back at the Fort or in a town hundreds of miles away…"

White Horse vigorously shook his head no, not even allowing me to finish.

"Sweetheart, Red Hawk, who is not even in this band, has gone all the way to the Cheyenne to tell them what happened. They too are joining the search at their end. These men will not escape. There is nowhere they can go that we will not find them.

You put a Cheyenne and a Sioux together, and we are unstoppable."

That I believe, at one time, the Sioux and the Cheyenne were bitter enemies. It wasn't until recently that they formed an alliance and became one in fighting the Blue Coats and keeping the settlers off the land. Unfortunately, the Cheyenne are getting the bad end of the deal and suffering the most losses. White Horse, followed by many other Chiefs, are retaliating along with the Cheyenne to keep the land. I am not surprised that the Cheyenne are returning the favor and helping us. It did make me stop and wonder just how far everyone is going to go in revenge, because of two soldiers who are believed to have abandoned their post. Although White Horse denies it, I do wonder if this is all because I am the wife of a Chief.

"You still believe that they are in Sioux territory?" I ask him.

"Yes, I do. They are running scared, and they are running in circles. I do not believe they are going back to the Fort. Blue Thunder and Koawa have tracked them, and they never showed up there."

"How can you be so sure?" I state.

He placed his hand in my hair, tangling it around his long fingers.

"You need to trust me on this. I understand your fear. I truly do, but let me handle this. I only want you to heal."

White Horse is right. My fear is talking. I have never doubted that White Horse knows what he is doing, and I realize I am an emotional wreck. I need to pull myself together and start to cope with my darkness. Curling myself around White Horse and feeling his strong arms around me, I evidently fall asleep.

Koawa and his warriors come upon the abandoned mine as the great darkness fills the land. Carefully looking around, he notices the men have left in what appears in a hurry. He orders his men to start looking for tracks in which direction they may have gone. Kikimo, remembering everything his father and uncle taught him on tracking, comes down on all four and touches the land. He notices within the darkness how the prairie grass has broken off at the tips and is lying flatter on the ground. He calls for Koawa, who rushes over to join him.

"Look," he says, "it keeps going that way."

Koawa widely grins and rubs the top of Kikimo's head. "You are well on your way to becoming an excellent tracker," he says.

Kikimo is so proud of himself. Finding such a small track in the daylight probably would not have fazed Koawa too much, but finding this track in the dark from an inexperienced brave like himself is a reason for him to feel proud. This is far better than killing any huge buck, he thinks to himself. He cannot wait to brag to Eagle Scout.

I awaken with a start with yet another dream. White Horse is quickly awake, and I am in his arms.

"It is alright, my Love," he consoles.

"Just hold me, "I whine.

White Horse does exactly as his wife wishes and holds her tightly in his arms until she falls back to sleep.

Two days have passed, and no word on any of our warriors, and all local searches are turning up nothing. I am growing more and more depressed and becoming more isolated. The women are wonderful, watching me and taking care of me. I cannot ask for a better support team, but nonetheless, I just want to be left alone in my own world. Feeling comfortable that I am in good hands, White Horse has joined on several local searches and has been responsible for many raids on wagon trains, if they get in the way of his path. When he is not out fighting or searching, he is in the smokehouse planning his revenge. He is totally and completely obsessed with it.

Two posts have been pounded into the ground halfway between our lodge and the clearing. These will hold our prisoners when they arrive. White Horse carefully positioned them here so that no matter where you are in the camp, they will be visible. They will be given water several times a day, but will be offered no food. I have asked him nothing about his plans, and in return, he has said very little except that he will keep them alive for several days here, and they will encounter a long and painful death.

I spent most of the day in a remote area at the lake, away from many. Little Foot and Morning Dove are the only ones I care to be with. With them gone off playing with the others, I am totally alone and have fallen into a deep sadness. I rubbed the stone that Minoke gave me back and forth between my thumbs. I know it is not going to do anything, but it gives me something to cling to as I continue in my darkness.

"There you are." I hear from behind. I see White Horse out of the corner of my eye, sitting down on a rock beside me. He notices me rubbing the stone between my thumbs.

"What do you have there?" he asks. I handed it to him.

"Minoke told me that if I rub it, it will keep the evil spirits away. But it is not working very well."

"It is not working because you do not believe in it." He then hands it back to me.

"I guess you are right." I feel him move my hair free from my face.

"The women have told me you have been isolated today. Are you alright?" I shake my head no.

"Do you want to talk about it?"

"I have been thinking, and I want you to know that I will completely understand if you wish to take another woman to your pelt."

White Horse is surprised and a little perturbed that I would even mention it.

"I am insulted that you would even think I would consider it. Why have you come up with such foolish words?" I shyly shrug my shoulders.

"I just thought you would want someone who hasn't been spoiled." He quickly turns my chin to face him.

"Now you listen to me. You are not spoiled. You wash that thought out of your mind."

"But I am. I have been with someone else."

"You were raped Carrie. It was not by choice."

"You deserve better," I say.

"I deserve you!" he yells. "Why would you think any different?"

"I thought because we have not been together since you have been home, you didn't want me anymore," I whine. "I mean, I don't blame you."

Now he understands how his poor Prairie Dawn is feeling. He puts his arm around my waist and tucks me into his side. "I did not think you would want anything. I was only thinking of you and not what I wanted."

"I thought I lost you," I cry.

"Never, ever will I ever take another woman to lie beside me that is not my Prairie Dawn." I wipe a tear. "I love you, Carrie, and nothing will ever change that."

"I love you, too, White Horse, and I am worried about you as well."

"I will admit I am very angry, but not at you."

"At the soldiers?" I question him as I come out of his arms.

"Not just them but Red Hawk and my scouts, too."

"Why?" I wonder.

"My scouts for not seeing you leave. They let me down, and I plan on telling them how I feel when they return from bringing in the soldiers."

"And Red Hawk?"

"Carrie, he had you in his grasp. I don't care how he felt about you sassing him. He should never have allowed you to pass. I blame a lot of this on him."

"Honey, he did try to stop me, and he was the one who found me and brought me to Koawa. He stayed with me all night. I saw a very different side of Red Hawk that night. White Horse, he saved my life."

"And for that I am grateful; however, that does not excuse him for allowing you to pass. Red Hawk is very arrogant and very mean to women and enjoys punishing them. I am certain Red Hawk allowed you to pass in the hopes something would happen to you and you would learn your lesson."

"That's cruel," I say.

"Yes, he is, that is why I have always told you to stay away from him. Red Hawk is a very good warrior and loves to fight. I respect him for that, but I do not trust him, and neither should you."

White Horse respects and honors all his warriors and others from different bands and has always welcomed them into his camp as if they were family. I have always known that White Horse is not really fond of Red Hawk, but he has never told me why. It is very clear to me that White Horse does not like him. I also know that Koawa despises him and never allowed Running

Water near him. Being that Koawa is out there with Red Hawk to look for these soldiers and White Horse is allowing it, tells me that there is some respect for him. However, I cannot help but wonder if Red Hawk was not Lakota, that White Horse would have anything to do with him.

"Ok, I will keep my distance," I assure him.

"Good. One more thing," he begins.

"What?"

"Minoke told me that this morning, when all the women and children were bathing, you refused. She thought this odd, and so do I. Was there a reason?"

I nodded my head yes. "I didn't want to show my body."

"Why not? It has never stopped you before. I for one enjoy seeing your body," he teases.

"At one time, it never bothered me. I was proud to show it, but not anymore."

"Is it because of what happened?" he asks.

"That and my welts," I conclude.

He leans forward motioning for me to turn around. "Let me see them."

"No, White Horse," I beg." They are so ugly."

He is not taking no for an answer. "Let me see them," he adamantly says.

I turn around and he moves my dress out from my back and peaks down.

Instant rage fills his souls when he sees the damage these men did to his Prairie Dawn. He holds his rage in and begins coming to his feet taking my hand into his.

"Where are we going?" I ask him.

"To take our baths," he answers.

"Now?" I say.

"Yes, now." I watch him remove his tunic and lay it on the ground.

"Come on," he smirks.

"No, not now," I protest.

No is not a word that White Horse is familiar with, and I am quickly stood up and on my feet. By the devilish grin on his face, I know I am in trouble.

"White Horse," I laugh.

He quickly scoops me up in his arms, rushing me teasingly into the water where he carefully, not to hurt my healing ribs, would toss me in a few feet. He then dives in behind me. I resurfaced in his arms. "You are terrible," I joke giving him a splash.

"Terribly in love with you," he smiles.

He is impossible, but God how I love him. I teasingly splash him again and fall into his lips.

Chapter Seventeen

Faces in the dark

Another evening falls on the Lakota camp. I need my husband close. I nudge up alongside him on our pelt and start playing with his manhood, as I am kissing his chest. This is usually a start to our love making, and he normally gives me no complaint, however, he is a little cautious tonight and rolls over on his side.

"Sweetheart, trust me I ache for you, but I do not want to hurt you if you are not healed."

"That part of me is healed. I need to feel you close," I softly say.

He faintly grins, giving him all the reassurance he needs, his kissing grows harder and our lovemaking begins. With one final hard thrust, White Horse empties inside of me, ending our evening of romance. I reached for the cup containing the baby herb and take a few sips. I then put it down and came up on top of him.

"Thank you," I mutter.

"For what?" he wonders.

"I have been so crazy lately and you have never stopped loving me." He lifts his hand and strokes my hair.

"You have no idea how much I love you," he huskily whispers. "You are not part of my life, you are my life. I am the man I am because of you. I could never stop loving you."

I am the only one that has ever seen the soft side of White Horse. There is very little he does not share with me when it comes to his feelings. I have always known that White Horse loves me, it is something we tell each other every day, but like the wind it will fly by with its meaning. Tonight, he is speaking from deep within his heart, words he has never spoken this deep to me before. I truly feel his love and at this moment there really is not a whole lot I can say that will top that. I rub his chest as I smile down at him.

"Where do you think they are at?" I finally ask, changing the subject.

"I am not real sure. I am certain they have made it to the mine by now. But being that my scouts have not seen them, leaves me to believe that the men were not there and they are most likely tracking them."

"They could be gone for a long time," I conclude.

"I do not think so. Not with Koawa on their tail and Red Hawk at the other end. They will be found. I think within a few days they will be here."

"I hope you are right," I conclude.

I then come off White Horse and reach for more tea. It is then that a chilling thought crosses my mind.

"White Horse."

"Hmm," he says.

"Do you know if Koawa gave me the baby tea in the cave?"

"I am sure he did."

"He gave me something to drink. It could have been the root to control the bleeding. He does not know I take this," I argue.

"Koawa is no fool. He is aware of the herb. I am sure he gave it to you," he reassures. I turned around and leaned on his chest.

"The baby tea must be taken almost immediately for it to work. White Horse, I was in no condition to drink it. If he did give it to me later, it is not as potent."

I then started to panic. "Oh my God, White Horse what if I conceived?"

White Horse comes up on his elbows, looping his hand into mine. "Don't talk like that."

"It could be possible," I frantically whine. "Lord knows they did it enough."

He sits straight up, bringing me into his arms. "Shh, it's going to be alright. Tomorrow morning, I will ask Flying Hawk to make the herb stronger for you. It takes longer to work, but if you feel nothing within a week then you did not conceive."

"And if I do?"

"You will miscarry," he kisses my forehead. "Do not worry about it. Everything will be alright."

Kikimo's skillful eye at picking up the little trail paid off. Two men fitting the description are spotted ten miles out, around a campfire, sleeping. Koawa and his men creep in. Both men are quickly overpowered with knives to their throats.

A sleepy White Horse reaches across to put his arm around his Prairie Dawn, only to find her gone. Puzzled at where she could be, he rises to his feet, slipping on his breechcloth and moccasins. He then goes to the flap and into the night air. He peers around the camp, searching for all her usual spots to find her nowhere in sight. After an intensive search of the perimeter of the camp, he goes to count his personal ponies. Noticing that there is none missing, he knows she must be on foot and therefore cannot be too far. He jumps on his faithful steed and starts looking for her.

Koawa gave Kikimo the honor of tying the men around a tree. There they would stay for the duration of the night. Koawa takes his nephew aside and speaks to him in his tongue.

"You will guard them tonight," he tells him.

"Alright."

"You do not speak to them in English, or let on that you understand them," he warns.

"I understand."

"Your father wants them returned alive. So do not hurt them."

"Alright," he reassures his uncle.

Koawa then hands Kikimo a rifle. "Do you know how to use this?" he asks him.

"Kind of."

Koawa shows him how to hold it, so Kikimo looks threatening. "Now go stand over there and remember do not talk to them."

"I won't." Kikimo does as he is told and finds his spot close to the men.

"I told you they would find us," the big man cries.

Kikimo just glares over and looks away out of ear shot. "Shut up," Frank bawls. "I have an idea." Frank starts messing with the tie around his wrists. "That boy over there, he is in training. That one over there is the leader."

"So," the big one says.

"Do I have to spell everything out for you, stupid? When he tied me, I cut me some slack. I will be out of here in no time."

"And you think we are just going to walk out of here with four warriors guarding us?" he argues, "and you call me stupid."

Frank grumbles at Horace's stupidity and asks himself why he ever met up with this man and take him under his wing.

"You really are as dumb as you look," Frank spats. "They will fall asleep, and then we will make our escape. I can charge the boy while you make a run for it, and before they wake up, the boy will be dead, and we will be gone."

"They will just come looking for us again," Horace says.

"But they will never find us. Trust me on this. I know what I am doing."

What was Horace to do but to trust Frank, who never stirred him wrong? He sits patiently and waits.

White Horse finds one of his scouts coming out of the darkness, approaching their Chief.

"Have you seen Prairie Dawn?" he asks.

"No, I have been on the ridge; she has not passed me."

"Go get Long Tail, tell him to search for her by the plateau. I will go back to the lodge and see if she has returned."

"Yes, Chief."

Kikimo looks over at the other warriors; all but Koawa are sleeping. He, too, is growing tired. He yawns as he fights to stay awake. He looks over at the men who did his mother wrong as they sleep. My, how he hates them and wishes he could kill them on the spot. He watches Koawa slip out into the woods, figuring he is probably relieving himself. Kikimo is thinking he needs to do the same thing. He squirms in place to hold it in. Growing sleepy, Kikimo yawns. I must stay awake, he tells himself. His eyes grow heavy. He turns his back and leans on a tree to rest his head.

Frank opens his eyes from a pretend sleep.

"Horace," Frank whispers. "Wake up."

"Huh," he says, waking up. "Oh, I'm awake."

"The boy is alone."

Frank removes his hands from the ties. He then very slowly reaches to untie Horace. "Just keep an eye on the other one. I saw him go into the woods."

"Hurry, Frank."

"Shut your trap before we are heard."

Both men are untied and creep to their feet. Frank motions for Horace to run as he comes up behind Kikimo. He grabs him from behind. Kikimo struggles to break free. Unbeknownst to Frank, who the boy's father is and how well he has been trained to fight, Kikimo surprises Frank with his strength.

The sleeping warriors, hearing the commotion, are awake and rush to Kikimo's aid. They quickly capture Frank. Koawa steps out of the woods with his knife to Horace's throat. He pushes him out in front of him and to the ground. Koawa speaks his tongue to Kikimo.

"Never turn your back on the enemy," he scolds him. "It could get you killed."

Kikimo is a little embarrassed. It is a hard lesson learned. He is relieved that his uncle and the other warriors were there to protect him. Koawa is now pissed. He is not taking another chance of these men getting free again. He spats out a command in his tongue. Kikimo watches on as his uncle takes his anger out on the men. Koawa goes to the one named Frank, ripping him free from another warrior, tossing him to the ground. He then gives him a swift kick in the groin. Frank bellows in pain. Koawa then shoves a gag in his mouth, tying it around his head. He is then handed a large rope. He ties Frank's hands together until his fingers are nearly blue. He then loops the rope around Frank's waist and brings him to his feet. The same action is repeated to Horace. Then each man is taken to a horse where the other end of the rope is looped around the horse's belly. Koawa then jumps on his horse, which is hauling Frank. He then gives another command in his tongue, and all the men mount and are on their way, with their captives walking behind them.

Prairie Dawn has not returned to the lodge. White Horse is extremely concerned. "Carrie, where are you?" he mumbles to himself. Just then, he hears his scouts. Prairie Dawn has been found. He rushes on his horse and follows his scout to the plateau. Long Tail points to the top of the bluff. White Horse grows pale when he sees his Prairie Dawn just inches from the edge. He rushes up there before she does something foolish and he loses her forever.

He comes up behind her with the wind in his hair. "Carrie," he calmly says. "Honey, come away from the edge." He can tell she has been crying. He reaches his hand out. "Come on, Love. Reach for my hand."

"I can't do this anymore, White Horse."

"Honey, we will talk about this. Give me your hand."

"I don't want to do this anymore," I sob.

White Horse must do something; his Prairie Dawn is talking crazy in her head. He watches the uneven ground moving below them. One slip from either one of them could be disastrous. He spots a strong tree limb just inches from his Prairie Dawn. He rushes over to scale the tree. He slides himself across the lower limb overlooking the straight drop. He is just inches from her head. He hears her sob. He holds his breath that the ground stays intact under her feet, as he scoots as far out as he can go.

"Sweetheart," he says to her. "Give me your hand."

He sees his Prairie Dawn shake as she comes out of her trance. She takes a step when the ground moves below her. He hears her scream. With no time to think of himself, he wraps his strong legs around the limb of the tree and leans over to pull her up. He swings her to safety in front of him. He sighs deeply as he rushes to hug her. "What were you thinking?" he barks.

"I couldn't sleep. I didn't want to wake you, so I went for a walk. I didn't realize how far I went. The breeze was so refreshing from the plateau. I wasn't going to jump, White Horse. Honestly, I wasn't."

White Horse is just relieved nothing tragic happened, but he has had enough with his Prairie Dawn being so callous with her own life. Tonight, it is going to stop. "I don't know what those men did to your mind," he states," but I will be damned if I will allow you to continue trying to hurt yourself."

"I wasn't going to jump," I argue.

"Then what were you doing so close to the edge?"

"Just looking out," I defend. White Horse sighs to keep calm. He rubs my shoulders. "I wish I could figure out what has gotten you so terrified."

The frustration in his voice is very apparent. White Horse is a problem solver and a damn good one. It is very clear he is frustrated because he cannot solve what is going on in the mind of his Prairie Dawn.

"You are not in my head, White Horse. You don't see them. You don't hear them. You can't smell them."

"Oh, honey," he soothes.

"Every time I close my eyes, they are there. They haunt me. They possess me. They are my demons." He watches as I dry a tear. "Sometimes I wish Red Hawk had left me in that ravine to die." White Horse snaps. He grabs my shoulders and shakes me.

"I don't ever want to hear you talk like that again. You understand me?" He releases his grip. Out of frustration, I watch him push his hair over his head, and it falls free. "I will not allow these men to destroy you!" he barks. "Fight them, Carrie. Fight them."

"I can't," I sob.

"Yes, you can. You must!"

"I can't do it anymore. Don't you understand that? I cannot beat them."

"You are strong, Carrie."

"Not anymore. I have no more strength."

White Horse gazes down into his very fragile Prairie Dawn's eyes.

"Lakota never lose their fight, never lose their strength. When one is down, another is right there to pick up where the other left off. You are not alone in this, Love. For I am Lakota, and when you fall, I will be right there to pick you up, but you cannot give up, for we never give up."

His words hit me like a rock landing hard on the ground. He is right. I cannot give up. I cannot let these men win. I must fight. I must regain control of my life. I fall into my husband's arms and hold him tightly as I cry my last, and hopefully, final tears.

Chapter Eighteen

The Little Warrior

The Lakota warriors have been riding for nearly a day with both men trailing behind them. Both captives are drenched in sweat and tired from their walk. Koawa needs them returned alive, so he stops at a watering hole for the men to drink and for a brief rest. Both men welcome the water and are getting their fill. Word of their capture has gone as far as Blue Thunder and Night Owl. They arrived at the watering hole along with several other warriors.

Horace's eyes grow huge as the size of the warriors has nearly doubled.

"This isn't good," he whines to Frank. "Why so many?"

"Shut up!" Frank barks as he cups his hand with water, pouring it over his head to cool himself off.

"Do you think that is her husband?" Horace cries as he sees Blue Thunder glaring at him.

"I'm not sure. They have no proof that we did anything. She is dead."

Kikimo has overheard everything and gives a quick glare to Frank.

"Then why do they want us?" Horace wonders.

"Because they think we are Blue Coats dumbass. They are too fucking stupid to know any different. Now silence. Here he comes."

Blue Thunder fiercely looks over at them as he jumps off his pony. He made a promise to Prairie Dawn when he left her, and he intended to keep it. He remembers the first time he met the woman with the golden hair, when their Chief carried her into the camp when she was attacked by a bear. He was confused why a man who he has always looked up to would fall for a white woman, who are known to be rude and lazy, but then he saw the love she had for his Chief when he took a bullet for her, and he saw her courage, and power for standing up to a town of ridicule and the knife of Minoke.

He then remembers her best friend, the one he called Rose Pedal, better known as Stella. He, too, had fallen for her. He will never forget their night of romance, how experienced she was, and how fulfilling it made him feel. How angry he was when she refused to follow him and how close he came to kidnapping her. He has not yet been able to fill that void and has only taken a few women quickly to his pelt.

He feels drawn to Prairie Dawn but not as a lover, more like a sister that he needs to protect. He brings his attention to the man with the big eyes. He squats right down in front of him and sees him shaking. He is going to have a little fun with the man Prairie Dawn says raped her. He speaks his tongue, and of course, Horace does not understand.

"What is he saying, Frank?"

"How the hell am I supposed to know?" he barks.

Blue Thunder motions with his finger for Kikimo to come over. He speaks his tongue to him.

"Koawa told me not to speak to them," Kikimo tells him in his tongue.

"I will deal with Koawa, now tell him," Blue Thunder snaps.

Kikimo obeys. "He said look at him."

Both men are surprised that the boy speaks English. Horace is too terrified to look. Blue Thunder speaks his tongue again. Kikimo translates.

"If you wish not to die a painful death right now, then look at him."

Horace does as the boy says. Blue Thunder has eyes of ice that pierced a hole in the big man's heart. Blue Thunder speaks his tongue again.

"He said, look into the eyes of the man who will kill you for what you did to Prairie Dawn."

Both men are now certain that the woman they thought they killed is alive, and their luck has run out. Frank is not as intimidated as Horace is and is much more arrogant. He knows he is going to die, so he has nothing to lose. He cannot stand Indians and loves to tease them, so he is just going to see how far he can push them.

"That bitch got what was coming to her," he growls.

Kikimo is enraged. He slams his foot down on Frank's hand, landing it painfully on a rock. Frank squawks in pain as he rubs it.

"That woman is my mother," he roars. "And both of you will die a great, painful death in the hands of my father."

Horace whines like a baby as Frank gives him a dirty look.

"I thought he was the husband," Frank says, nodding over at Blue Thunder.

"He is nothing to what you will face when my father rips you apart with his bare hands."

Koawa has heard enough and comes up alongside Kikimo. An arrogant Frank just doesn't know when to stop.

"Let me guess," Frank growls. "She must be his whore too."

Kikimo lost all control. Like a bolt of lightning, he roars as he pounces into the water, pushing Frank's head under. He lifts it up as Frank gasps for air before repeating it again. Kikimo's strength is stunning, even to the warriors watching on. Blue Thunder starts to come to the young brave's aid when Koawa stops him and together they watch Kikimo, as he continues pushing the man's head underwater. After several pushes of the red-haired man's head under water, Koawa stops him. Kikimo is full of rage and extremely winded when Koawa pulls him off.

Blue Thunder comes into the water, bringing Frank to his feet. Koawa hears him chuckle as he looks at Frank realizing what a mere boy did. How proud his Chief would be with his son he thinks, as he forces the man out of the water. The men are pushed back behind their horses and tied back up. Kikimo, still very angry, is coaxed on his pony by Koawa. As Koawa turns to mount his pony he nudges Frank, nearly knocking him over. Against what he told Kikimo he speaks in a language the man will understand.

"This is your lucky day, for today you live," he spats. "But your days are ticking away. Tick! Tick! Tick!" he teases and goes to his pony. On his command they are off.

The light of another day is on us. I awake feeling less sore and more mobile. Flying Hawk gave me a stronger herb to drink. If I have conceived, this will terminate any child that may be inside of me. He explains to me that it is slower acting and may take a few days to work. If I do not experience any discomfort in a few days, then I will feel nothing and most likely never conceived. This is one thing I truly hope never happens.

Feeling confident that his Prairie Dawn is in good hands, White Horse has been out with his warriors for most of the day patrolling and scouting. They are ready to head back in when White Horse spots a lone rider running in hard.

"That's Kikimo," he says.

In a flash he runs to catch up to him with his warriors close behind. When Kikimo sees the others coming he slows his pony down to a trot. He watches his father come up alongside him.

"Is everything alright son?" White Horse asks.

"We got them Father," he smiles.

White Horse is very pleased. "Where are they now?"

"Koawa is bringing them in. He is a few miles behind me. He told me to run in to let you know."

"I am proud of you son."

"How is ma?" he asks.

"She is back at camp. Why don't you go tell her."

"You coming?"

"No. I am going to go meet up with Koawa."

Kikimo looked at his father. "I kind of lost my temper with them," he admits.

"What did you do?" He smiles, as he can only imagine.

"We had stopped for water. Blue Thunder and the others had met up with us. Blue Thunder got into his face and the red-haired man didn't like it too much. That red-haired man is nasty. He started talking bad about ma, and I pushed his head under the water several times until Koawa stopped me. I also smashed his hand on some rocks."

White Horse couldn't help but chuckle and wished he could have seen it. "It's alright, son. They are going to wish that is all that is done to them when I get my hands on them." Kikimo agreed.

"I am going to see my ma. We will wait for you by the post."

White Horse nods and watches his son leave. It didn't take them long to catch up with Koawa. He finds them just as they are crossing the creek. White Horse rides up right in between the two exhausted, sweaty men. He speaks his tongue to Blue Thunder and Koawa to stop, and he gets off his pony.

An exhausted Horace falls to his knees. He takes one look at White Horse and starts to whimper and plead to the great warrior for mercy. For a few seconds, White Horse stares down at him and then suddenly, in a flash, he kicks him with all his might, forcing him to stand up. He then lunges forward, grabbing the man around his throat. He squeezes, leaving very little air as he comes eye to eye with the man who raped his wife. Horace nearly urinates on himself when he sees the fiery eyes of White Horse.

White Horse fixes his eyes on Horace as he begins to weep. "You cry now while you can. Because by the time I am through with you, there will be nothing left."

He then releases his grip as Horace gasps for air. He then turns his attention to the man with hair of fire. The man whom Kikimo just moments ago told him insulted his wife. He finds the man standing arrogant and cocky, less afraid and bold. White Horse knows this is the man he is going to focus on until he wipes that smirk off his face. This is the man who tied his wife so she couldn't fight, gagged her so she couldn't scream, and beat her so she couldn't run. It is now his time to see how it feels. The only problem is that White Horse is twice his strength and can inflict twice as much pain. He nods for both Koawa and Blue Thunder to start walking. White Horse then grabs the back of his red hair, nearly bringing him off his feet. He kicks him, forcing him to walk. They move a few feet.

"You like to fight women, huh?"

White Horse then tosses the man down into the rocky creek by his hair. All the while, Blue Thunder continues walking on his pony, dragging the man behind him until he comes to his feet. He shuffles his feet to keep up with the pony, only for White Horse to toss him down again. This is repeated several times. White Horse, still wanting them alive, lets up and starts walking behind them all the way to camp. If one man is to stumble or fall, they are at the mercy of White Horse until they come to their feet.

When they enter the camp, he sees his Prairie Dawn next to Kikimo watching on. He catches a glimpse of Minoke and Songbird making their way to stand beside her. He is pleased with this, and it allows him to handle the men as he sees fit. The men stop in front of their post. White Horse waits patiently for them to be set free. He then rushes in, grabbing each man by the back of the shirt and pushing them into the post headfirst. A loud thud followed by a holler from each man is heard. On their Chief's order, the men are then tied up. White Horse looks over at his Prairie Dawn. She appears to be a little timid. He motions for her to come. She is a little hesitant but obeys. When she is within his distance, he grabs her hand and walks her over to face them. He feels her tuck her head into his chest as they approach.

"You have warriors surrounding you. There is no way these men will ever hurt you again. If you want to face your fears, you are going to have to face them."

He brings me in only inches to the one named Horace. He tells Koawa to lift his head so I can see him. When he sees me, his face turns white. He is filled with fear and knows he is a dead man.

"That's him," I say.

White Horse nods over to Koawa, who elbows the man, knocking him out cold. We now turn to the one named Frank. He is the one I fear the most. Blue Thunder picks up his head. He takes one look at me.

"Why won't you die?" he growls.

White Horse is livid. He gently moves me away behind Blue Thunder, and then with all his brute force, he lifts his leg up and slams it into the man's chest. I hear the man bellow in agony. White Horse has no choice. He wants these men alive for at least a few more days. He is going to make them pay the Lakota price for violating me. He is going to make them an example for all of what he can do when you mess with him. Despite his enormous rage, he nudges my arm to follow him, and we walk away.

Chapter Nineteen

Eye for an Eye

White Horse awakens early. He had a very restless night, and it was not due to his Prairie Dawn, who had slept her best in several weeks. His insides burn, his veins pulsate with rage; all he could do last night was think of his revenge. No matter what he does, no matter how spiteful he will be, nothing will bring the justice his Prairie Dawn deserves. He steps outside his lodge feeling cynical and ornery, the foulest mood he has been in for a very long time. He sees his two captives asleep at their post. He arrogantly walks down to the red-haired man, whom he despises the most. Towering over him as he sleeps, he pulls out his shaft and starts urinating on his head. The man awakens with a squint, as White Horse is in midstream. He growls as he turns his head to avoid any further humiliation. White Horse finishes adjusting himself back in and gives the man the wickedest smirk. He then notices the big man still sleeping and thinks it only fair to wake him up as well. A swift kick in his groin should do it. He hits his mark, smiling when the man awakens, whimpering in agony. That will do it for now, he tells himself. The rest will come in due time.

Later that day, White Horse joins Koawa and Blue Thunder under a tree, looking out at his captives. He watches his Prairie Dawn scrapping hides with Minoke and Songbird not far away. He notices that she is moving better, and her ribs seem to be healing. He also notices a little smile on her face from time to time. He is very pleased to see his wife starting to get better. His thought is interrupted when he suddenly sees his warriors riding in along with a few guests.

I stop a moment from scraping a hide to see who our guests are. I am not surprised when I see one rider being Red Hawk. I am certain White Horse invited him to join in the taste of Lakota justice. I see White Horse come to his feet and make the short walk to my side. We both watch as Red Hawk gets off his horse and starts his walk to us, bringing a gift behind him. He greets White Horse and then looks at me. In his tongue, he speaks.

"This is for you." Behind him, he is leading a horse. I am speechless. In my years as a Lakota woman, I have only received two horses as a gift, and both were from White Horse. One he gave to me when Sugar Foot died one winter from old age, and the other was on our fifth-year anniversary. This is a rare occasion that a warrior who is not my spouse-to-be is giving a gift as priceless as a horse.

"Your pony was killed. So, I found a new one for you," he says.

I am flattered beyond words. White Horse owns many horses, more than anyone else. I am welcome to take any of them. This is something that I know Red Hawk is aware of. I glance over at White Horse. I am not really sure what to do. If I do not take the horse, it could be an insult to Red Hawk. White Horse nods his head for me to take it. I take the lead from Red Hawk.

"Thank you," I tell him in his tongue. "I will ride his big back with pride."

I smile. I am certain I see him grin. I then leave the men to do their business, taking my horse to the corral with the rest of them. I found some apples for my new horse, which I have decided to name Shadow, due to his solid black coat and white ankles. I am planning on taking him out for a ride today and hope White Horse will join me.

On my way back from the corral, I notice the fun has already started from Red Hawk, as he is picking on the heavy-set man. I come in closer, standing next to Kikimo and watching on. The man has been dragged out to the center clearing. Red Hawk, Blue Thunder, Yellow Hawk, and Night Owl are kicking the man as he cowers on the ground. I can only imagine the agony this man is enduring as four of the toughest warriors are inflicting their pain. I catch a glimpse of White Horse making his way to the clearing. Koawa is right behind him with the red-haired man. He tosses him on the ground as if he were a rag doll. I watch White Horse kick him, rolling him into a ball. It is then that I noticed that his hands are tied at his wrists. I faintly grin, an eye for an eye, I think. The camp watches on as both men are kicked and beaten by the six toughest and most vindictive warriors I have ever met. After several minutes of the men being beaten, I put it upon myself to walk out to the clearing. I hear White Horse speak his tongue, and the men stop. I look over at White Horse and speak his tongue.

"Allow me entrance," I tell him.

I am allowed. I make my way to the big man, just as Red Hawk gets him to his knees. The man sees me approaching and starts whining like a baby.

"I'm sorry," he cries. Begging, pleading with his eyes to make these men stop. "Don't let them kill me," he begs.

"Why shouldn't I? Did you stop when I wanted you to?" I spat.

The man is in tears, pleading from the heart for mercy. "Please! I beg you! I never wanted to hurt you."

"Then why did you do it?" I wonder.

"You, you were just lying there, you were so, so purty."

That is when I snapped. My eyes immediately turn to ice. I lunge forward in rage, taking everyone by surprise. I dig my nails into the eyes of the man. Red Hawk releases his grip and the man falls to the ground screaming in pain. I am uncontrollable with rage.

"You destroyed my life!" I scream, as I kick him in the face.

The man whimpers and rolls in a ball. I look up at Red Hawk, no words are spoken. Only White Horse has ever seen my temper and both men are caught off guard and slightly amused to see it come out. I then appear in front of the red hair man. White Horse has the weight of his foot on his head, so he cannot move. He lifts his eyes to me.

"Fuck you, bitch," he spats.

I am probably bolder than I normally would have been, but I am so angry, and I know there are enough warriors around me that I feel safe. I kick the man in the face. I then come down on top of him, forcing him to swallow some dirt.

"I will enjoy watching you rot," I hiss and come to my feet.

As I am walking back to the lodge, I hear the beatings continue. I step inside to cool off, closing the flap behind me.

Later that afternoon, White Horse orders that the men receive a small amount of water. He wants me nowhere near them and gives Minoke the honors. I watch her only a few feet away. Two warriors join her, for her protection, although by the looks of them, either one is in much shape to do anything. Little Foot joins me by my side. He is just starting to understand who these men are and what they did. We watch together as Minoke finishes. She gently touches my shoulder as she walks by and heads back into camp with the other two warriors. I look down at my son. I can tell he is trying to be brave. I watch him pick up a stone, weighing no more than a few ounces. He then tosses it at the red-haired man, just ever so gently hitting him. Little Foot then turns and starts walking away. I begin to join him when I see the red-haired man smirk. He thinks it comical. I think it is insulting. I glare at him.

"You think that is funny," I bark.

I picked up a stone. This one much bigger and heavier. I toss it with all my force hitting the man in the chest.

"No one makes a fool out of my son."

I grab another rock and toss again. I move in closer to make a harder hit, several of them land. The commotion is heard throughout the camp. White Horse and a few other warriors are sitting under a tree just watching, ready to pounce if need be. I am now joined by several other women and children, all of us are tossing stones at each captive. We continued this for many minutes. I pick up my last rock before I call it quits, right in front of the red-haired man. I glanced up at his buckle on his belt. A capitol letter H is engraved on the buckle. An immediate flashback occurs. I gasp. "Oh, dear God."

I waste no time and quickly find Koawa, who is sitting in a circle along with White Horse and other warriors under a tree. I stop next to White Horse. He knows by my face something is wrong.

"What is the matter?" he asks me. I hold onto White Horse's shoulder as I come down on my knees.

"I just remembered something."

"What?" he asks. I look over at Koawa.

"The day Running Water died." It is a day he will never forget. He grows still as he listens on. "I heard the soldiers coming so I took some of her blood and wiped it on me and played dead."

Blue Thunder is extremely curious about what I am saying and asks his Chief to translate. It is then I switch and speak the tongue everyone knows. It will take me longer to tell my story, but I feel all should hear what I have to say. I continue.

"When I was lying there, I overheard two soldiers talking about how they got us good. One soldier commented on my hair color. Before he could turn me over, they were called away. Hatford. He was called Hatford. The day I was attacked, before Red Hawk found me in the ravine, I overheard them talking again. One said that he was sure this time I was dead. Just now when I was picking up a rock in front of the red-haired man, I saw his…" I had to stop for a moment as I couldn't think of the word. I turn to White Horse for help.

"Buckle," he translates.

When all is comprehended, I continue. "On his buckle there is a Capitol H." Koawa is not following me. "H, for Hatford. Koawa, these are the same men who killed Running Water. I am certain of it. Why else would they say anything about my hair and about me being dead if they were not the ones who were there that day we were attacked?"

Koawa grows instantly with rage. "Which one!" he growls.

"I cannot be sure, but I think it is the heavy-set man. I recognize the voice and the laugh."

"The revenge will be even sweeter. Thank you, Prairie Dawn."

"Finally, both of us will get a closure," I tell him. He faintly grins.

I then start to come to my feet when I am hit with excruciating pelvic pain. I bellow out and nearly fall into Blue Thunder's lap. White Horse is quick to react and stops me from falling as another pain hits, bringing me to my knees. All warriors are on their feet when White Horse jumps up.

"What is it?" he asks worried.

My eyes fill with tears from the pain. I grabbed his hand and tried to stand.

"The tea," I cry out.

White Horse knows then exactly what is going on. He scoops me up in his arms, walking me briskly to our lodge. Minoke and Songbird are ordered to follow. He places me down on our pelt just as another pain hits and I start to miscarry. Songbird and Minoke are rapid with their aid on helping me.

White Horse watches on as his blood begins to boil beyond control. He hears his Prairie Dawn cry in pain as another contraction is felt. His rage explodes as he yet again sees what these men have done to his beautiful wife. It is more than he can control. He grabs his whip and claw and storms out of the lodge.

Stomping down to the post, all eyes turned to him. There is not a soul in that camp who does not see the rage on their Chief's face. Several of his warriors follow behind him as he comes to the first post of the red-haired man. He literally rips him free of his bonds, tossing him out to the clearing. He tears open the man's shirt, trampling the man with his strong legs until he cowers. Giving a quick flick of the whip that is heard throughout the camp, he smacks it on his back. The crack is heard throughout the valley. The man screams in agony. White Horse takes his foot, pushing the man to a crawl. When he does, White Horse hits him again. The action is repeated several times, with each crack becoming louder and louder as it hits the back of the soldier. After receiving nearly twenty whips and the man falling limp on the prairie grass, is it then when White Horse stops. He grabs him by his feet, dragging him harshly across the ground to his post. He is tossed there where Night Owl will tie him back up. Still full of astronomical rage, he rushes over taking the other man from the post. The man pleads with him as he just witnessed what he did to his friend. As big as this man is and as much as he weighs compared to White Horse, he is no match to White Horse's brute strength and incredible rage that is making him even more lethal. In no time, White Horse has him overpowered and into the clearing.

Koawa has come into the clearing followed by Red Hawk and Blue Thunder who are on their horses. The man's shirt is ripped open. He is nearly disrobed. White Horse then takes the rope, already looped around Blue Thunder's horse, and ties it around the wrists of the man. He then smacks the rear of the horse and it takes off. Blue Thunder runs the horse hard. The man bops up and down the plains, hitting hard with every bump. Red Hawk gallops alongside the big man, blowing dust up from his horse into the man's face. Blue Thunder runs several yards and then turns around and comes back.

Upon turning around, Red Hawk takes his club and smacks it hard on Horace's back until he comes to his feet. Blue Thunder then takes off again. Horace is unable to run behind the speed of the horse and is tossed to the ground where he is again dragged across the prairie. When Blue Thunder arrives back, the man is cut free and kicked by White Horse to get to crawl. When he refuses to crawl, Koawa gives him a kick in the abdomen, forcing the man on all four. It is then that White Horse takes his bear claw club and smacks it on the back of the man named Horace, allowing the claw to grip under the surface of his flesh. White Horse then slides the claw down, tearing open the man's skin. The man screams in agony. Koawa kicks the man, forcing him to get up and walk. A few steps are taken, and White Horse repeats the action, making the man fall to the ground. This is repeated numerous times until the man is limp and filled with blood. White Horse straddles the man as he lies on the prairie ground on his belly. He lifts his head by his hair, forcing the man to arch his back, bringing him complete agony. White Horse then squats down in front of him.

"You have brought enough torment to my wife and people. A quick death is too good for you. You rest, you son of a bitch, because I have only just begun." He then pushes his face down into the ground and comes to his feet, leaving the man where he lies. He makes his way back to his lodge as his warriors drag the soldier back to his post. He enters the lodge and Songbird and Minoke leave. He comes down on his knee stroking my cheek. I turn my head.

"How are you feeling?" he asks me.

"Songbird gave me the root. I will be alright," I tell him.

He faintly grins. "You are so strong my woman. You have suffered so. I fear my justice will not be enough to heal your wounds."

"I heard what you did. How I wish I could have seen it."

He strokes my hair leaning in to kiss me. "Soon, but for now I want you to rest." He then comes to his feet and leaves. The remainder of the day I will rest, sleeping off and on. Minoke and Songbird are taking excellent care of me. I lie on our comfortable pelt and think of White Horse, how he looked so different and distraught. It makes me wonder if he is taking this as hard as me

Chapter Twenty

The Unselfish Love

White Horse awakes just before the sun. He leans across to give his Prairie Dawn a kiss on her cheek before rising to his feet. He quickly dresses as he debates on whether he wants to take an early ride to clear his racing mind or a walk to his favorite spot overlooking his camp. He decides on the walk. He has much on his mind and his heart weighs heavy. He has always been able to clear his mind on a good walk.

He opens the flap leaving his family to sleep and starts his walk, just as the great circle in the sky begins to rise. He stops a moment to look at his captives sitting asleep bound to their post. He watches the toll of each man as he realizes how brutal yesterday's beating really was. He has to give these men some credit, most men would not have survived it, but these were not any ordinary men, he thinks, these men are demons.

He continues his walk at a leisure pace. He has much to think about, much too clear away. He touches a few tree branches as he walks by, noticing that the season is changing. He spots a doe as it comes out to graze, not at all threatened by his presence. It watches him as he passes by. He thinks back to the first time that he took his Prairie Dawn out to the woods when she spent a few days at his camp after being attacked by a bear. He remembers how much he impressed her when he was able to approach the deer and pet it. He has not done it since.

He gazes at the heavens and spots a hawk in flight soaring across the bright sky. How he wishes he could just fly away right now at a time when his heart is so heavy. He comes to the hill where the great tree stands, nearly reaching the clouds. He begins the steep incline overlooking the camp. He finds his usual spot and sits down. It is there where he closes his eyes and begins his morning worship. He prays for his people and to the Nation as a whole. He gives thanks to Mother Earth for their survival and wellbeing. He will remain here in his thoughts and prayers for several minutes.

I am awake to a tug by my six-year-old son, who is in need of relieving himself. I slip on my moccasins and together we make our way to the bushes at the edge of the camp. We stop briefly and look at our captives, seeing for the first time what our Chief and our warriors have done. I am amazed that either one is still alive. We move away quickly when one stirs awake.

Little Foot and I make it to the bushes. Although he is very capable of relieving himself without my aide, I always come with him to check for snakes that occasionally call these bushes home. When he is all clear of any creepy crawlers, I leave him to do what he must do and find my own spot.

"Mama snake," I hear my son say, as I begin my flow.

"Oh, guess mama missed one sleeping under the rock," I tease him.

"Yeah, mama missed one."

"Let it be." I tell him.

"Mama, it is coming closer."

I can hear the distress in his tiny voice and know it is bothering him. Most of the snakes around here are harmless and until I met White Horse I was scared to death of them. I quickly finish and come to my feet. Dusting my dress off, I step into the bushes where my son is squatting. My hunch is correct, and the snake is harmless.

"He is just hungry son," I tell him as I watch the snake slither closer to us.

"Hungry for me," he says.

I find a stick and allow it to curl itself around it. If White Horse was here, he would have just picked it up with no stick, but I on the other hand, haven't yet received the courage to be that close to one yet.

"No son, you are too big for it. It will find a mouse." I comment.

"Father can eat it for breakfast," he says.

"Yes son, he probably would."

I walk further in the bushes and release the snake. "But for today it will live." I watch it slither away. Little Foot finishes his morning movement and joins me outside of the bushes.

"Mama look," he says as he points to the hills.

I follow his finger. "Father." Sure enough, sitting under the great tree is White Horse.

I figure he went up there early this morning to pray, but I am certain by what I can see, he has finished as he is gazing out into the horizon, unaware we are down here.

"Can I go run to him, Mama?" Little Foot asks.

"No son, leave him be," I say.

White Horse was acting very differently last night and was very restless in his sleep. I need to make sure he is alright.

"Son, go back with the others. I will join you in a little bit."

"Alright mama," Little Foot says.

I then watch him as he runs off and back into camp. I am feeling stronger today with just a nagging pain in my lower stomach. However, the hill looks steep, and I am not sure I am strong enough to make such a climb, so I find a different way up, coming up behind White Horse. He is clearly deep in thought when I see him. His face is thick with obvious turmoil in his mind. I wonder what is so heavy to bring this strong powerful man down. I hear him deeply sigh as I slowly walk my way over to him. He hears the movement of my feet and quickly turns his head my way. He rushes to his feet.

"Sweetheart you should not have climbed such a hill," he says as he grabs my arm to lead me the rest of the way, helping me down to a comfortable sit. He then came down beside me.

"I am worried for you and wanted to make certain you are alright."

"Do not worry for me Love, for I am fine." I do not believe him.

"Your face tells me different," I say. He faintly grins.

"You have been married to me too long, for you know me well," he teases.

"Yes, I do and I know when your mind is deep."

I watch him lean back against the tree and hear him sigh. He reaches for my hand gently squeezing it.

"You are a good woman my wife. You have been there for me, followed me, loved me. I sometimes ask myself why? Why do you love someone who is so selfish?"

His words surprise me as White Horse is the most unselfish man I have ever met.

"Why are you thinking that?" I ask him.

He grows still, just gazing out at the horizon. "White Horse, talk to me," I tell him.

"Carrie," he mumbles tilting his head back against the tree. "Sometimes I wish you were more selfish like me."

I came closer to him, placing my hand on his cheek. I look deep into his eyes, seeing how heavy they are with emotion.

"You listen to me," I begin. "I love you White Horse, with every ounce of my blood. You are the strength that keeps me strong, you keep me living. It is your unselfish and unconditional love that keeps me going every day." He faintly grins as he strokes my hair.

"Carrie, you have given up so much for me, your life, your brother, and your friends. You followed me, laid with me. You nearly died to give me a son. You have been ridiculed, shot at, beaten, and raped, keeping your pain and suffering to yourself so we can have peace, all because of your unselfish love for me."

"No White Horse, don't think like that."

"It is true my Love. My selfishness has brought you a lot of pain."

"How can you figure that?" I ask him.

"White Fawn warned me of great danger to you before I left, but I ignored it. I was too involved at the task in hand to give her old mind a second thought." I am confused.

"I don't understand," I say.

"My mother warned me of danger lurking over you. She stressed for me to keep you nearby. I should have told you. I should have told Koawa but instead I left. I left and because of your love for me, you left in the night to save my mother's life. You were attacked because you refused to give me away. Me Carrie, you did it for me. You always do it for me."

I can tell this is really bothering him. I can see the pain in his eyes as he turns his head. This powerful and very strong man is near tears. He feels responsible for my attack, for all the wrong and bad things that have ever happened to me. I feel he thinks he has failed me in some way. I must get through to him. I must assure him that he is wrong, that I do not hold him at fault. I have no regrets about marrying him. This is where I belong, and nothing would ever change my mind. White Horse is my life.

"White Horse," I start as I take his hand into mine. He looks my way as he composes himself. "Everything I did, I did it because I had too."

Perplexed, he looks at me. "It is because of your enormous love for me that I felt compelled to disobey Koawa and leave. Because I felt I owed it to you for all the love you have for me, I had to return it back to you. I had to prove my love to you."

"Oh, honey," he mumbles as he caresses my hand.

"No, sweetheart."

"White Horse, let me finish, please," I beg him.

He sits back, allowing me to finish. "Every day, every breathing moment, I feel your love. It is wrapped all around me.

It is in the air I breathe. You give me so much and you never complain. I give you so little, that is why I left. I wanted to give you something back. I wanted to prove to you how much I love you and how much I need you."

I can feel my tears coming. He grabs a tear as he leans forward, placing his hand on my cheek.

"There is never a day Carrie that I do not feel your love. We are one and together we are whole. When you hurt, I hurt. When you cry, I cry. Every emotion you feel is a part of me." He wipes another tear. "Sweetheart, I do not want you to ever think that you owe me anything, for I love you and without you beside me I am dead. For as long as you are happy then I have done everything right. That is why this is shattering me to a million pieces, because no matter what I do to these men it will not be enough to mend the deep hole in your heart that I feel as well."

I faintly grinned as I stroked his cheek. I love this man more and more every day.

"You have a good start," I smile. "I saw the soldiers on my way here. There is not much left of them."

He shakes his head. "When I saw you in all that pain and realized that one of those men did it, I completely lost it. I wanted to rip their hearts out and shred it into a million pieces. I have never been that angry in all my life."

"It is understandable White Horse."

"Yes, Koawa feels my rage as well. If it was up to him, they would have been beaten until they were dead."

"Why didn't you?" I wonder.

"It is too good for them. They deserve a long painful death, and they are going to get it. Tomorrow, I finish it."

I faintly nod, relieved that is nightmare will finally be behind us. "But they will not die here," he adds.

"Where at?" I wonder.

"I have asked Red Hawk to take me back to the canyon where he found you. The men will be taken there where I will finish them off."

"I want to go with you," I say.

I can tell by his look on his face that he does not think it is a good idea.

"Please White Horse," I beg. "I need a closure to this just as much as you do. Please allow me to go."

"Honey, it is not going to be pleasant, and I will be gone over night."

"I don't care. I need to go. Please, White Horse. Let me go."

He strokes my hair as he thinks. "You are a warrior within, my love," he smiles. "I will allow it, but if you ever get to the point where you cannot stomach it, you need to tell me, and I will take you away."

"I will, I promise."

That right there tells me that this is going to be very gruesome. I only hope I do have the stomach. For a few moments he just gazes into my eyes, stroking my hair. He then ever so slightly grins.

"I love you Prairie Dawn, I know I do not say it often enough, but I do."

Never have I doubted that he doesn't. He is correct that he does not say it very often, but he has never had too, just by the way he treats me I am always convinced that he loves me. He leans in and kisses me. It is a deep kiss that is allowed to linger. We hear someone walking behind us. Our lips part as White Horse lifts his eyes up and sees his brother.

"Have I ever told you, you have lousy timing," White Horse growls.

Koawa grins. "Sorry, but we need to talk."

"What is the matter?" White Horse asks him.

Koawa glances down at me. This is a sign to me that this conversation is private, and it is time for me to leave. White Horse is a man with a dual personality that can change in a blink. The few tender moments of him being a husband are gone, and he now has to be a Chief. This is something that rarely ever comes between us, as I have learned over the years how to deal with it.

I start to come to my feet. White Horse takes my hand helping me up as we both come to a stand.

"Let me get her back," he tells Koawa. "Meet me in the smokehouse."

Koawa then walks away. Hand in hand White Horse guides me down the hill. We make our way into camp, stopping briefly a few feet from our prisoners. Both men are awake but neither one has the strength to stand and are limply sitting on the ground attached to their posts. The red-haired man looks up at us. I glance up at White Horse anticipating what he might do as I am trying to attempt the difficult task of reading his mind. White Horse remains stony-faced, almost as if in a standoff. He then touches my shoulder, nudging me to move along. I pat his chest and walk the rest of the way into camp by myself. I watch him walk up to the red-haired man, slightly kicking him, just as my boys greet me.

"One more day," he growls down to him. He glances over at the other man before walking away himself and disappearing in the smokehouse.

Chapter Twenty-One

Sioux Justice

White Horse exits from the smoke house with the most unpleasant news. Blue Coats have been spotted less than a day away. He orders his men to go out and fight them off, hoping to stop them from coming in any further. He is pretty sure that his cousin Running Bear is already aware of the situation but sends Red Hawk off to warn him and help with fighting them off. Fearing that his Prairie Dawn will not take this well, he decides to stay back and not join his men in the fighting and not to tell her about the Blue Coats being so close, due to her fear of retaliation. Although he has never spoken with a fork tongue to his wife, under the circumstances and for now he feels it best to keep this information to himself. It will be almost night fall before his warriors will return. He makes his way to his captives, squatting down in front of the soldiers, gripping the back of the hair of the red-haired man forcing him to look at him.

"Your friends are moving in. They found me once, but they will not find me again," he growls, "because unlike you, I know how to disappear into the hills. But fear not, you will be found. I will lead them right to you, but it will be too late as you will be dead. But my message will be clear as they will know what I will do to them, if they ever cross my path again." White

Horse then releases his grip, slamming the head of the red-haired man into his post.

I am preparing my husband's evening meal when I see several warriors returning. I look up just as White Horse is stepping out of the smoke house. I watch our warriors as they cross the creek and make their way into camp. I notice several of the warriors are carrying scalps. I know then that they fought in a battle. One by one I watch the warriors as they ride by. I then spot Koawa with blood all over his chest. I gasp and run over to him, just as he brings his horse to a stop.

"You are hurt," I tell him. He glances down at his chest.

"It is not my blood. It is the blood of a Blue Coat," he says.

I am shocked. I had no idea that Blue Coats were this close. I glare over at White Horse, who has made his way over to us.

"You knew about this, and you said nothing," I spat.

Koawa slides off his horse, handing me its lead. "It is alright Prairie Dawn," he says. "They are gone, and we lost no one."

"For now," I huff. "What about next time?"

Both men say nothing. I yank the lead of Koawa's horse as I huff. I glare up at White Horse before stomping off.

"I knew I should have told her," White Horse tells him.

"Leave her. We have another problem," Koawa says.

"Now what?" "Pawnee scouts," he tells him.

White Horse lifts his brow. "Two Pawnee scouts were seen with them." White Horse curses under his tongue. The Army has outsmarted him and has recruited Indian scouts. He knows this is not good as Pawnee are excellent trackers. "Did you get them?" he asks.

"No, Blue Thunder and I followed them as they made their run, but they got away. We found their tracks heading towards Running Bear's camp before they cut their trail and we lost them."

White Horse is not happy as not only are Pawnee good trackers, but they are excellent warriors and arch enemies of the Sioux. This causes him great concern.

"Red Hawk has warned Running Bear," Koawa starts. "He will not move his camp. He says if Pawnee want him, to come get him."

Running Bear and White Horse are complete opposites, in so many ways. It is amazing they even get along. He is not pleased that Running Bear is refusing to move his camp and wishes he would stop being so stubborn. He cannot understand why Running Bear would chance it and will not move his people north into the sacred hills where they are more hidden, as he has lost nearly two thirds of his camp in a year due to Blue Coats.

But he cannot worry about that as he must think of himself and his people and what he will do next.

First order of business is the disposing of his captives at first light.

"Have our men expand their patrol to fifteen miles, cutting the trail as they go to lead them away from us. First light, we leave to dispose of the men. We then move ourselves further into the hills. Soon our Chief will sign the treaty with the Blue Coats that may buy us some time before winter."

Nothing further is said, and Koawa leaves to clean up. White Horse now must find his Prairie Dawn and only hope she is not too upset with him. He finds her in their lodge kneeling by the fire. He can tell by her face that she is still very angry and can't help but find that attractive. He comes down on the pelt beside her. White Horse says not a word as I sit and sulk in my anger. He faintly grins as I know seeing me angry has always turned him on.

"I knew something like this would happen," I spat.

"I know."

"Why do you have to be so stubborn?" I bark.

"You knew I was stubborn when you married me," he says.

I huff as I glance over his way. I become even more perturbed when I see he is finding this amusing. In all the years that we have been married, only one time have we exchanged harsh words to each other and then White Horse felt so foolish and apologized afterwards, taking me to our pelt where he made mad passionate love to me all night and showered me with gifts for a week. I feel White Horse take my hand into his.

"My Love, I understand you are angry and I do not blame you. I should have told you, but I did not want any more fear or pain on you, that is why I kept it to myself." He strokes his wife's beautiful hair that lies freely off her shoulders. "Try to understand my thinking, for I truly do not like it when you are angry with me."

"I never would have guessed by the way you are smiling at me, as if this is a joke."

"I cannot help it you are even more beautiful when you are angry," he teases.

This man is truly impossible and makes it terribly difficult to remain curt with him. I teasingly hit him gently on his arm.

"Your impossible," I smile. I see White Horse grin. "I am not angry with you White Horse," I finally say. "I am just worried about everyone."

He squeezes my hand. "I know love, I know you are. Come, let me hold you. Let me take that fear away." I grin over at him. It is truly impossible to be angry with this man as my love for him is too deep. I go into his lips and fall into his embrace.

We awake bright and early. Our captives are hooded, gagged, bound, and draped over two horses. We are well on our way to the canyon. White Horse keeps several of his best warriors back in the event we are ambushed when we are gone. He asks Blue Thunder to join us because he was there the night I was lying in the cave and wants the blood of Blue Coats on his hands as well. White Horse thinks it is only fair that he come along and participates, and I agree. Koawa and Red Hawk are with us as well. Although White Horse swears, he will kill these men with his bare hands, he is heavily armed, as well as are the other warriors, in the event we meet up with Blue Coats.

I sit proudly on the back of my new horse Shadow, as we travel in silence for quite some time. I smile across at my husband who is riding directly beside me. We exchange a loving grin as we continue in silence to the canyon. A few minutes later Koawa comes up beside us.

"Just behind those boulders is the cave where we took you," he says.

White Horse and I both look up. I, of course, do not remember this and am amazed at how high up it is and how far Koawa had to carry me from his horse.

"So, it is not much further?" White Horse asks.

"No," he answers. "Just a few more miles is where I met up with Red Hawk carrying Prairie Dawn."

White Horse glances over at Red Hawk, who is riding next to Blue Thunder on his right. Although he does not care for this man and still blames him for my attack and not using more force to keep me from going, he did save my life and for that he is thankful.

"I never did properly thank him," White Horse states. "I will have to make sure I do that when we get home."

We continued the next few miles in silence. As we get closer to the canyon, it is then that I start to remember. I start receiving flashbacks as I relive my attack. I look down at the canyon floor and remember running down it to the ravine.

"Are you alright, honey?" White Horse asks.

I look to the left of Blue Thunder at a line of trees.

"Right there," I say, failing to give White Horse a response. "That is where I first saw them." I point. "We are close, we are really close."

I am beginning to get anxious as I flash back on my memory of being chased down this canyon. A knot develops in my stomach, as I am certain that at any moment, I will find the remains of my beloved horse, as I hear the gunshots in my head. Just then, Red Hawk confirms that we are close.

We continued our slow walk. White Horse and Red Hawk are in front of me. Suddenly, they both stopped. "Sweetheart, don't look." I hear White Horse say, but it is too late. I nudged my way by and came face to face with the carcass of my horse. I gasp.

"Oh my God." I turn my head to look away as I fight the tears. I take a few deep breaths and ride by. All the men follow me. I stop as I come to the place that I adamantly remember.

"Right here," I say. "This is the spot." I then slid down off my horse's back. Everyone else follows me. White Horse is quickly beside me as I make my way up the embankment. I pause several moments as I flash back again looking down at the ground. I knew by coming here I was going to be opening some licked wounds that I am desperately trying to forget. I feel White Horse grab my hand. "You do not have to do this," he says.

"Yes, I do." I wipe a tear just as the other warriors come up the embankment beside us. I can see and feel the remorse that each one has as they watch me dry my tears. I switch to their tongue and point out.

"Down that ravine is where I was drug, until right about here." I walk a short distance. "Here." I sigh as I can feel my eyes welding up again. "This is where it all happened. This is where I was raped."

White Horse puts his hand on my shoulder as Red Hawk speaks his tongue. "That thicket over there is where I found her."

White Horse has seen enough and is starting to think that bringing me along was not a good idea. "Go get the men," he orders Koawa. "I need to get my Prairie Dawn away from here."

"No, White Horse please," I beg him.

"Carrie you are getting too upset. I never should have brought you here."

"I need to be here. I need the closure. Please don't push me away," I beg him.

I understand why he feels he needs to take me away, but I need to heal and to do that I need to face my demons. He reaches for my hand.

"I do not like seeing you so upset," he says.

"I will be fine. Please just let me stay," I plead.

"Alright," he finally agrees. "But if I see you getting upset again, I will take you away."

"Thank you. I will be fine."

I watch as I sit on the rocky embankment. The warriors remove the men from the horses. I then watch them remove their hoods and each man squint as the bright sun glares down at them. I observe each man as they look around. It did not take long for them to figure out where they were.

"Look familiar," White Horse growls, as he pushes the red-haired man to the ground.

I see the big man whimper as I am certain he is aware this is not going to be good. He too is pushed to the ground by Koawa. I then watch as each man is tied by their wrists and ankles to four stakes pounded into the ground by Blue Thunder and Red Hawk. I hear them scream in agony as they are stretched to the stakes just out of a comfortable range and secured down. Then White Horse takes the honors of completely disrobing them. I hear cries and whimpers from both men before their gags are replaced over their mouths. Here they will remain for several hours, until our warriors return to move the stakes further out of comfortable range, forcing the men to stretch even more. Little by little the men will be stretched throughout the night. They will receive no water, no food, and no protection from any wildlife that may come up during the night and pick them off. If they are unlucky enough to survive the night, they will face the remaining torture of White Horse in the morning. Either way, White Horse has assured me that by this time tomorrow night we will be in our own lodge.

We set up camp further down the canyon in the trees. Our captives remain close with a short walk between us. Each warrior takes there turn at watching them from nearby. Blue Thunder took the honors of hunting for dinner. I finish preparing it and hand it out to all the men. White Horse has left to check on the soldiers, so I start with the closest warrior to me, which is Koawa, then Blue Thunder and last Red Hawk. He briefly hesitates before removing it from my hand to look up at me. I hand it off and walk away. Koawa chews as he watches Red Hawk. He does not like the way he looks at his Chief's wife. In fact, he is not real fond of Red Hawk altogether. He sees Prairie Dawn walk out into the trees holding her husband's meal. He glances back over at Red Hawk again and watches him follow Prairie Dawn with his eyes. This really burns him, and he quickly realizes he needs to warn Prairie Dawn to watch herself around Red Hawk.

I find White Horse leaning against a tree watching out at his captives, deep in thought. I come up beside him to hand him his meal.

"I thought you may be hungry," I smile.

He grins and takes the meal. "How are they doing?" I ask him, as I look out in the darkness at the men.

"They are still alive," he says.

"You think they will make it until morning?" I wonder.

"The red-haired man, unless something comes in the night and eats him, I think, will make it. The other one has lost his will to fight. I do not see him lasting much longer." He looks down at me as he swallows.

"How are you holding up, my Love?" he asks.

"I am just fine. I will just be glad when it is over."

"As will I."

White Horse is very quiet, and I am certain I interrupted a thought. I reach up to kiss his cheek before heading back to camp. He grins down at me before turning his attention back to the captives.

I find an area away from the three warriors that are gathered around the fire and sit down. I rest my head on my knees and close my eyes. I am not there long before I see Koawa come down beside me.

"Are you alright?" he asks.

"I just feel uneasy. This place, it is evil."

"You are just remembering," he consoles.

"I reckon you are correct," I state. "I am so scared Koawa."

"You have nothing to fear. I told you I will not allow any harm to you. You know that."

"When I saw that blood on your chest, I got really scared."

"I know you did."

"I can't shake the feeling that something really bad is coming."

"You cannot let your fear control you."

"Everything I am worried about, I fear is coming true. The Blue Coats are close. They are coming. I can feel it and I cannot get White Horse to understand that."

"He understands, he just doesn't tell you."

"There is a lot he does not tell me," I huff.

"It is only because he does not want to worry you. Prairie Dawn, you mean everything to him. This has been very hard on him as well."

"On you too," I tell him "I owe you so much Koawa. I have given you so much grief."

"Stop talking like that. I did nothing special."

"Yes, you did. You were there for me and I will never forget it." I see him faintly grin. Koawa has the cutest smile when he allows himself to do it. I see him glancing out towards the campfire at Red Hawk.

"White Horse is not the only one who finds you beautiful."

I look over at him. Surely Koawa is not hitting on me. I mean, I love Koawa to death. We have grown considerably close within the last few years. But I am his brother's wife. Koawa respects that. He grins, he knows what I am thinking.

"I am not talking about me," he smiles.

"Then who?" I wonder.

"Red Hawk," he smiles, because he knows I find him repulsive. My eyes grow huge.

"Red Hawk!" I belly ache.

"Yes, I see the way he looks at you when your back is turned."

"I never would have guessed."

"I do not believe it has always been there. I believe only since your attack. Something intrigued him about you, most likely the same thing that White Horse and I see." I am speechless.

For one thing Koawa has never mentioned to me that he finds me intriguing, and two that it is Red Hawk, who I still find very rude and hateful. Yes, he was there when I was attacked and part of his heart came out, but I figured it was because of the shape I was in, and I am White Horse's wife and thought nothing more of it.

Red Hawk has never been married, nor does he have any children. White Horse says it's because Red Hawk believes a woman will make him weak and therefore, he refuses to marry. I know he has had many women on his pelt and most of them only make it one night. Several have been from our camp; even Minoke was one of them before she married Qutoh.

"You just be careful and do not be alone with him," Koawa cautions.

"Does White Horse know?" I wonder.

"White Horse is no fool I am sure he sees it but has no worry as he knows Red Hawk is leaving tomorrow to go back to his camp. You will not see much of him then, but until then I will keep an eye on him for you and my brother."

I can always count on Koawa. He is about as loyal as they come. He gently smiles as he comes to his feet. I watch him walk off just as White Horse comes out of the trees.

"What was that all about?" he questions me as he joins me by my side.

"He saw me over here alone and wanted to make sure I was alright," I tell him.

"And are you?"

"Yes, I am just fine."

A tender moment is shared between White Horse and me. I look over my husband's shoulder as he is nibbling my ear, at Red Hawk off in a distance looking at me. I am glad that Koawa is looking out for me and more grateful that Red Hawk will be returning to his own camp where I will seldom ever see him. I giggle when White Horse finds my ticklish spot and Red Hawk looks away.

Morning is upon us. I stand on the embankment looking at the warriors below me. Both of our prisoners are still alive. The heavy-set man is the worst of all, barely clinging on to life. He will be the first to die. Although White Horse said he would kill them with his bare hands with a quick flick of his knife, the man is deeply castrated. The shock to the body is enough to kill him.

White Horse then goes to the red-haired man, who is looking up at White Horse as he comes to terms with his fate. His eyes widen as he tries to scream through his gag, when he too is castrated. I turn my head as my stomach turns.

The warriors watch as the man bleeds out. He is stronger than the other one and is putting up one hell of a fight to the end. Little breath is remaining in him. The warriors watch as he slowly starts to die. I grab a tree limb as my knees begin to wobble. I feel as if I am about ready to puke. I feel a presence behind me. I turn my head to see Red Hawk. He says not a word, only nodding his head, assuring me everything is alright. Remembering what Koawa told me, I make haste, running behind some trees where I will sit down and bury my head.

The red-haired man closes his eyes as his last breath is only moments away. Feeling that Sioux justice has been done, White Horse finishes him off by removing his scalp.

There is a deathly silence in the canyon when White Horse walks up the embankment. I know it is over. Finally, my madness has come to an end. I bury my head once again into my knees and weep. White Horse finds me behind the trees and squats down in front of me, rubbing my back.

"It is alright Love. It's over," he consoles.

"I want to go home," I cry.

White Horse comes to his feet, wrapping his arms around me as I stand.

Red Hawk watches on from a short distance away as the Chief consoles me. He watches him whisper something tender in my ear. He sees me faintly smile. How he wishes she was his. One day he says to himself, she will be. He turns and walks away when he sees the Chief and his wife go down the embankment.

Chapter Twenty-Two

The Honeymoon

Seven days pass since the killing of the soldiers. White Horse has moved us further into the hills. Running Bear moved very little, despite White Horse's efforts to convince him to go further north. Blue Coats are still being seen nearby but so far, our men have been able to keep them away, either by skirmishes or cutting of the trail. I am still having nightmares but not about my attack. In these dreams I am always running away from the red-haired man. It makes no sense but wakes me up every time in a cold sweat. It has White Horse very concerned as I don't sleep or eat much and am keeping more to myself. He is growing frustrated, and it has led to several arguments that have left him leaving the lodge before too many harsh words are spoken.

Today White Horse is finding sanctuary in the smokehouse where he is in deep thought over his wife. His thoughts are interrupted when the flap is opened and Flying Hawk steps in. White Horse fails to look up at him as Flying Hawk stops in front of him

"My Chief," he starts. "I wish to take a moment of your time and speak with you as my mind is heavy with concern."

White Horse is always eager to offer whatever advice he can when called upon, so he offers Flying Hawk a seat across from him.

"What troubles your mind?" he asks after Flying Hawk is comfortable on the hide across from him.

"My mind is not the one that is troubled," Flying Hawk says.

White Horse looks at him as he raises his brow puzzled at what the old man means.

"Then who?" he asks.

"You," Flying Hawk answers.

"Me?"

"Yes, my Chief. It is you who is troubled. I can see it in your eyes."

"Old man, I can assure you I am fine," he grins.

Flying Hawk just shakes his head.

"I knew your father very well," he says. "He was my best friend. He told me everything, even when he became Chief. Many times, we would pass the pipe and speak of many tales and many problems. You are exactly as he was. His eyes told the story, as yours do."

White Horse lowers his eyes as he remembers how great and powerful his father was and how much he misses him. He shakes his head as he knows Flying Hawk is right and White Horse is not in his right mind.

"I see your Prairie Dawn," Flying Hawk continues. "She is still in great pain."

White Horse lifts his eyes to the old man as he nods.

"I do not understand why," he says. "I thought by killing the men who hurt her, it would find her justice and peace, but I fear it has only made it worse." He shakes his head. "I fear I have lost my Prairie Dawn."

"My Chief, she has suffered greatly, and she just needs more time," Flying Hawk assures.

"How much more time can I give her?" White Horse barks. "She is wasting away. She will not eat. She will not sleep. She isolates herself from me and our children."

"Have you tried to talk to her?"

"Yes, but she gets angry with my words. I cannot talk to her anymore as her ears are closed. She is fading away, and I do not know what to do to stop it."

White Horse is a very strong man and shows little emotion to anyone except his wife and brother. Flying Hawk knows this is hitting his Chief very hard, for him to show this kind of emotion. White Horse needs a father figure to talk too, and Flying Hawk is up to the challenge.

"When your father and your wife passed away, I took you and Koawa in as my own. I provided for your mother and you both. I welcomed you into my family." White Horse just nods as he remembers.

"And I am grateful," he says.

"I did not do it to get gratitude. I did it because I loved your father. I gained two sons that day. I promised your father I would care for you and Koawa and I have. I have no sons of my own. It was an honor then as it is an honor now. You are not only my Chief, but you are also my son."

White Horse's eyes weld up as he lowers his head. He has always been very fond of Flying Hawk and holds him very close to his heart. These words mean everything to him. Flying Hawk leans forward, putting his hand on White Horse's shoulder.

"Many moons I saw the darkness in your eyes after you became Chief. You were so young, barely a man yourself. You grew up so fast. It was very difficult on you, as you were grieving so. Even after you mourned, there was still this void that was missing. You were very lonely. You could have had any women of your choosing, but you had a vision of a woman with golden hair that would bring you wealth in your heart and love to your soul. You hung on to that vision. You fought to keep it alive. One day your vision came true, and Prairie Dawn has brought you great love. It was not easy. You had to fight for her. You had to get her to love you. You fought to keep her. You fought to love her. You must keep fighting for her now."

"I am afraid my fight is gone. Nothing I do is helping her."

"You both need to find each other again. I believe you both need a sacred purification."

White Horse is very aware of what it is and has thought of it himself. Flying Hawk has the power to perform it on White Horse, but his Prairie Dawn must be purified by a woman and the only one here with a great enough power to do it was White Fawn and she is gone.

"I thought of this myself, but there is no one here with great enough power to perform it on Prairie Dawn."

"Yellow Bird," Flying Hawk says.

Yellow Bird, of course, he thinks to himself, why didn't he think of it? Yellow Bird is a very powerful woman and the wife of Running Bear.

"We will leave in the morning," he says.

White Horse grabs Flying Hawks arm, gently squeezing it. "Thank you," he tells him.

"You are welcome son," Flying Hawk says.

White Horse smiles at the word son. He has not been called a son for nearly ten years. It has a sound that White Horse likes. Both men come to their feet. Upon leaving the smokehouse, out of the blue, White Horse gives Flying Hawk a hug. He is feeling hopeful that this will work and he will get his Prairie Dawn the help she needs. As he walks to his lodge to give Prairie Dawn the news, he comes up with another idea and quickly rushes inside to find her.

White Horse and I leave early in the morning to Running Bear's camp. He spent a great deal of time last night explaining to me what we were doing and even more time convincing me to go. I am still very hesitant about it, but it is important to him and I know he has my best intentions at heart so therefore I will trust him and speak no more of it. I have been advised to pack some blankets. Running Bear's camp is only a day away so I am unsure why we would need them, but again I do not say a word and trust him.

We are riding at a leisurely pace. White Horse is not worried about Blue Coats as our warriors are cutting our tracks, leading them away from us if they get to close. A few hours into our ride White Horse and I stop at a stream to allow the horses and ourselves to drink. I watch him jump off his horse's back and come over to me. He reaches for me lifting me off. He stops for a moment before putting me down to gaze at me. He has not done this to me since we were courting. I know then something is up.

"What are you up to?" I ask him as he takes my hand into his.

"What, I cannot look into the beautiful eyes of my wife?" he smirks.

He then turns away and walks to the stream where he sits down. I come down beside him.

"It is just you have been very closed mouth about this whole thing," I tell him. I see him grin, as he reaches up to stroke my hair.

"I just wanted some time alone with you." He glances up at clouds. "The sky is changing its color. Soon it will get very cold which means our Little Foot will soon be seven."

"I am not following you."

"It is simple love. We have another year onto our marriage."

"Yes, that is true."

"We never got a honeymoon."

"Well considering what we were going through and my father's death, I never thought twice about it."

"Well, I have and know it is the time to take that long awaiting honeymoon."

"Are you serious?" I ask in amazement.

I have been asking for this moment for many years. He just never had time or something would always interfere with it. After being let down so many times I just evidently gave up on even asking him. I am thrilled.

"Why the change of heart?" I wonder.

"I have just finally had time to sit down and see what is important to me and see how much it would destroy me if I lost it." I blush.

He is so sweet. He leans over and gives me a kiss. "I love you Carrie," he huskily says after our lips part. "And I don't ever want to lose that love."

"I love you too."

The rest of the day we ride in a leisure pace. We found a place near a brook and set up camp for the night. We are only a few hours to Running Bear's village. Here White Horse feels we are safe as we are remote enough to be left alone, but secure enough as there are also warriors from both bands not far away if we got into any trouble. He catches us some fish and we both get our fill. The evening air has a chill in it, as we are well into autumn. I now understand why he wanted to pack the blankets. Nestled near the fire, we snuggled under the blankets. It is so peaceful and quiet.

"This is all I have ever wanted," I whisper, "right here with you."

I glance over at him, and when I do, he kisses me. He lifts to rest on his elbow, placing his hand on my face. He gives it a gentle stroke.

"I have been thinking," he says.

"About what?"

"Having another child."

"Are you serious?"

This is better than a honeymoon. I have been trying to get him to have another child ever since Little Foot was a year old. He has never been willing to sacrifice losing me after I nearly died giving birth to him.

"There is an abundance of root here, come spring, that blossoms well into early fall. If you take the root early on, I believe you will be fine."

I am ecstatic. This is the news I have been waiting for.

"But, if we do not conceive right away, we will have to wait until next winter, as we have only a few months to work with," he cautions.

I completely understand where he is coming from. He is only willing to take the risk so far. I do not mind, as I will do whatever I can on my part to conceive.

"Thank you, White Horse. Thank you."

Before anything else is said and before he can change his mind, we quickly go into baby-making mode.

Red Hawk hides in the trees nearby. He has been watching the Chief and his beautiful wife for nearly an hour. He knows he should not be here, especially now when the romance has begun. If he were to get caught, he could be severely punished by both Chiefs, but he doesn't care. He is too mesmerized to move. His groin aches as he watches Prairie Dawn perform a task on her husband that every man enjoys. He gazes on as he visualizes it being him. He watches on as moments later the Chief, pressing his hands against his wife's luxurious thighs, lifts his head from getting his meal and enters her.

For a brief moment, he sees the reflection of her breasts as the Chief gets into position. How could he have been so foolish all these years? Why didn't he take her back in Willow Creek when the Chief nearly died? He remembers the first time he saw her when she came out of the cave and stepped into the garden of paradise, when her people came for the foreign children. He thought she was pretty then. Why did he let her skin color get in the way of the woman that lies within? Why did he let her go to the soldier camp that night? Why was he so harsh in his words to her when all he wanted to do was scoop her up in his arms? Maybe if he did, she would never have been hurt. She probably would have fought him. How he would let her. He loves her flare and her fight, which he has never seen before in any other woman, and how it turns him on. He has not looked twice at a woman for many years. He has found none that are worthy of him or that deserve him. He wants this, Prairie Dawn. He wants her badly. But how? How will he do it when she belongs to the Chief? He will get her to trust him. He will be nice. They will become friends. He will start there, and then he will make his move. Then he will take her, take her far away. His thoughts are interrupted when he sees the Chief pull out and roll over onto his side, taking the blanket covering up Prairie Dawn and himself.

I am so fulfilled with what was the hardest love making we have had in a very long time. It is something we both needed, the closeness we both have been longing for. I kiss his chest as I lay my head down on it, reflecting how much I love this man. How badly I need him. How I pray nothing will ever take him away. I held him near, resting my arm across his solid chest.

"Do you think Running Bear will join us further in the hills?" I ask.

"I don't know Love. He is so stubborn."

"Like you!"

"What do you mean like me?" he teases.

"Isn't that why you are not joining the head Chief in the signing of the treaty?"

"No, I am not signing the treaty because I do not trust the White Man Chief. Many lies have come out of his mouth. Many of his men are corrupt."

"Not all of them are bad," I add.

He raises his head, and I look up at him. "How can you think that? How soon have you forgotten what they did to you?"

"I will never forget it, but White Horse, there were two men who left their post. They never really were true soldiers."

"Did you not say that they had Blue Coats on?" he argues.

"Yes, they had Blue Coats on."

"Alright then, they were Blue Coats. Whether they went back to their post or not afterwards, I do not care. They were still Blue Coats, and for that reason, I will not sign."

"Honey, do you remember back in Willow Creek when we were being attacked by One Eye and his renegades?"

"Yes," he answers.

"You told me then that not all Indians are bad. That there were good Indians and bad Indians."

"Yes."

"Well, it is the same thing here. There are good White Men and bad White Men."

He shakes his head as he rests it back down. "At one time, I would have believed that, but not anymore. Now all they want is to push us into a hole, making boundaries on where we can roam, prohibiting us from how much we can hunt, taking land that is ours and not allowing us to keep it pure and sacred. I will not do it. I will not be told how to live." He strokes my hair. "I'm sorry, Love."

"Don't ever be sorry for what you believe in," I state.

He gently smiles as he leans in to kiss me tightly. We would unite one more time before falling asleep in each other's arms.

Red Hawk remains in his watch in the darkness of the trees, watching Prairie Dawn as she comes on top of the Chief and they make love again. He sees it all as she drapes her blanket off her back. He watches every curve, the roundness and fullness of her breasts, and the smoothness of her skin. He sees her hair freely bouncing behind her as she rides her Chief. He briefly closes his eyes as he feels the heat between his legs. He visualizes her and what beautiful sex they would have. He will remain there for the duration of the night, watching her as she sleeps, keeping her safe as the Chief slumbers beside her. Soon, the great circle in the sky will appear, and he will run back to his camp, arriving before them. He can hardly wait to see her again.

Chapter Twenty-Three

The Purification

We are quickly greeted by Red Hawk and other Lakota scouts as White Horse and I are nearing Running Bear's camp. I fail to look at Red Hawk as White Horse greets him, but feel his eyes upon me as we are riding in. Running Bear is welcoming us with open arms as both White Horse and I dismount. A little girl around the age of eleven years takes both of our reins and walks off. White Horse, being a Chief and incredibly handsome, is gawked at by several women as we walk to meet up with Yellow Bird. This is something he is used to and pays little attention to. This is not my first time at Running Bear's camp, and everyone here knows who I am and knows I am his wife. The women who are gawking at my husband see me beside him and turn their eyes away.

One woman seems more interested in White Horse than the rest. Her eyes are following his every move. The little girl who took our reins comes up beside her. I am assuming this is her mother; however, I cannot recall ever seeing either one of them before when I have been here. White Horse looks over at her and turns hard in the face. The woman quickly takes her child and walks away. I am taken by the hand by Yellow Bird and head towards a lodge, as White Horse follows behind. He turns me around as we come to Yellow Bird's flap.

"Now, sweetheart, you may find a few of her rituals strange, but it is important for you to heal properly that you do everything she tells you."

"Where will you be?" I ask, as I am hoping he will be with me.

"I will go with Running Bear into our own sweat lodge. I will not be far, Love. I promise," he assures, as he strokes my cheek.

"You are not going to go in there with me?" I whine. I am quite nervous about this and am really hoping he will join me.

"Sweetheart, as much as I wish I could, it is forbidden. If I thought Flying Hawk could have done it, we would not have come. It must be done by a woman of great power, and Yellow Bird is the only one."

He then removes from around his waist a little pouch and hands it to me. "When you are finished, you place this by the rocks to thank the Great Spirit for healing you," he instructs.

I am uncertain what it is and can only trust that White Horse knows what he is doing. "Alright," I tell him. I turn to go in and briefly stop. "I love you," I tell him. I see him grin. He holds the flap open and I walk in to join Yellow Bird.

I have never undergone a Purification and am clueless about what to expect. I enter a lodge heavy with smoke. The smell of incense is very strong. In the center of the lodge is a circle of steaming rocks. The lodge is very humid and moist. Yellow Bird instructs me where to sit. She then wraps a blanket around me. Unlike White Horse will be when he enters his sweat lodge, I am not disrobed. She then finds her place to sit and begins to pray.

Yellow Bird is great in age but younger than White Fawn by a few years. She is very round in the face with deep-set wrinkles and long grey hair. In her youth, I can only imagine how beautiful she must have been, as many of those features are still within her. I know little about this woman, despite her being a Chief's wife as well as I am. One would think we would have been close as we are kin, but like me, she rarely leaves camp.

I remember the first time I met Yellow Bird. I had been married to White Horse for less than a year. She came to the camp along with Running Bear to bless Little Foot, who was three months old. Even though White Fawn and Flying Hawk had already blessed him when he was just a few days old, she insisted on doing another one and was upset that the snow was so heavy for so long that she couldn't get there sooner. It was not until several years later at the annual Sun Dance that I would meet her again. Sitting here, I reflect and wish I had taken the time to have known her better. As she finishes her prayer, she has me inhale some sage for several moments. I am now really beginning to sweat. She starts to chant in a language that I do not understand. My sweating is more profuse, and I am becoming lightheaded.

White Horse is undergoing his own ritual and is joined by Running Bear and Red Hawk in the lodge. Deep chants are heard as White Horse goes into a trance to clean his soul and mind.

The time arrives, and my purification is completed. I place the pouch that White Horse gave me as an offering next to the hot rocks. I am then allowed to stand up and leave the lodge. Yellow Bird joins me just outside the flap. She hands me a feather that is hanging freely off a beaded chain. She then speaks her tongue.

"I want you to have this. Hang it over the pelt you share with your husband. It will protect you and bless you."

"Thank you," I tell her. She faintly grins and walks away.

I look around at the camp in front of me. White Horse is nowhere to be seen. I can only assume he is still in the sweat lodge. Feeling very awkward, as a few eyes turn to me, I find a remote tree and sit down under it to cool off. The camp is quiet despite the many people working. As I look around from face to face, the bond with everyone is not as tight here as it is with ours. Several women are working on their own, and young children are playing alone. It is more like a village than a huge family. Running Bear's camp is not as big as ours; it never has been. I believe part of the reason is that Running Bear is more aggressive than White Horse and will instigate a battle with the enemy.

This has resulted in him losing many of his warriors and his camps being raided. He also refuses to run and hide, and does not move as much as White Horse. If provoked, White Horse will fight. Running Bear does not need to be provoked, and his band is responsible for more attacks on Forts, wagon trains, and homesteads than White Horse's is. Some say that White Horse is too soft and afraid to fight, but White Horse is a peaceful man and, up until recently, would go out of his way to keep peace with the White Men.

My thought is interrupted when the little girl who had taken our reins earlier comes running up to me.

"Hello," I greet her in her tongue. She shyly smiles. "What is your name?" I ask her.

"Rising Sun," she answers.

"That is a beautiful name for a beautiful little girl." She giggles.

Before anything else can be said, her mother hastens up and quickly scolds her away. She gives me a look of more curiosity than friendliness while she remains still in her stance. I greet her in her native tongue.

"Hello!"

For a few seconds, she remains still, only looking at me. She is about ready to speak when she sees White Horse coming up. I watch him as he glares across at her. I think this is very odd coming from White Horse, who I have never known to glare at a woman. She cowers and quickly runs off.

I watch White Horse sit down beside me. He kisses my cheek.

"How do you feel?" he asks.

"I am not sure," I tell him. "How am I supposed to feel?"

"More at peace," he answers.

"Then yes, I feel better," I tell him. "And you?" I ask him.

"I feel much better as well."

"Good."

"Running Bear has offered us a lodge for tonight, but I told him no."

"Why? Are we going home now?" I wonder.

"No, we will stay here and leave at first light, but I have another idea on where we will sleep."

"Where?"

"I know of a place next to the lake, not far from here, that overlooks the prairie. The stars light up the sky. This will be our last night alone. I thought we could enjoy our rebirth together."

"I would love that," I smile.

"We will still be close enough to camp to be protected, but far enough away to be alone," he reassures.

"It sounds wonderful," I smile.

White Horse and I make the short ride to our camp overlooking the prairie. He starts a fire as I set out our blankets. Tonight, we both agree that we will fast and no food will go into our bellies. White Horse is accustomed to fasting and can go several days without eating. I have never done it, but I will give it a shot at least until the morning when my stomach growls.

"White Horse, why does Yellow Bird have no children?" I ask him.

"The great spirits never gave them any," he answers.

"So, who would be next in line for Chief if something happens to Running Bear?"

"Running Bear has always taken a liking to Red Hawk and took him in when Red Hawk's parents died when he was just a boy. I would imagine it would be Red Hawk."

A chilling thought. Red Hawk as a Chief, God help us all. White Horse must have read my mind.

"He is not as bad as he appears. He would make a good Chief," he grins.

"I thought you didn't like him?"

"I don't, but I know a good warrior when I see one," he states.

White Horse has me all confused about his feelings for Red Hawk, and I reckon it doesn't really matter to me or that I really care.

"Yellow Bird gave me this," I tell him, changing the subject. I hold up to White Horse the feather that Yellow Bird gave me. I hear him chuckle to himself as he comes to his feet and walks over to join me on the blanket.

"She told me if I hang it over our pelt, it will protect me and bless me."

He chuckles again.

"What?" I wonder, as White Horse is definitely amused.

"That my Love is not only used as protection, but it is also believed to help with conceiving. That is what she meant by being blessed."

"Oh," I am certain I am blushing. "But she does not have any children, so it must not work very well."

"I do not believe she personally used it. I believe she gave it to as a gift."

"But I did not give her anything in return."

"I do not believe she wanted anything in return. She is aware of your condition and I believe she gave it to you so when you do conceive, both you and the child will be protected and blessed."

"Do you believe in this?" I ask him.

"It does not matter what I believe in. It matters what you believe in, for it can only work if you believe. It was just like you being purified. It will only work if you believe and my darling, I do believe it worked."

"Why do you say that?"

"Because you have light in your eyes again that I haven't seen in many weeks." I smile as he leans in and kisses me. "We have one more thing we both need to do to complete the ceremony," he says after our lips part.

"What?" I wonder.

He takes my hand, pulling me to my feet. "To the water we go."

The lake is within our view, just a few yards from our campfire. Hand in hand we walk down there. White Horse takes off his shirt.

"We bathe," he says.

"Yellow Bird never said anything to me about bathing," I argue.

He just glances over at me as he continues to undress.

"What, do you doubt me?" he teases.

I truly do believe he is bluffing as White Horse is always teasing me, but I remove my dress anyway and come into the water with him. I watch him as he scoops up some water and gently rubs it on my chest. His eyes are thick and full of lust. The little rascal is bluffing me. I playfully hit his chest as he smiles.

"You are terrible," I laugh.

Chuckling, he pulls me into his arms and we passionately kiss.

As the sun falls, White Horse and I splash in the water. He is an excellent swimmer and can hold his breath for a very long time, making his teasing under the water very unpredictable. On several occasions, he would sneak up underneath me and tickle my feet or come up behind me and scare me. I am having the time of my life, with no care at all in the world. When our playtime is finished in the water, we come to the shore and nestle under the blanket. We gaze up at the stars. He tells me stories that he has never shared before. I feel so close to him and so full of love. Before we call it a night, White Horse and I make love. I hold him tight and I hold him close as I sleep.

Red Hawk is keeping a watch over the Chief and his beautiful wife. He saw from a distance as they played in the water. He, too, enjoyed the laughter. He watches them curl up into the blanket and end their night in romance. It is then he walks away and goes to his own fire, not far away to leave them be. He lays there looking up at the stars, wishing he had someone there with him. But not just anyone, he thinks, he wants Prairie Dawn. She looks so happy with the Chief, so full of love. He knows he will never have her as long as the Chief is around. He closes his eyes to catch a few winks before the sun comes up. He will awake early so he can ride along secretly behind the Chief and his wife and keep them safe. He will then turn around and come home. Come home and plan when he can see her again and take her away from her Chief.

Chapter Twenty-Four

Lakota Blood

I feel a gentle peck on my cheek. "Sweetheart, it is time to wake up," I hear White Horse say. I open my eyes to a beautiful day and my husband looking down at me. "If we want to make it home before the children slumber tonight, we need to get moving," he says. I quickly stretch before coming to my feet.

My morning routine of having to void comes across me and I step out into the trees to do what I have to do. White Horse starts packing up the horses and tying my bag and blankets on Shadow's back.

"You hungry?" he asks me from the distance.

"I will eat when you eat," I joke.

I hear him chuckle as White Horse is used to not eating for several days if need be and I am not.

"We will eat later," he says.

I finish and come to my feet, brushing off my dress. We both jumped upon hearing gunshots.

"What was that?" I ask in a panic. We hear them again.

"I smell smoke," White Horse says.

We then quickly race up a hill and look down to the prairie below us, and freeze in horror. Running Bear's camp is being attacked by Blue Coats.

"Oh my God!" I gasp, as we watch in shock the attack going down in front of our eyes. White Horse has no time to waste. He must help his cousin fight. He takes my hand and rushes me over to the tall grass and pushes me into it. "You stay down!" he orders me. He then jumps on his horse and races off.

I cower low as I hear the shots echoing. I start to cry in horror, as there is nothing, I can do but pray. After a few long minutes, the earth finally grows still. The gunfire ceases. I know the attack is over and the Blue Coats have left. I crawl out of the tall grass, being careful not to be spotted in case some Blue Coats are still lingering around.

"White Horse!" I cry. "I have to find White Horse."

I quickly rush and jump on Shadow's back, giving his ribs a nudge, and run off through the prairie grass. I am unclear where exactly the Blue Coats are, and for that reason, I am very cautious as I near the camp. The smoke is thick in the air as I enter the ghastly sight. The first thing I see is a warrior lying dead on the prairie grass in a pool of blood. I slide off my horse and continue on foot. I gasp in horror. My stomach curls over as I gaze around at the death surrounding me. There is no lodge standing. Not one that has not been burnt. There are bodies lying everywhere. The land is covered with blood. I slowly walk through the field of bodies, both young and old. I nearly cried when I saw a woman still holding her child by the hand, both dead at my feet. I lower my head as I try not to cry.

Through the thick smoke, I make my way further into the camp revealing more of the horrific attack. I check as many bodies as I can, in hopes someone has survived. I soon realize that all my hopes are fading fast as the camp lies in complete silence. I continue my way in utter dismay as I stare around at the gruesome sight. I then quickly rush to my knees when I see among the dead is Running Bear. I stroked his cheek as I felt a tear begin to surface. I then noticed Yellow Bird not far away. I gasp again as my tears flow. I sob softly as I gaze at all the death. All the innocence destroyed because of greed, because of hatred. I fill with rage. I have so much hate for the people that I was born into, whose color I share. I cannot take it anymore. I am so angry, so upset that anyone would have so much hatred for one culture. I literally scream out in rage, as I outburst my anger, I fall to my knees again and weep.

Out of the thick smoke I hear movement. I see the silhouette of a horse approaching. "White Horse!" I say as I rush to my feet. I see him slide off his horse. I rushed into his arms. For a few moments we tightly embraced. He then sees Running Bear over my shoulder and rushes to his side.

"No!" he whispers, as he lifts his cousin's head up in his arms. "Why? Why wouldn't you listen to me?" he tells him in his tongue.

He then lowers his head to hug him as he repeats in his tongue. "Why?"

It takes a few moments for White Horse to compose himself and come to his feet. I hear him deeply sigh as he chokes back his tears. I then saw the rage surface in his eyes.

"We will go home and get my warriors. We will come back here and collect the dead, and then we will fight." He rushes to his horse. I ran after him and grabbed his arm.

"White Horse no!" I shout. He whisks his arm free from my grasp. He is furious. "You cannot fight them anymore. You must find peace, White Horse. You must!"

White Horse is trying to stay calm but is clearly annoyed with my comment. "Look around you, Carrie. Look at what we have lost. Look at what our peace means to them. They do not want peace. They will not stop until we are all dead."

"White Horse, you are just angry. You are not thinking straight."

"You are damn right I am angry," he yells. "I am done with being nice. I am done with talking peace. The big men in Washington want a war; they got one."

"And what has it solved? White Horse, the more we fight, the more we kill, and the more they do. It goes around and around, and it solves nothing. I told you this was going to happen. I knew something like this was going to happen when you killed those soldiers."

"Is that what you think? You think all this happened because I killed those soldiers?"

"Yes!" I cry.

"How soon you forget that our camp was destroyed months before you were attacked. How many lives were already murdered by army guns? How our land was rutted by wagon wheels and our buffalo killed for their tongues and hides. Carrie, I didn't start this war; they did."

I grow very still. I know White Horse is right. This is not his fault. Our Nation has been fighting for years to keep what is ours. Our constant struggle to live in harmony with the white men and our futile efforts to get along with them have been tiresome. It seems the more we give them, the more they want and the more they take.

"Prairie Dawn," he continues, "you told me the night after our attack not to stop fighting and not to stop believing in who we are." I nodded my head as I remembered the conversation as if it were yesterday. "We will never be free. We will be told where to put our lodges, where we can hunt, and what we can eat. We will never roam free. We will never live the life we want. I, for one, will not be told how to live my life. I will fight for who I am."

White Horse's words hit home. We have no choice but to fight. We must maintain what dignity we have left. We must honor those who have died and stand strong and proud.

"I'm sorry," I tell him.

He reaches for my hand and strokes my cheek when I look out into the horizon. "White Horse look," I say, pointing out. White Horse turns around, just as the little girl known as Rising Sun is seen in the dust. I quickly rushed to her side, scooping her into my embrace. I faintly hear her cry as her head is buried in my chest. "Shh," I console. "It's alright, sweetheart." I wipe her dusty tears away. "It's alright sunshine," I tell her. "It's alright." She softly speaks her tongue between her sobs.

"I run. I run away." My embrace around her is harder.

"Oh, sweetheart, I am so sorry."

"We ran as fast as we could. I take as many as I can, just like Chief Running Bear said. We hide and do not come out until the big booms stop."

I look up at White Horse. His eyes are hard and callous as he looks down at the little girl.

"Are there more survivors?" he huskily says.

"Yes," she answers. "We hide in a hole."

"Can you take me to them, sweetheart?" I ask her.

She nods her head yes and grabs my finger. She walks me to a place just outside of the camp next to the bluff. She then moves some trees branches to reveal an opening to a very small hollow crevice in the side of the mountain. Cramped inside there are six children. Each one of them is terrified. I am truly amazed that this one little girl was not only able to save herself, but six very young children from the ages of two to six. White Horse removes the children from there hole as he consoles the only survivors of his cousin's camp. Everyone is filthy, covered with dust and dirty streaks down their faces from crying.

"White Horse," I whine. "What do we do? These children are alone. Their parents are dead."

"We will take them with us and give them new homes. We need to leave Carrie, as there is nothing more we can do here."

Just then Rising Sun sees her mother among the dead. She runs over to her, falling on her knees and wails on her chest. "Mama," she sobs.

She tries to shake her mother awake. "Mama."

I rushed to her side, pulling her away from her mother. She struggles to break free from my hold as she cries out to her mother. White Horse yanks the girl out of my arms.

"Stop your wailing!" he barks.

I am dumbfounded at White Horse's behavior. Never have I ever seen him so cold and harsh to a child.

"White Horse, she just lost her mother!" I snap.

"We all lost," he snarls. "Blue Coats may still be close. Her cries could be heard. You need to shut her mouth."

"How can you be so callous!" I ask. "She is just a child."

"Carrie, we do not have time for this. We need to get these children out of here."

I watch as White Horse turns to the other children. His demeanor instantly changes. He is consoling them, being very gentle with his words and touches, White Horse that I know. Why? I ask myself. What has this child done to him? Rising Sun clings onto me around my waist. We walked together to my horse. I reached down to help her up. White Horse is quick at pulling her down.

"She walks," he barks. Now I am getting annoyed.

"What the hell is your problem?" I bark at him. This peaceful man glares over at me.

"She is not of ours."

"What do you mean?" I ask.

"Her mother was Crow. She is a half breed."

"And this is her fault, why?"

White Horse ignores the question and lifts a smaller child up onto my horse. "She is old enough to walk," he grumbles.

"If she is Crow," I begin, "then we can take her back to her family."

"She has no family," White Horse snorts, "and her father is Sioux."

"Then she does have family if she is Sioux," I snap back.

With a face of stone, White Horse looks over at me. "Go get the rest of the children together as I gather what horses I can. We leave now." He then tosses me the lead.

I watch White Horse as he walks away. I have never seen him act this way before, and I am clearly not liking this side of him. Although White Horse said that Rising Sun will walk, enough horses are gathered that I will give her mine. I take another child, put him in front of me, and jump on another horse. With all the other children on horses, we are ready to leave.

White Horse rides up alongside me. His eyes turn thick as if he is trying to apologize for being so curt. I would have bought it if it were not that his look at Rising Sun was one of disgust. This totally pissed me off and I kick the side of my horse and leave.

Chapter Twenty-Five

The Fallen Warrior

Our ride is very slow and quiet. We are heading home the way of the canyon; however, we are in an area that I am unfamiliar with. White Horse is taking this way because it is more isolated, as we are unsure where the Blue Coats are and fear that they may still be close. The children are very well behaved, which most Sioux children are; no cries are being heard, and nearly all eyes are looking ahead. The older three children are in control of the reins on their horses, as the smaller ones are riding in front and hanging on. Rising Sun keeps looking over at White Horse. I am not sure as to her reasoning, but I am assuming she is memorizing the face of what is now her Chief. After several hours of riding, White Horse breaks the silence when he sees something on the ground and motions for us to stop. We watch him as he jumps off his horse and squats down, touching the earth.

"What is it?" I ask him.

"Pony tracks, and they are fresh," he answers.

"Blue Coats?" I question.

"No," he mumbles, "they are one of ours."

He then looks out, coming to a stand. He walks a few feet and squats down again. I watch him as he wipes his fingers in some dirt. I then see what he is looking at. It is blood.

"It is very fresh," he says, as he smells it.

"Could it be a wild animal?" I ask. He shakes his head no.

"I don't think so. I think we have a fallen warrior."

He stands back up and continues tracking. Usually, White Horse's hunches are correct. It is almost as if he has a sixth sense. We slowly follow behind him a few yards until he stops again. We then see the horse. I gasp, as lying on the ground next to it is Red Hawk. White Horse rushes over to him as I jump off my horse. He quickly realizes that Red Hawk is still alive but bleeding heavily from his side from being shot. As I come to my knees next to White Horse, I see that Red Hawk is in bad shape. He tries to speak.

"I see Blue Coats when I…"

"Shh," White Horse says. "Don't talk, my friend."

Rising Sun quickly joins us, taking Red Hawk's hand. "Papa," she cries.

I am speechless. Rising Sun is Red Hawk's daughter.

"My precious…" he mumbles.

Red Hawk is profusely perspiring. I know he is struggling to hang on.

"White Horse, we have to do something."

White Horse is aware that I have some knowledge in this area, thanks to my brother Roger. "Can you help him?" he asks.

"I think so," I nervously say. "I need to remove the bullet."

"What do you need?"

"Give me my bag on my horse."

White Horse is quick to obey. I speak his tongue to Red Hawk.

"I need you to trust me. I need to remove the bullet." He faintly nods as White Horse returns with my bag.

"You always complain that I take this everywhere with me," I tell him. "Now you know why." I reach inside and grab what I will need.

Over the years, I have always traded for White Man medical supplies when everyone else was trading for blankets or flour. I would only grab the basics that were small enough to carry with me. This has always infuriated White Horse as he considered it a waste. I have never been able to trade for medicine, which is why I had to leave for White Fawn's medicine, but nevertheless, I bet White Horse is changing his mind right about now.

"This is going to hurt," I tell White Horse.

He finds a stick and puts it between Red Hawk's teeth. He then speaks his tongue to him. Rising Sun holds her father's hand as White Horse holds him down. I then begin. I hear Red Hawk grunt when I apply the cleanser.

"I am sorry," I tell him. I look up at White Horse. "Hold him as still as possible." White Horse softly speaks his tongue to him as I go in with my knife to dig the bullet out. Red Hawk is feeling a great deal of pain, but is remaining still as he fixes his eyes on his daughter.

"I got it," I say.

I grab White Horse's hand, placing it down on a cloth to apply pressure to the wound. "Hold it there," I instruct him as I dig in my bag for the bandages.

"I will wrap him in hopes to keep it clean. I got the bullet, but I am still worried about his bleeding, even though it has slowed down."

"Flying Hawk will be able to help him."

"White Horse, he can't ride that far," I argue.

"Well sweetheart I am not leaving him here."

I stop and think for a moment about where we are. "How far away are we from the cave where I was when I was attacked?"

"A half mile back maybe," he answers.

It is still further than I want to go, but at this point I have no other choice. I remember the day that Koawa took me home. We left with only the blankets, leaving everything else behind. If we can get Red Hawk, there I have a suspicion that everything else will still be there that I need to take care of him.

"Can you get him there?" I ask White Horse.

"If you can handle all the children, I can get him there."

"Rising Sun," I look across at the little girl who is still holding Red Hawks hand. "Your Chief is going to move your father to a place where he can rest. I need you to help me with the others at getting them there."

"I will help," she softly says. White Horse just looks at her briefly before turning away. I am not sure what this child has done to him or why he has so much animosity for her? It is clear to me that White Horse does not like this child and I do not believe it is because she is part Crow.

We are making the walk to the cave. Thank God White Horse is strong, because Red Hawk is dead weight over his shoulders. He decides against laying him across his horse, due to the risk of him sliding off when we climb, or the bumpy ride of the horse's back making him bleed more. Rising Sun and I have no problem with the other children, who have been so well behaved. We are both on foot, guiding the horses along, which has not been an easy task. Including Red Hawk's, we have six horses that we are trying to climb with.

Rising Sun is the oldest. The next behind her is Little Eagle, who is six. He reminds me of my own six-year-old, with the exception that he rides better, which is fortunate for me. He is holding a two-year-old girl who is nearly asleep, curled up in his arms. I am told by Rising Sun that this is his sister. We are approaching an area that I am starting to recognize. The cave is seen up the ridge. White Horse is starting to slow down, and I am certain his endurance is being tested.

"You need to rest, Love?" I ask him.

"No, we are almost there. I can make it."

The last little bit is steep for the ones on foot. I am beginning to wonder if White Horse is going to make it, as I am certain his thighs are burning as he moves up the steep hill. Normally, this climb would have been nothing for him, but with Red Hawk's weight on top of his shoulders and carrying him for as long as he has, I can only imagine the discomfort his body must be feeling.

Finally, we make it to the top. White Horse gently lays Red Hawk down inside the cave. With a quick look around, I realize my hunch is correct and everything is still in place from when I was brought here a few weeks ago. A quick flashback occurs as I know remember being carried in here by Koawa.

"Are you alright?" White Horse asks me.

"Yes," I say. "It is just sort of eerie that I would end up in here again helping the man who helped me."

"I wish I had been here then. You needed me."

I gently stroke his chin. "You are here now, that is all that matters."

I make my way to Red Hawk, who is awake but in a great deal of pain. I speak his tongue to him.

"We meet here again," I smile. He faintly grins. Rising Sun again is holding her father's hand. I am still amazed that this is his daughter. I am unclear why no one ever mentioned it. I begin the task of checking on how badly Red Hawk is really bleeding and reapply some clean bandages. White Horse takes a few minutes, and looks around at the remains from when I was here.

This cave is telling him a story, a story of darkness and pain. He sees my dress torn to shreds in the back of the cave. He sees the slices of the material from the belt that tore it open. He sees the water basin and the bloody rag lying beside it. His heart sickens as he sees firsthand everything I have been through. He looks over at me as I tend to Red Hawk. He reflects on how much he loves me. How empty he would feel without me. He thinks back to when we were first married, how little I knew about their ways, and how fast I have learned. How quickly I earned everyone's respect when I delivered Morning Dove in the woods when Running Water had left after a spat with Koawa, and how far I have come in such a short time. He smiles faintly down at me as he thinks of how proud he is of me, how proud he is to call me his wife, so proud to call me Lakota. He walks over to me, gently pecking my cheek as he squats down.

"Sweetheart, we need to get these children out of here. Red Hawk is going to have to hold his own. We can leave Rising Sun with him if he needs anything. I will send my men to come back and get them."

"Absolutely not," I argue. "I am not going to leave him here. He is in no condition to take care of himself."

"That is why Rising Sun will stay here."

"No, no White Horse. I will not leave him."

"Carrie, I need your help with the children. And I am not going to leave you alone."

"Rising Sun can help you. She knows the children better than I, and besides, she does not know how to properly take care of him if he were to bleed out, and I do."

"Then I will stay with you as well."

"Honey, I know you are worried about me, but I can handle myself. Koawa will have the scouts further out, so you will only need to get the children to them, and then you can come back and get me. You will be here by tomorrow night, and by then he should be strong enough to at least move."

"Then we all wait together," he argues.

I normally do not make it a habit to argue with White Horse as I usually lose, but I clearly feel White Horse is being selfish by thinking of only me and not the children who are scared and most likely hungry.

"White Horse, you know as well as I do the temperature around here at night is bone chilling. We have only two blankets, and there is not enough room here for everyone to sleep. Not only that, White Horse, but you also must warn everyone about the Blue Coats and tell them about Running Bear."

"Koawa is not stupid, he will see the smoke high in the air and know something happened," he states.

"And we are not back yet, can you imagine what he must be thinking?"

I can see the wheels turning in his head. He knows I am right, but the stubborn man he is, he is refusing to give up.

"He will see the smoke," he begins. "When he does, he will go to it, and when we are not among the dead, he will start looking for us. By then, Red Hawk should be able to move."

"That could take days, and the children don't have days. White Horse, you have to go."

White Horse hates it when I make a good argument. He tries one final plea. "Carrie, this just doesn't sit well with me. I worry that Blue Coats will show up on you as I am certain they are not far away, that is why I cannot signal Koawa for fear it will be seen by them."

"That is why you need to get these children home. I worry for you."

"No, I will take the hills home where I can hide, but Carrie, you are lower and defenseless."

"You saw how high this cave is. Koawa never would have brought me in here if he didn't think it was safe."

I understand why White Horse is so apprehensive, and normally, I would not even suggest this, but we have no choice. Red Hawk cannot be moved, and we have to get these children to safety and warn our scouts.

"Sweetheart, I have never told you this, but Red Hawk and I have a very bad history, and he did something to me many years ago that has caused some very harsh feelings between us. I worry about what he will do to you when no one is here to protect you from him."

"White Horse, look at him, he is in no shape to do anything to me. When I was alone with him here and I was hurt, Red Hawk was there for me. He saved my life, and I will not turn my back on him when he needs me. Please, White Horse, these children need you, as do your people. I can manage on my own. You and Running Water have taught me well. I will be fine."

"Alright," he finally says, "I don't like it, but I will go."

"I don't like it either, White Horse, but I don't see another choice."

"I will leave you with a rifle, and I will cover our tracks. You only leave to get water and hunt. I will be back here as quickly as I can."

I leave briefly to help White Horse with the children and explain to Rising Sun how she will need to help her new Chief.

"I will take good care of your father," I tell her. "I promise."

I then turn to White Horse to give him a hug. This is the part of being Chief that he does not like. He has to put his own selfishness behind and think of his band and the children who are more vulnerable than I. I know this is tearing him up, but he has no choice. "You be careful," I tell him.

"You too." He pecks my lips and jumps on his horse.

"You be nice to her," I warn him.

He faintly grins and leaves. He will take all the horses with him, as leaving us two here would have increased the chance that we will be seen. This leaves Red Hawk and me virtually on our own and extremely vulnerable. I watch him cover our tracks before heading back inside.

Chapter Twenty-Six

Secrets of the Past

"How are you doing?" I ask Red Hawk in his tongue as I come down beside him.

"I am alright," he faintly answers.

"You are a good liar," I joke. I see him faintly grin. "You sleep," I tell him. "I am going to build us a fire."

"Rising Sun?" he mumbles.

"She went with our Chief. She will be alright. You just rest now."

"No, I must get to her," he says as he painfully tries to sit up. I gently stop him by pushing him back down to rest.

"Rising Sun is fine," I assure him. "You need to rest."

Red Hawk is a little reluctant, but I am able to persuade him that his daughter is fine and White Horse will keep her safe. He is still not convinced and wants to go for her, but soon realizes he is too weak to give me any more of an argument and finally calms down.

While Red Hawk sleeps, I build a fire and prepare the cave for the cold night ahead. I looked around at what was left behind when I was here. I momentarily flash back as I can remember Red Hawk and Koawa cleaning my welts in front of a similar fire that I have now. I look over at a sleeping Red Hawk, thinking that he is lying in almost the identical spot that I was. I noticed in the back of the cave a piece of my dress lying on the ground that Koawa tore off me. I see the cup that I drank out of and the old, burnt stick that was used to clean my wounds. The memories of my vicious attack and the frantic effort to save my life are scattered everywhere throughout the cave. With Red Hawk still sleeping, I make my way down the hill to find the stream, which I am certain is not far away, to get all the water I can carry back before the sun sets. I follow the cluster of trees to find the stream that is just below the cave. Looking up at the Bluff, I can see the entrance to the cave as plain as day. I am aware that my assumption is not correct and can see why White Horse was so concerned. From this area of the river and hills, the cave is very well seen, and we are not as well hidden as I previously thought. I now must be even more careful about keeping us hidden and keeping the fire low. I fill the basin of water and head back up the steep hill. I stop briefly when I see yet another potential problem, the paw prints of a big cat.

"Great," I say to myself. "That is all we need." I can only hope that the cat has moved on and has found another home.

When I enter the cave, Red Hawk is awake. I kneeled beside him. "I went to get some water. I need to clean your wound," I tell him in his tongue. He only nods as he watches me start to work. I am very pleased at how well it looks. Except for a little oozing of blood, the bullet hole looks clean, and there is no sign of infection. I believe that Red Hawk will be alright and just needs his rest. I feel his eyes thick on me as I wipe his wound down. Out of the stillness, I suddenly, gently feel his hand caress my cheek. It completely takes me off guard. I stop what I am doing and look down at him. I then remember Koawa's warning. I quickly move my hand away and stand up.

"That should be good for a while," I tell him. He says not a word as he watches me sit down next to the fire before closing his eyes.

Many hours go by, and Red Hawk sleeps through almost all of them. The cave is starting to get cold. I take the only blanket we have and cover Red Hawk up. I start to think of White Horse and wonder if he has made it to his scouts yet. I know he will have to ride slowly because of the children, and I fear he will not make it home before dark. I only hope because we have failed to return at our scheduled time that Koawa and our scouts are heading this way to find us, but even then, if White Horse took a route that no one ever heard of, it could be morning before he is spotted. I am now wishing I had not taken a blanket and had given both to White Horse, as I am sure the children are cold. I then think of Rising Sun. How come I have never seen her, and why are there all the secrets that Red Hawk is her father? I think of my husband and his animosity towards her. Why? I wonder. What has this child ever done to White Horse, and why would White Horse be so cruel to a child, even though she is part Crow? I curl myself around my legs in front of the fire in an attempt to warm up. It is then that I feel a presence behind me. I quickly turn and jump to my feet when I see a huge cougar walking in. She sees me and growls. This, in return, wakes up Red Hawk. I see him painfully try to sit up as the cougar is ready to pounce on him.

I spot White Horse's rifle propped up against the cave wall entrance. I quickly decide against using it when I think of the Blue Coats and the echo the shot would give throughout the canyon. I only had one other choice. I have to use my knife. Red Hawk's eyes are huge as the cougar charges in. I charged behind it and started stabbing the life out of it. Finally, the cougar falls dead. I come to my feet and catch my breath. I look over at Red Hawk, who is just as relieved as I am. "You hungry?" I asked him, winded. I hear him chuckle as he lays his head back down.

I have never skinned a large cat before, but I treated it like all the other animals I have. Red Hawk watches on as I gut the cat and remove some meat, putting it on the fire.

"Here you go," I tell him after the cat has been cooked. "I am not sure how it will taste. I didn't have much to work with."

He didn't seem to care and picked off a big piece of meat from my knife. I come back down in front of the warmth of the fire and start eating. As I am chewing, I think to myself about the first time I met Red Hawk in Willow Creek when I stepped into the garden of paradise to rescue the foreign children. How scary he looked with all his war paint on his face. I think back to the first time he ever spoke to me. It was the first time I went to Sundance with White Horse. He said two words to me for the entire three days. I found him rude and incredibly heartless. I have always avoided him and was thankful he was from another band. It was not until the night of my attack that I lay here in his arms that I saw another side of him. It is the same side I am seeing now. We are now going to be in the same band as I am sure he will follow White Horse, now that Running Bear is dead. I wonder what this will do to Koawa, as he too is not really fond of him. I think of Rising Sun how my heart goes out to her. What is this child going to do without her mother? How difficult is it going to be for her to start over with complete strangers? I then decided to try to get to know Red Hawk better and see for myself if he is everything that his reputation says he is.

"She sure is a pretty little girl," I say to Red Hawk in his tongue. He looks confused. "Rising Sun," I clarify. "She is such a smart little girl."

He nods his head yes as he chews another bite. "Why did you not tell me you had a daughter?" I ask him.

"She is not my daughter," he answers.

"But she called you Papa," I say, confused.

"Yes, she is such a beautiful child and so smart. Her real father wants nothing to do with her, so I provide for her as if she were mine."

"Her mother, were you in love with her?"

He shakes his head no. "White Horse said she is part Crow."

"Yes, she is. She Who Stands was Crow."

"Was that Rising Sun's mother?"

"Yes."

"How did she come to live with your band?"

"Many years ago, a Crow warrior, He Who Runs, came into our village when we were all asleep and stole some of our horses. We found our horses the next day when we rode into their camp. Chief Running Bear wanted the man killed for what he did. He Who Runs Chief asked if She Who Stands could be traded as well as six of his ponies in exchange for his son's freedom. One of our warriors wanted another wife and agreed to take her. He was shortly thereafter killed."

"Is this Rising Sun's father?" I wonder.

"No," he answers.

"What happened to She Who Stands?"

"After he died, his first wife never accepted She Who Stands, because she was Crow, and his first wife was very mean to her. She would have the other women beat her and say mean things to her. She was given no place to live. She had to fend for herself. She tried to return to her family, and their Chief would not allow it as he was afraid Running Bear would kill his son if she returned, so she came back to us. She then turned into a beggar and a whore. She would lie with any warrior, just to have a place to stay for the night. Even I gave in to her. I would have taken her in, but she had eyes on someone else, someone who was next in line for great power. He wanted nothing to do with her and turned her down many times.

One night, he comes into our village with many of his warriors to celebrate a huge victory against our enemies, the Pawnee. Much firewater was spread throughout all the warriors in celebration of our victory. He had too much and got very drunk. She Who Stands took advantage of his drunkenness and seduced him. When he woke up the next morning beside her and saw he was naked, he knew what she had done and was furious with her for taking advantage of him and wanted her dead. Chief Running Bear calmed him down, and as a punishment to She

Who Stands, he ordered her to remain in her lodge, and he made her his slave for the rest of her life.

A few months later, she found out she was with child, and by this time, the man was happily married and had a child of his own. She was hoping he would have had a change of heart, but he did not and had his Chief banish her from his band, as well as the child, and told her if she ever mentioned to anyone about the child, he would order them both killed. So, she returned to our camp, and the child was born. Running Bear and Yellow Bird took the child in. Several years later, this man would lose his wife, and the Chief would die, and he would then receive great power. She tried again in hopes he would reconsider, but again she was banished and told that if she returned, she and her child would be killed. I could not leave the child behind, as there is Sioux in that child. So, I provided shelter and food for her and her mother. I never took her to my pelt again. She would not break my heart again. I love Rising Sun, but I hated her mother."

Wow, I am truly amazed at this story. My heart goes out to Red Hawk and Rising Sun. "What are you going to do now that her mother is dead?" I ask him.

"I will continue raising her as mine. She does not need to know that her father disowned her."

"Red Hawk, I will help you. She will never be alone. There is not a woman in our band who will not take part in Rising Sun. She will want for nothing."

"Prairie Dawn, you do not understand. Her father is still alive, and he is aware of who she is. He could cause many problems for her now, and that would cause death between him and me, as I would die for her."

"White Horse would not allow any harm to come to anyone in his band. You do not need to worry about her Red Hawk. She will be fine."

I can tell he is really concerned about this, and I feel as if there is more to the story than I am being told. I do not know much about Red Hawk except he has a short fuse, so for that reason I dropped the subject.

"Do you want more?" I ask him.

"No, I am full," he grins.

Red Hawk is looking so much stronger. Although he is still seeping in his wound, it looks so much better, and I expect after a few more days he will be on his feet and well on the mend. The chill in the cave is getting intense. I curl my legs up pulling my dress over my knees to warm myself up.

"Are you cold?" Red Hawk asks.

"A little," I answer.

"Come," he says. He opens his blanket. Koawa's warning of me avoiding on getting too close to Red Hawk is haunting my mind.

"I am alright but thank you."

Seeing my apprehension, he puts his hand out.

"I know you have been warned about me, but with everything you have been through, I would not dream of hurting you."

I can see the sincerity in his eyes and I am getting extremely cold. I gave in but remained cautious as I slid under the blanket beside him.

"See, Red Hawk behaves," he smiles. I chuckle.

"I am sorry about Running Bear," I tell him on a serious note.

"Running Bear was a good Chief, and he was very good to me, taking me in when my parents died when I was boy. His name will be remembered for a very long time."

"You have lost a lot and for this I am sorry."

"Red Hawk did not lose everything. I will start again. Rising Sun and I will be fine."

"I meant what I said. You are not alone. I will help you with Rising Sun, if you wish."

"I would like that," he says. "I would like something else as well."

Laying here beside him I am almost afraid to ask. I look over at him. "I want to learn your language," he says.

I am a little surprised that he says this out of the blue, and I am embarrassed that I was thinking what I was.

"Why would you want to do that?" I finally asked him.

"I have my reasons. Will you teach me?"

"English is not an easy language," I say.

"I do not care, if I can learn how to be a warrior then I can learn the White Man's words." He looks over at me. "Will you teach me?"

"I would be honored." He faintly smiles.

I have never taught anyone how to speak a language. White Horse already knew it before I met him, and he taught me his language. I am not real sure how to start. I think for a moment and then point to myself.

"Woman," I say.

Red Hawk looks at the way I move my mouth as I repeat it. He then says his first word. "Wwooo.. man."

"Very good," I smile. I then point to him.

"Man."

"Mman," he repeats.

I will admit I am impressed. I try something else. I hold up my hand.

"Hand," I say. He repeats.

"Hhand." I couldn't help but laugh. Red Hawk has a very deep voice when he speaks English. He tells me in his tongue, "stop laughing at me."

I of course laugh harder, which in return makes him laugh. He holds his stomach as the movement of his laughter gave him pain. I go to another word. I lift my hand, taking it to my chest and holding it straight out when I say the word. I say it in his tongue first.

"Good." I then repeat it in English. He takes my hand and repeats the action as he says the word.

"Good."

For the next several hours, this is all we do. I am very impressed with how quickly he is catching on. He has a long way to go, but he is well on his way to learning my language.

Another day is on us. I help Red Hawk get on his feet and go outside because he has to void. I left him and went to find my own place. On my return, I find him sitting on a rock just outside the cave.

"Good day," he says in English.

"Yes, good job," I smile.

He is so proud of himself. He remains there on the rock as he watches me pull out the cougar from the cave. I need to dispose of the carcass as I am afraid the smell of it will attract wolves or other cats. I want it to be as far away from us as possible. I remove more meat that we will eat off later and start dragging it out.

This is the biggest female cougar I have ever seen. It must be at least one hundred pounds. This is not an easy task for me. I consider myself strong, but dragging this thing is becoming a challenge. I am able to drag it to the edge of the ridge. It is then Red Hawk, seeing my struggles, provides me with what help he can by kicking it and helping me push it over the ridge. I am totally exhausted when I watch it go rolling down the hill. I dust my hands off as I turn around.

"You are a strong woman, Prairie Dawn," Red Hawk says in his tongue.

"Thank you," I tell him. "Now to get you back inside and to bed."

I help Red Hawk get back inside the cave by putting my arm around him and helping him sit down. He is looking so much better today but just that little adventure has worn him out. I will let him rest as I go down to the stream for some fresh water.

White Horse makes it with the children as far as his scouts. It was a very long and cold night, and he is grateful that all went well. The word is spread about the death of Running Bear and the attack on the camp and what has happened to Red Hawk. With the children nestled comfortably with the women, he focuses on returning for his wife and Red Hawk. He takes about a dozen warriors and starts their way back to the canyon.

Chapter Twenty-Seven

On the Run

The water is crystal clear. I can literally see my reflection as I fill the basin with fresh water. I glance up at the cave entrance just above me where Red Hawk rests. I think of Rising Sun and all she has gone through. My heart goes out for her, and I hope the women will welcome her in our band with open arms, despite her being part Crow who are bitter enemies of ours. I think of White Horse who must manage the children by himself and how vulnerable he is if he is seen by the Blue Coats. I worry for him so and can only pray he has made it to our scouts safely and is on his way back here with his warriors. I am almost certain he is just as worried for me as I am for him. With the water basin filled, I take a few extra moments to splash some of the cool water on my face and clean up. I glance out at the nature around me and back up at the entrance to the cave. It is then I see off in the distance something blowing in the wind. I stand up to get a better look. I watch it as it moves just over the ridge. I notice it is the top of an American flag. It is then that I panic as it can only mean it is Blue Coats. I glance back over at the entrance of the cave and the direction that the Blue Coats are coming. It is then that shear fear enters my mind as they will cross right in front of the cave entrance. I then started to run, keeping close to the ground so not to be seen as I crawled up the hill and into the cave to warn Red Hawk. I rushed to his side and woke him up.

"Blue Coats!" I frantically say.

"Where?" he says.

"Just over the ridge."

"Hurry, cover the smoke from the fire," he orders as he struggles to get to a stand.

I rush to the fire and start kicking dirt over it as Red Hawk is on his feet with White Horse's rifle in his hand. He peers outside to see how close they are while cocking it, as I start tossing the rocks around the fire and over the dirt to stop it from smoldering. Red Hawk then rushes over and grabs my hand.

"There is no time. Come on!"

We quickly make our way outside the cave. Red Hawk is in no shape to be running and is holding his side as we slide down the hill. We both look back and see the Blue Coats coming around the hilltop approaching the entrance to the cave. Red Hawk pushes me down low to the ground as the Blue Coats are right on top of us. We remain motionless and wait for them to pass. The One Who Kills Many, one of the Pawnee scouts for the United States Army, is one of the last to pass the cave entrance. He sniffs as he passes by. He stops his horse, speaking his tongue to the army translator. He motions for everyone to stop as he dismounts his army horse. He sniffs again as he makes his way inside the cave. A soldier of the highest rank follows him in. The One Who Kills Many sees the fresh fire and the blood from the slaughtered cat. He squats down and spots fresh tracks.

"There are only two," he says to the translator.

He sees the blanket that covered Red Hawk and the blood on the ground near where he lay.

"One is injured," he adds. "They have not been gone long."

"Are they Indian?" the translator asks.

"Yes," he answers.

"How long have they been gone?"

"We missed them by just a few minutes."

"Then they can't be far," the officer says.

The One Who Kills Many stands up and speaks his tongue to the translator. "I saw no pony tracks when we came in so they must be on foot."

The one who is highest rank orders his men, who are in a small group of roughly ten men, to comb the area. I nudge to Red Hawk that we need to get out of here. We slowly crawl backwards the rest of the way down the hill, until we get to the backside of the cave, where the incline is steeper and easier to find a place to hide. We can hear the movement around us over our heads and then suddenly a shot is fired as we are seen by one of the Pawnee scouts. The shot just misses my head, bouncing off a rock. Red

Hawk is quick to react and has us up against the rocks out of sight. He then takes a shot at the scout, hitting him.

"Nice shot," I tell him.

He faintly smiles, but our celebration is cut short when another shot is heard from a soldier and I hear orders being told to climb down after us. I quietly speak my tongue to Red Hawk on what was said. We have no time to think. We keep it low as we sneak down the rocks and into the trees. By the time we hit the trees, Red Hawk is not doing well and has started bleeding again.

"You are bleeding," I tell him.

"Not too much, I am alright," he says.

Before we can catch our breath, we hear them as they enter the trees. Red Hawk again has me by my hand and we run to find a place to hide. He finds a hollow in an old tree and quickly pushes me in there. He then comes in next to me, plastering himself up against me as the hollow is barely big enough to fit us both. I can feel Red Hawk's heart beating on my chest. I have no choice but to press myself up against him as we patiently wait for the soldiers to pass. We both hold our breath as we hear them go by. I deeply sigh when they disappear out of sight.

"That was too close," I say.

We wait a few more moments to make sure they are indeed gone. I look up at Red Hawk whose eyes are thick on mine.

Red Hawk gazes into the eyes of Prairie Dawn. He sees how beautiful she is and visualizes how good they would be together. For a moment, he is enjoying having Prairie Dawn so close to him but now is not the time to lust for her. He must keep her safe, he must keep her alive. He is aware how close the Blue Coats are and fears for her safety. It is time to move on. He blinks and steps out of the hollow.

"We will walk back to my camp," he says in his tongue as I step out of the hollow.

"It is closer than yours. We will stay there until Chief White Horse returns."

"That is a good half a day's walk," I argue. "The cave is closer. White Horse should be here soon."

"No, the Blue Coats will remain close as they know we are near. It is too dangerous to stay. We go back to my camp. They will not think to return."

"If the Blue Coats are going to remain close, then that means they could find White Horse. We must warn him."

"White Horse will not come alone, and he is already on his guard. He will see the haste with which we moved and know we are on foot. He will track us. I will make it easy for him to find us."

"If White Horse can track us, then so will the army."

"No, they won't. I will make tracks that only White Horse can pick up. We will go back higher up in the hills where Blue Coat ponies will not go. Then we come back down where it will lead us into Running Bear's camp. It will take us longer, but it is safer."

I am skeptical and not sure if I can trust Red Hawk, but right now I have no other choice as I am clueless about where I am or even how to get to safety. My bag was left at the cave, and Red Hawk is bleeding. He needs me as much as I need him, so I wrap my arm around his waist to help him walk and we disappear into the woods.

We walk in silence for what seems like hours. Red Hawk is slow at moving and I am certain he is feeling the pain with every step, but he is a true warrior and fighting every inch along the way. I try to help him as best as I can, allowing him to lean on me, which in return wears me out, but like him I am determined to get us up this hill and to safety. I try to get his mind off the task at hand and start another lesson.

"The grass is green on the prairie," I tell him in his tongue. He then repeats it in English.

"The grass is blue on the prairie."

"No," I chuckle. "Grass is not blue. It is green."

"I am new at this, why did you give me something so hard?" he says in his tongue. I chuckled again. "Ok I'm sorry, try this. I have many horses." He repeats it in English perfectly.

"You never did tell me why you wanted to learn English?" I ask him.

"No, and I won't," he says.

"Why not?" I ask him.

"Because I want to be difficult," he teases.

"Aw I see, well just because of that I will give you a hard one," I joke.

"Nothing is too difficult for me," he comments.

"Oh," I am arrogantly amused. "Ok, smart ass, try this. The flowers grow abundantly across the prairie."

He hesitates for a moment to think as we continue our slow walk. I can hear that his breathing is getting harder as his fatigue is setting in. That makes two of us as I too am exhausted.

"I do not care about flowers," he says in his tongue.

"Chicken," I tease.

Thank God he has a sense of humor and is not taking any offense by me playfully putting him down.

"I am no chicken," he comes back.

"Then try it. I used to mess up your language all the time. I still do from time to time, but I keep trying as you must too."

I hear him deeply sigh as he stops catching his breath. He proudly looks down at me. "The flowers grow across the prairie," he says.

"Abundantly across the prairie," I correct.

"Who gives a shit," he smirks.

I chuckle as his English was great. It is then that I conclude he understands the foul words of the English language. I assume White Horse or Koawa has something to do with it.

"You understand more than I thought," I say.

"Some, but not too much," he says in his tongue.

We continued our walk for many miles. Fatigue and thirst are on both of our minds as our energy levels are going down. We continue our hiking in silence for some time. Red Hawk breaks briefly to sit down and catch his breath. I take a moment to look at his seeping wound through the bandages.

"I don't like the way it looks," I tell him.

He glances at it. I can tell by his face he is in pain.

"I will be alright," he tells me.

"Red Hawk, it is seeping more. You should not be walking. We need to set up camp so you can rest."

"No," he says. "It is not safe. We move on."

"But if this gets infected it could kill you," I plead.

"I do not care about me. All I care about right now is getting you to safety."

"I understand that, but soon the sun falls, and the threats of Blue Coats will stop for the night."

"No, Prairie Dawn," he argues. "I will not chance it. They know we are close, and they have a scout who knows how to track."

"I thought you were covering them?"

"I am but I cannot cover the scent of blood that is coming from me. A wild animal or a skilled scout may come up to us at night and kill us. We must move on."

"We have a rifle. I will guard you as you sleep," I suggest.

He faintly grins. "You are brave woman, but I cannot allow it. We walk."

Enough was said, if this was White Horse I would have pushed it harder as I am not afraid to state my opinion to him, but Red Hawk is a different story and I don't want to push my luck and have him turn on me, so I remain quiet and help him to his feet and continue.

"Give me another hard one," he says after we have walked a little further on.

"Alright, umm," I say as I think for a moment. "The horses run quickly."

"You are getting tired," he teases in his language. "This is easy." He then repeats it in English perfectly.

"You are a fast learner," I tell him.

"You are a good teacher," he says, "and a beautiful one as well," he grins.

Red Hawk is a huge flirt. I never would have guessed he had it in him. Before I can come back with a smart comment, I see off in a nearby distance, a cabin.

"Red Hawk, look," I say as I point.

"This just might be our lucky day," he says.

From where we are standing the cabin appears to be abandoned.

"I am going to go check it out," I tell him.

"No, we go together."

With that said Red Hawk and I make our way to the cabin.

Chapter Twenty-Eight

The Guardian

My assumption is correct, and it appears no one has been in the cabin for years. The place is in rough shape and extremely run down, but at least it will provide us with the shelter we need for the night from any wildlife and Blue Coats and give us the warmth from a fire. I found a place near the fireplace for Red Hawk to rest. He watches as I start a fire, keeping it low so it does not smell. I take a few moments and look around at the contents in the cabin to see if there is anything I can use to collect water in or any sort of blanket for warmth, as everything was left behind in the cave, including my bag.

"What are you doing?" Red Hawk asks as he is watching me go through cabinets, drawers, and chests.

"I am trying to find anything that we can use," I answer him. "Ah ha!" I smile as I pull out of the cabinet a water bucket.

"Prairie Dawn you are not leaving this cabin," he warns.

"Red Hawk neither one of us have had any water all day."

"You could go miles before you find water," he says.

"Someone at one time had to have lived here. There must be a well or a stream nearby. They wouldn't go without water," I argue.

"Then we search together," he stubbornly says.

"Red Hawk you need your rest. You are still bleeding."

"I told you I do not care about me. I will not allow anything to happen to you."

"Well, I do care what happens to you," I argue. "I won't be gone long."

As I am turning around Red Hawk grabs my arm. I look down at him.

"We are in this together."

"Then I suggest you let me go."

I watch him as he grabs his stomach and comes to his feet.

"You should not be walking," I argue.

"I do a lot of things I am not supposed to do," he snarls.

This man is truly impossible and about as stubborn as they come. He is definitely one of a kind and I can understand why he is single as he must be the most unpredictable, domineering, and egotistical man I have ever met, nothing at all like my husband.

"Alright, the sun will soon be down and we need to find food and water before it gets to dark."

"Unless you can kill something with your bare hands we cannot hunt as we cannot chance the shots being heard by Blue Coats," he says.

"White Horse showed me how to spear a fish once. I can do that."

"Again, you may walk hours without finding a stream. I will find us food. You go get the water."

"How are you going to hunt when you can barely walk?"

"I will find a way," he snaps.

I deeply sigh as I know I am getting nowhere, and I do not have time to argue with him as dusk is already upon us.

"We will go together," I say.

I am not crazy about the idea of leaving the protection of the cabin any more than he is but, we have no choice. I am clueless where I am and I need Red Hawk to get me out of here, so for that reason I am staying with him. I am suspicious there is a stream nearby as I cannot imagine anyone living here without some sort of water supply. Coming in, I do not remember seeing a well anywhere around the cabin, so therefore there must be a stream and where there is a stream then there will not only be water but most likely fish as well.

I walk with Red Hawk through the dense trees and in just a few minutes he finds the stream. It is then that I realize how great his tracking and sense of smell is as I am not certain I could have found it so tucked away in the trees and this close to dark. He finds a log and sits down watching me as I fill the bucket with water.

"See there is a lot of fish here," I tell him as I watch them swim abundantly by me. He removes his knife from his waistline and hands it to me.

"Use it as if it was a spear," he says.

I reluctantly take his knife. It has been seven years since White Horse showed me how to spear fish and then we were courting at the time and he did most of the work himself, only instructing me on when to throw it as I was tucked in his arms. I wasn't sure I could do this and wish I hadn't bragged to Red Hawk that I could.

"Come on," he orders. "It is almost dark."

"Don't push me," I snap. "I haven't done this in a while." I hear him faintly chuckle as he is watching the fish swimming around me.

"That one over there," he points.

I watch the fish that he is pointing to and follow it with my eyes until I feel comfortable enough to stab it.

"Hurry up," I hear him say, "Before it swims away."

"Stop pushing me!" I bark.

I hear him huff and come to his feet. He reaches down and grabs the knife out of my hand as he is holding his side and goes out into the water. I watched him a few seconds before he tossed the knife into the water and stabbed the fish. He made it look so easy. I roll my eyes as he gives me an arrogant smirk. I walked out into the water to get the fish and hand Red Hawk his knife back. He then repeats it and kills another fish. We now have our dinner. I come out of the water along with him with the fish in our hands and make our way back to the cabin.

White Horse and his warriors have returned to the cave just before the sun sets on the great canyon. He rushes in to meet his wife only to find her gone. He sees the heavy bloodstain on the ground and his wife's bag. His heart sinks as he knows she would never leave her bag behind. He is certain something bad has happened and fears she may be dead. Koawa comes into the cave behind his brother.

"There is a dead Pawnee scout by the ridge," he says.

"The Blue Coats were here," White Horse tells him.

He holds his wife's bag closer to his chest. "She left her bag behind. They moved fast."

Koawa, seeing the bloodstain on the cave ground squats down as White Horse's mind does circles.

"There is much blood here," he says. "Something really bad happened here." White Horse kicks some dirt up out of frustration. "Those sons of bitches, I never should have left her. They got her! They took my Prairie Dawn!"

"No, White Horse," Koawa says racing up beside him. "Look, smell," he tells his brother as he waves his fingers in front of his nose.

"This is animal blood, probably from the cat prints we saw when we were coming in. It most likely came in, and she killed it."

"Or it killed her!"

"No, my brother, we would see the remains as it cannot drag them both off. They saw the Blue Coats and they ran. Red Hawk most likely killed that scout when they were making their escape."

"We have to find them. Soon it will be dark, making the tracks harder to find," White Horse says.

Koawa puts his hand on his brother's shoulder. "We will find her. I do not trust Red Hawk either, but he would never allow anything to happen to her. She is fine, I am certain of that."

White Horse deeply sighs as he thinks of his Prairie Dawn out there alone and vulnerable. He is certain Red Hawk will keep her safe, but can only hope he behaves himself and keeps his hands off her. He vows to himself that if Red Hawk touches her in any way that is inappropriate, he will kill him and take Rising Sun back to the Crows. He has no time to waste as nightfall is approaching quickly. He rushes to his horse and soon everyone is tracking in effort to find them both.

Our bellies are full of fish and fatigue is starting to set in. I find a place close to the fire near Red Hawk and curled up. I hear the thunder rolling outside as the sky opens across the prairie. I start to think of my husband, who I am certain has made it back to the cave and is worried sick about me. I wonder if indeed Red Hawk did leave tracks for only White Horse to find as I still at times question his motives and wonder if he is not up to something to keep me away from my husband.

I worry about the second Pawnee scout that is tracking for the Blue Coats and wonder if Red Hawk covered our tracks enough that he couldn't pick it up. I started to think of the conversation in the cave with Red Hawk regarding Rising Sun. How her mother, She Who Stands, seduced her father. I could understand why he would be so upset, but why take it out on a child and order her killed as well? I then think of White Horse and how harsh he was with her, is it really because she is part Crow? It angers me that he would feel that way as Little Foot, his own son, is a half breed as well. My thoughts are interrupted when Red Hawk stirs awake.

"You are still awake," he says in his tongue.

"I cannot sleep," I answer him.

"Do not fear for we are safe tonight," he reassures me.

"I am just thinking of White Horse. I am sure he has made it to the cave by now and is worried sick."

"He will know where to find us, I made it very easy for him."

"If you made it that easy, then that Pawnee scout could find us too."

"No, what you need to understand Prairie Dawn is we have many ways of communicating with each other that only we know. Our enemies cannot figure out what we are saying or where we are at."

"You mean like a code?" I wonder.

"That is exactly what I mean. Rest assure Prairie Dawn, when we reach Running Bear's camp your husband will be there."

I only hope I can trust Red Hawk and that this is not one of his wicked ploys to keep me to himself. I take his advice and make myself comfortable and try to get some sleep.

The wind and rain are harsh on the prairie and trees. White Horse is having no luck on tracking and can only assume if Red Hawk did leave a trail that the rain has washed it away. With the wind in his hair and the rain pushing down on him, White Horse deeply thinks where Red Hawk may be taking her. Koawa comes up beside him.

"Brother we must seek shelter," he says.

"They are close Koawa, I can feel it."

Just then Blue Thunder calls his Chief over. White Horse races over to join his warrior who is pointing down to the ground.

"They were here," White Horse says as he looks at some stones that form a circle in the soil. He is very aware of what it means and is certain where Red Hawk and his wife are heading.

The morning sun rises on the prairie. The smell of last night's rain fills the air. Red Hawk and I are making our way to Running's Bear camp in silence. Last night's rain provided us with a great deal of puddles that are soaking the souls of our moccasins as we walk through them. We are entering an area that I am now familiar with and am certain, in just a few hours, we will be in the big boulders overlooking where Running Bear's camp once proudly stood. It has been an incredibly long two days, and my feet and back are throbbing in pain. Red Hawk is holding up very well and is helping me get across certain areas of the land that I am having trouble with.

I must admit that I am impressed with Red Hawk and am starting to believe he is not as bad as he lets others believe. He has been a gentleman by keeping his hands to himself and holding any rude comments or thoughts to himself that he may have about me as I am certain I am slowing him down.

Finally, after hours of hiking down the rocks and crevices, we made it to the ridge overlooking the camp. For several moments Red Hawk remains still in his thoughts as he gazes out at the mass destruction and the dead bodies still lying there. I squeezed his shoulder as I saw the sadness enter his eyes. The amount of pain he must be feeling and the sudden knowledge that he is the only warrior who survived this massive ambush from the Blue Coats must weigh heavily on his mind. I watch him as he sits down on a rock, gazing out at the destruction below.

"I told Running Bear that we were too open. That is why I told Rising Sun what to do in the event we were attacked. She knew where to hide." I watch him as he shakes his head. "Why wouldn't he listen to me?" I come down on the rocks and sit down beside him.

"You cannot feel responsible, even White Horse tried to warn him. Running Bear just would not listen."

"He was used to things that had been and not what is now and look where it got him."

My heart ached for him. The emotion is thick in his eyes, although no tears were shed, it is all over his face, Red Hawk is devastated. I put my hand on his shoulder, gently rubbing it.

"You will come and join us. We will be your family."

He grins my way. "Thank you," he says.

We come to our feet and look back out at the horizon.

"Red Hawk look," I say excitedly.

Just off in the distance we see White Horse and many warriors approaching the camp. Red Hawk grabs my hand.

"Let's go," he says.

Slowly we start to descend to the camp, inch by inch making our way down. We hit the last landing before getting into the prairie. Red Hawk helps me down from the steep jump, as we are walking down, we both abruptly stop and gasps. Coming in from the opposite direction we see Blue Coats. We both look over at our warriors on the other side of the hill.

"They are heading right towards them," I say. "Red Hawk, we have to do something."

Red Hawk is quick in his thinking and has us covered behind some boulders. "Keep your head down," he orders before cocking the rifle and shooting.

The shot is heard throughout the valley and all the Lakota warriors abruptly stop and look up at the canyon where the shot came from.

The army soldiers, upon hearing the shot as well, are taking cover. Red Hawk runs over to me, handing me the rifle.

"I am going further down to signal White Horse, if the Blue Coats move any further to them, shoot!"

"Alright."

I get myself to a position that is in between two boulders that overlooks the prairie below. I am in perfect position in seeing the Blue Coats, but they are unable to see me.

Red Hawk is quickly running down to the prairie below in the direction of White Horse and the Lakota warriors. He knows he must signal them and warn them of the danger ahead. He rushes down on his knees, quickly scooping up some twigs. He gets some rocks and sticks and starts to try to get some smoke. The army Sergeant orders his men to move ahead. I take a shot to hold them back. I see them look up at the rocks where they believe they come from. A soldier shoots back. I hear it ricochet off the rocks in front of me.

White Horse and his warriors are now in battle mode and rush in towards the gun fire. This is making me more nervous as he is still heading directly towards the Blue Coats.

"Damnit, White Horse," I curse.

Red Hawk is having a hell of a time at getting smoke due to last night's rain making everything wet, but he knows he doesn't need much and is nearly there. He hears the shots from Prairie Dawn and then again as someone is shooting at her. He must hurry, he thinks to himself, as he has left Prairie Dawn extremely vulnerable. Finally, he gets his spark and is able to make enough smoke to signal the warriors below.

Blue Thunder is the first to spot it and stops his Chief from advancing to the rocks. "It's them," White Horse says.

The warriors look out at the signal that Red Hawk is giving them.

"Blue Coats!" he yells at his men. "Everyone charge in!" he orders.

Satisfied that his signal has come across, Red Hawk races back up to help me. The Blue Coats have seen the signal as well and know that Indians are ahead. They too are instructed to advance by their sergeant and head directly into the Lakota warriors. The last Pawnee scout ignores the sergeant's order to advance and turns his horse around and heads up to the rocks where the shots were heard. Red Hawk is quickly upon me and has me by my hand and we are running down to the ground below us.

The Lakota warriors have made it to the Blue Coats and a full-blown battle is emerging between them. Red Hawk and I can hear the battle around us. I am absolutely terrified but showing no emotion as I continue holding Red Hawk's hand allowing him to escort me down. We slide down a steep, rocky incline as the gunfire is going over our heads.

One by one the soldiers fall to their deaths as our warriors have the upper hand. I can hear the cries from a soldier as I am sure he is being bludgeoned to death just below us by one of our warriors. Red Hawk and I have made it to the bottom and approached a cover when I feel the air of a bullet just missing me. I scream! Red Hawk grabs me by my waist and has me down on the ground and shielded.

"It is alright Prairie Dawn," he whispers to me in his tongue. "Just stay down, it should be done in a minute."

Red Hawk could have easily left me to help the others, but he remains with his body on top of me, shielding me from gunfire for several seconds. Suddenly, Red Hawk sees the Pawnee scout. Ignoring his own injuries, he is quickly on his feet and in a run to chase after him. Sheer terror fills my soul as I know Red Hawk is not fully healed and ready for a fight. I come up on all four, crawling over to the rifle. I am quick at cocking it when I hear a horse coming in fast. I aim up and am ready to shoot. As the horse and rider come into my view, I see that it is White Horse. I rush to my feet just as he reaches down, grabbing my wrist and swinging me on behind him. We are now in a dead run.

Red Hawk has found a horse belonging to a fallen army soldier. He jumps on his back and gets in a run chasing after the Pawnee scout. Blue Thunder is right behind him. White Horse is keeping me safely behind him by keeping his distance from the battle. We sit on his pony as we watch the last few soldiers fall to their death. We then see Koawa raise his rifle in the air and let out a victory cry. It is over. The battle has ended. I smile as I watch my husband repeat the victory cry. I am so relieved that for today, all our warriors are still standing proud. We slowly started to walk towards the battle ground. Red Hawk and Blue Thunder return, making our victory short lived.

"We lost the scout," Blue Thunder says.

"I am not going to worry about it," White Horse says. "It will take him days to get back to the Fort and regroup and by then we will be long gone and our dead will be gathered."

He removes my bag over his head, reaching behind him he then hands it to me. I am a little surprised due to his animosity towards me having it, that he rescued it from the cave.

"I thought you objected on me carrying it?" I questioned him.

"Well, I changed my mind," he smiles.

I put my arms around his waist and embraced him.

"You are a softy," I tease.

I hear him chuckle as he reaches around and squeezes my leg.

"Let's go home Love," he says.

"Amen to that," I agree.

The Pawnee scout sits high on his horse on a hill away from any Lakota warrior's view. He watches the great Chief and his warriors ride through the plains. So far, he thinks to himself, they have been lucky but soon their luck will run out. He will find their camp. He will tell the White Man army where they are at. He will be highly rewarded by the White Man Chief. Enjoy your freedom for now he thinks to himself, because soon it will end.

The End

Stayed tuned for the third book in the Prairie Dawn series Whispers Through The Wind. When White Horse is among the missing and presumed dead, Koawa, now Chief, must honor his brother's wish and take the grieving Prairie Dawn in as his own. Her grieving is stopped short when Koawa realizes another man wants the beautiful widow as well and will stop at nothing to get her. Koawa must defend Prairie Dawn and honor his brother's name, as his love for her grows. A deep secret will be revealed that will bring much turmoil to the Lakota camp. When White Horse is found alive, a shocking discovery starts to unravel as White Horse slowly starts to regain his memory from the accident. A face from the past will return and call on White Horse for help that will put Prairie Dawn and Koawa in a strange and twisted adventure. Many more secrets and deceptions will be made. This is a must-read, action-packed romance that is filled with many twists that will leave you guessing until the end.

9 798889 976595